*H*

*D*

AND

*Flower in
the Snow*

WORDSWORTH ROMANCE

# Highland Doctor

AND

# Flower in the Snow

## MARGARET ALLAN/JULIA HAMMOND

WORDSWORTH EDITIONS

The paper in this book is produced from pure wood
pulp, without the use of chlorine or any other substance
harmful to the environment. The energy used in its
production consists almost entirely of hydroelectricity
and heat generated from waste materials, thereby
conserving fossil fuels and contributing little to the
greenhouse effect.

First published by Robert Hale Limited

This edition published 1994 by
Wordsworth Editions Limited
Cumberland House, Crib Street, Ware,
Hertfordshire SG12 9ET

ISBN 1 85326 517 9

*Printed and bound in Denmark by Nørhaven*

# Highland Doctor

# *ONE*

It seemed to Katrina that she had been on the train for ever watching the soft green landscape of England flash past until at long last it had been replaced by the more rugged grandeur of Scotland. Her injured arm throbbed relentlessly, reminding her that it was hours since she had swallowed her last painkilling tablet. She would take one as soon as she got to Castle House, and that would be quite soon now because there were the familiar mountains, there was the shining stretch of river that would join the loch close to her home, and there at last was the little station where her father would be waiting for her. A rush of emotion filled her as she caught sight of him. Then she was hoisting her travel bag awkwardly on to her uninjured arm and jumping down to the platform and into his arms.

'Oh, Dad, it's so good to see you!'

They hugged each other, then he frowned as he indicated her bandaged arm. 'What have you been doing to yourself?'

'Crashing my car,' she confessed.

'When? You didn't say anything when you rang me last night.'

'I didn't want you worrying. I thought I'd wait

5

until I got here to tell you.'

'Were you fit to travel? Did the hospital say you could? You don't look too good.' He was surveying her anxiously as he said that.

'I'll be fine, once I've had a cup of tea and a painkiller.'

She did not answer his other question. The hospital doctor had told her to stay at home and rest for a couple of weeks, but after a couple of days spent on her own in the flat she shared with two other girls she had had enough and decided to do her resting up in Scotland with her father.

'Let's get you home then. Mrs Muir has been making scones ready for your arrival.' He took her bag and put it into the back of his elderly but still elegant Jaguar while she took her seat in the front. 'Was anyone else hurt in the accident?' he asked then.

'No, Dad. It was just me and the car, and someone's garden wall.'

'How did it happen?' He was edging the vehicle carefully out of the lane that led from the station to the road which would bring them in a couple of miles to Castle House.

'A dog ran out in front of me. I swerved to avoid it. It didn't get hurt at all,' she told him.

'But you did.'

She shrugged. 'It could have been worse, though the car is a mess. Anyway, I won't be able to drive it for a while, so I thought I might as well come up and see how you were. How are you, Dad?'

It seemed to take him some time to answer that. She felt a small stir of disquiet as she waited, and a deeper one as she took a long look at his face.

'Not as well as I'd like to be,' was all he would say.

'What does that mean?'

'We'll talk about it later, over tea. We are nearly home now.'

Yes, there was the beloved grey stone building with its little round towers and its balustrade. The house which was so much like a small castle, and which took its name from the centuries old castle ruins which were closer to the edge of the nearby loch. Here she had been born and here she had spent her happy childhood; here one day she would perhaps bring her own family. Her throat swelled with the joy of being home.

Even before she was out of the car her father's golden retriever dashed down the front steps to welcome her with a wildly waving tail, followed at a much slower pace by her father's elderly housekeeper. Katrina patted the dog, then hugged the housekeeper.

'How are you, Mrs Muir?'

'The better for seeing you, my dear. It seems a wee while since you were here.'

'I couldn't come at Easter because I was in Italy.' She ought not to have felt guilty as she said that, but she did.

'Come away in and have some tea,' the housekeeper who had known her for most of her life urged her through the lofty hall and into the spacious drawing room where a huge window overlooked the garden and the acres of forest that made up the Kerrbridge Castle estate.

The house seemed very quiet, which indicated to Katrina that there were no paying guests staying at present. Some years ago her parents had started to provide sporting holidays for business men who enjoyed fishing, shooting or playing golf. It had been necessary for them to do this because of the ever-increasing expenses incurred in keeping Castle House in a reasonable state of repair. She was glad there were no guests; that she could have her home, and her father, to herself. As the thought crossed her mind he came into the room and sank into one of the big chintz covered chairs. He did not speak until the housekeeper had brought in a tea trolley and gone out again.

'Can you manage to pour, or shall I do it my dear?' he asked then.

'I'm getting used to doing things with my left hand,' she said with a smile. Then, after handing him a cup and saucer, she said what was on her mind. 'Why aren't you as well as you would like to be, Dad? What did you mean by that?'

He sighed before he gave her his answer. 'I'm not so good these days, Trina. In fact Daig thinks I ought to cancel the rest of the house parties.'

That gave her a jolt. Her father had been such an active man that it was hard to think of him being unfit. Yet Daig was not one to make a fuss about nothing.

'Then do,' she begged. 'You mustn't make yourself ill, Dad.'

Her father sighed as he set down his empty cup. 'I don't think you quite understand, my dear, about the paying guests. I can't afford to keep this place going without the money they bring in. The cost of keeping the house and estate going is increasing all the time.'

'What about the money Grandfather left?' she interrupted. 'I thought —'

'Death duties, and years of nursing home fees for your grandmother, ate into that so deeply that there wasn't enough left to keep the place in good repair. That's why we started the fishing and riding and golfing holidays. It was so much easier when your mother was alive. She had so much energy; so much enthusiasm for our visitors. I can't carry on without her. I find myself dreading each new arrival now,' Malcolm Kerr confessed.

Katrina felt a rush of sympathy for him. 'Oh, Dad, you must give it up then.'

'That's what Daig says, but I find the alternative hard to face.'

'The alternative?'

'Selling Castle House,' he said quietly.

'Oh no! It can't be as bad as that!' Aghast, she stared at him.

'It is. The repairs to the roof brought a huge bill last year, and now some of the windows need to be replaced. I don't know where to find the money for that.' His shoulders sagged as he gave her that news.

'Maybe you could sell more of the land? Or get a bank loan?'

'I've already sold more land to pay the bill for the roof repairs, and there's no chance of getting another bank loan.' Katrina drew in her breath sharply. The thought of Castle House belonging to someone else stunned her because she had always believed it would belong to her one day. That she would live here with the man of her choice and bring her children up here to enjoy the sort of wonderful childhood she had known herself. She did not know what to say, or how to come to terms with the idea of Castle House being sold.

'I've had a good offer,' she heard him say then.

'You've gone so far without even telling me?' she gasped.

'You know I wouldn't do that,' he rebuked her.

'So how can you have had an offer if Castle House isn't on the market yet?' she wanted to know.

'It was one of the people who came to stay here for the fishing.'

Katrina was incensed. 'You mean he actually asked you to sell him our home while he was a guest here?'

'It wasn't quite like that. I was talking to him about my problems with the upkeep of the place, and the possibility of having to sell. Before he left he said if I did decide to put the house up for sale he would like to be given the chance to buy it.'

'But you can't sell Castle House! There has to be some way we can keep it.'

'There is no way, Trina.' Her father's voice was unemotional. 'Believe me, I've been through it all until I'm weary of the whole business. The offer he made is a good one, so I'll probably accept it.'

'I can't bear to think about it,' she whispered, bowing her head so that he should not see the moisture that was gathering in her eyes.

Malcolm Kerr felt his own throat tighten. 'I'm sorry, my dear, that it's happened like this. Of course I hoped to leave Castle House to you, but as things are now I'd just be leaving you an enormous burden. At least we can take comfort from the fact that the house will be put to good use in the future.'

'What do you mean?' she mumbled without looking at him.

'Dr Dunbar intends to turn Castle House into a clinic for the treatment of depressive illnesses.'

She shuddered. 'I don't know about a good use. A home for hypochondriacs, more likely!'

'That's not fair, my dear,' he rebuked her gently.

Her tears were too near to the surface now and she did not want to distress him by breaking down in front of him, so with a muttered excuse about having to find her painkillers she ran from the room and up the stairs to her bedroom. There she stood for some time staring out of the window at the view of the loch and the mountains beyond, a view distorted by the tears that slid slowly down her cheeks. She could not imagine life without Castle House to come back to at Christmas and Easter, and for the long summer break from her teaching job in London. It was unbearably painful to contemplate. She was still standing there, lost in misery, when Mrs Muir tapped gently on her door.

'Did your father tell you there's a guest for dinner tonight?' she asked as she bustled into the room. 'I thought you might need help to unpack, or take your bath, with that bad arm?'

Katrina turned to face her and forced a smile. 'Thanks, Mrs Muir, you're an angel, but I can manage. Though I wish we were to be on our own tonight.'

'Your father didn't know you'd be here when he invited Dr Dunbar.'

With that, the housekeeper left Katrina to prepare for the evening meal, to freshen up and put on a kilt of blue and green tartan and an emerald sweater. The guest would probably be some old friend of her father's she decided as she brushed out her shoulder-length auburn hair and powdered her nose.

The grandfather clock in the hall chimed seven as she descended the stairs but there was no indication that her father's guest had arrived. No car standing at the foot of the steps that led into the garden. The guest was late in arriving, and her father would not like that, being a stickler for punctuality. Already he was pacing the hall floor, frowning. Then his face cleared.

'That sounds like Matthew now,' he called over his shoulder to her as he hurried towards the open front door.

Katrina listened, puzzled. She could not hear any approaching motor vehicle. All she could hear was the sound of a helicopter over the house. Her father did not seem to be at all disturbed, even though the helicopter was now coming to rest on the circular lawn in front of Castle House.

It was then that the suspicion entered Katrina's mind. This was no old friend of her father's! His friends did not arrive by helicopter to talk about fishing or golf or army days. The man who made his unhurried exit from the helicopter and advanced briskly towards Malcolm Kerr had to be this doctor who wanted to buy their home.

Her lips tightened as she surveyed him and found him a little above medium height and slender, with a lean clever face, a slightly hooked nose and arched eyebrows. She was certainly not going to allow him to talk her father into selling him their home. As soon as she had the chance to be alone with him she would tell him that he was wasting his time. She took a deep breath, ready for the battle she was certain was about to begin.

'Katrina, I'd like you to meet Matthew Dunbar. I mentioned earlier to you that he had stayed here for one of our fishing holidays. Matthew, my daughter Katrina.'

A hot tide of anger rose inside Katrina. When

the doctor held out his hand to her she quite deliberately indicated that her injured arm prevented her from shaking hands with him. This seemed to cause him some amusement.

'There's no law that says one can't use the left hand to make contact, as far as I am aware,' he told her in an unmistakably American accent. 'Certainly not in my country!'

'But we are not in your country now, are we Dr Dunbar?' The cleft in Matthew Dunbar's strong chin seemed to become more pronounced. His grey eyes mocked her as he surveyed her for what appeared to her to be a very long time.

Then he hit back. 'I don't think one could quite truthfully say that, Miss Kerr, since I am certainly of Scots descent and even more certainly determined to establish myself here in Scotland as soon as possible,' he informed her crisply.

So Matthew Dunbar was not going to waste any time in wresting the family home from her and her father! She would have to stop him, somehow, but how? She tried hard to control her feelings as she moved with her father and his guest into the drawing room, but her heart was thumping hard and she kept her hands clenched to stop their trembling. Because the evening had turned chilly Mrs Muir had lit a fire of pine logs and the scent of these was pleasing, but the cosy effect of the firelight was spoiled for Katrina by the presence of Dr Dunbar. His personality seemed to dominate the room.

'I didn't think I'd have the pleasure of meeting you so soon, Miss Kerr,' he said as her father moved away from them to pour sherry for her and malt whisky for himself and his guest.

'I didn't expect to be here tonight,' she replied tersely. 'I only came because I couldn't do my job with an injured arm.'

'So your misfortune has become my own good fortune.'

She frowned. 'I don't follow you –'

'I mean, we would have been certain to meet, sooner or later, and I'm very pleased that it turned out to be sooner. Though I don't suppose you are, under the circumstances?'

'No.'

'Your sherry, my dear.' Her father handed her the delicate glass of pale gold liquid.

She reached for it with her right hand, instinctively, then winced as pain caught her. Before she had recovered, Matthew Dunbar was taking the glass from her and placing it on a small table.

'That hurt, didn't it?'

'Yes.' She was angry with him for noticing, and for expressing his concern.

'Katrina was involved in a car accident a few days ago,' her father explained as he handed the American a cut glass tumbler containing a generous tot of whisky.

'I'm sorry to hear that. What happened?'

His perceptive glance seemed to be taking in all the grazes and bruises which still marred her fine pale skin. Taking in the evidence of her recent tears, as well, she guessed with resentment against him building up inside her again.

'I'd rather not talk about it. In fact I've come home to forget about it and get a bit of peace and quiet if I can,' she replied brusquely, and knew as she did so that she had displeased her father with her hasty dismissal of Matthew Dunbar's interest.

'In that case I'll drink to your complete and speedy recovery,' the American said as he lifted his glass.

When Mrs Muir entered the room a moment later to say that dinner was ready Katrina was surprised by the friendly way he greeted her. 'I'm very well, except for my arthritis, Dr Dunbar,' she answered in response to his enquiry about her health. 'I've made your favourite casserole of venison and mushrooms in red wine for dinner.'

'It was good of you to remember how much I enjoyed it on my last visit, Mrs Muir, but then I enjoy most things that you cook for me.'

Katrina's brows drew together as she heard that. It sounded as if Matthew Dunbar had been a frequent guest in her home while she had been working in London. Annoyance simmered within her as he waited for her to precede him through the door that led into the dining room. Once in there she found that Mrs Muir had placed him opposite to her at the oval mahogany table which was beautifully dressed with lace-edged linen, old silver and cut crystal, and a bowl of pink roses.

She eyed the portion of smoked salmon garnished with cucumber with little interest, even though it was one of her favourite dishes, and wondered how she was going to get through the meal. Matthew Dunbar, she noticed, was tackling his food with enjoyment and at the same time engaging in conversation with her father about the salmon fishing on the stretch of the loch which bordered the Kerrbridge Castle Estate.

'I'm looking forward to being able to fish more often when I come to live up here,' she heard him say, as though the sale of her home to him had already been concluded.

She scowled at him, which brought a quirk to his lips and a gleam into his grey eyes as he asked 'Do you fish, Miss Kerr?'

'I used to.'

'But you don't now?'

'I live in London now.'

'You must miss this place. Why did you choose London?'

'It was the only place where I could get the sort of job I wanted when I finished at art school.'

He was still considering that statement when Mrs Muir brought in the venison and dishes of vegetables. Katrina helped herself clumsily to these with her left hand.

'Your father showed me some of your paintings. I liked them.'

'They are not all that good.'

'That's a matter of opinion, I'd say.'

'They were the work of a beginner.'

'You are too modest, isn't she Mr Kerr?' He was determined to go on discussing her work. Was it a way of getting round her father, this praise of her work which she did not consider was justified?

'No, I'm just totally honest,' she put in before her father could say anything. 'You should visit the galleries in Glasgow or Edinburgh if you want to see good pictures.'

'I've already been to some of them, and I still like your style of painting.'

Talk moved on then as the meal progressed to the raspberry trifle which was one of Mrs Muir's specialities. As they were finishing this the housekeeper interrupted them to ask Mr Kerr if he would take a telephone call. Now was her chance, Katrina decided.

'I know why you are here,' she began hurriedly. 'My father told me.'

Matthew Dunbar smiled. 'It was very good of your father to invite me to spend these couple of quiet weeks with him. The last time I was here there were other guests and we did not have as much time to talk as I would have liked.'

'I mean – I know the real reason why you are here,' she rushed on.

He seemed amused. 'Do you?'

'Yes. You are here to try and persuade my father to sell you our home so you can make a lot of money by turning it into a sort of hotel for your rich hypochondriacs.'

He looked suddenly forbidding with those arched brows drawn together above his high-bridged nose. His voice had an edge to it.

'I find it hard to believe that such totally inaccurate information was given to you by your father, Miss Kerr. I may not have known him for long but I've certainly been acquainted with him for long enough to know that he would never speak in such a way about someone he had invited to be a guest in his home. In fact I am certain I would not be here at all if he did not feel a degree of sympathy for the unhappy people who need my help so badly, and who need a place as peaceful and beautiful as this to live in until they are fit enough to go back to their own homes. I can assure you that my patients are not hypochondriacs, and I find it extraordinary that you should feel so bitter towards them and me.'

Her cheeks began to burn. 'How would you feel, in my place?' she demanded. 'Having your home taken over by strangers –'

'There are strangers in your home quite often already, are there not? These businessmen who come in response to advertisements offering them sporting holidays, at a price!'

'They don't own the place, as you intend to do if you get the chance, Dr Dunbar.'

'I would not have made my offer to your father if he had not made it quite clear to me that he would have to sell to someone fairly soon.'

'So you saw your chance and made your offer before he could change his mind!' she burst out.

'You are quite wrong about that. At the time I was considering buying another property. It was only when that proved to be unsuitable and I came back here to think things over in peace and quiet that I came to realize I could do my work as well here as anywhere else. Maybe better.'

Katrina felt deflated. This man seemed able to supply a valid reason for everything he did, and at the same time to make her feel as if it were she who was in the wrong and not him. It was a fairly new experience for her, and one she found hard to come to terms with.

'It will kill my father, having to leave here. He loves the place so much.' Yet even as she said that Katrina was remembering what Daig had said about her father's health; that he should take things easier and give up running the sporting house parties.

'He won't be leaving here if he accepts the offer I've made to him,' Dr Dunbar's voice broke into her thoughts. 'Didn't he tell you what I'm proposing to do?'

She shook her head.

'So you don't know about the offer I've made to

convert three estate cottages into one good dwelling for him, and to allow free use of the estate to you and him for as long as you retain ownership of that dwelling?'

Again she shook her head. She was completely bereft of words as she took in the full implication of Matthew Dunbar's statement. How would her father feel about living in these cottages which had once housed his estate workers? Before she had sufficient time to consider the idea her father came back into the room.

'Sorry to have to leave you like that, Matthew, but I'm sure Katrina has kept you entertained in my absence.' The smile slipped from his thin, scholarly looking face as he became aware of the tension which had built up between Katrina and Matthew Dunbar.

'She has certainly done that, Malcolm,' Dr Dunbar told him grimly.

Katrina rose to her feet. 'I'll get some coffee, Dad,' she said before hurrying out of the room.

All at once she felt she must get away from Matthew Dunbar and his challenging glance that seemed to make a mockery of everything she said. Mrs Muir, whom she found stacking plates in the dishwasher, was inclined to comment favourably on the guest.

'A very nice young man, Dr Dunbar. Don't you think so, my dear?'

Katrina did not answer.

Mrs Muir was not put off by her silence. 'He's had a book published about his research into these awful depressive illnesses,' she said.

'I wish he'd never come to Castle House!' Katrina said with such passion that the housekeeper looked at her with disapproval.

'My, your father wouldn't like to hear you speak so about such a fine young man, and one who's a guest in his house!'

Katrina rounded on her so swiftly that the coffee slopped out of the jug she had just filled and scalded her fingers.

'You won't think Dr Dunbar is such a fine young man when you know the real reason he is here.'

Mrs Muir turned a troubled glance on her and sighed. 'I do know the reason he's here. Your father confided in me when he asked me to prepare for Dr Dunbar's visit.'

'Yet he never told me who it was coming to dinner!' Katrina knew she was sounding childish but she seemed unable to help herself.

'He only said he was thinking of selling.'

'He told me he was going to write to you about it. In fact I think he may already have done so because I posted a letter to you yesterday from him. Only you wouldn't have got it before you left to come here because I missed the last post of the day. I'm sure he didn't mean the news to come as such a shock to you. Try to see it from his point of view,' the older woman urged.

'It's Matthew Dunbar I'm angry with, not Dad. I'm annoyed at the idea of him persuading Dad that he should sell Castle House to him and go and live in one of the farmworkers' cottages. He'll hate that.'

'I don't think he will, my dear. I think he'll be relieved not to have to worry about keeping this place going any more, and what Dr Dunbar has offered him isn't just a single cottage. It's three made into one, so he'll have all the rooms he needs.'

'You are on his side, aren't you Mrs Muir?'

Katrina accused.

'I only want what is best for him.'

'How can it be best for him to leave his home?'

Mrs Muir looked at her sadly. 'You still don't understand that he just isn't well enough to cope with the worry this big house has become. You have to accept that, Katrina, as he has done.'

Katrina did not wait to hear any more. She made her exit with such speed that again the coffee slopped over her hand. Outside the door of the dining room she paused to take a deep breath and gain control of herself. Matthew Dunbar must not be allowed to see how upset she was. It would perhaps be best to let him think she had accepted the idea of him taking over her home, at least until she could think up some way of stopping him.

As she pushed open the door awkwardly with her uninjured elbow he came to her aid. 'Let me help you, Miss Kerr,' he drawled.

'I can manage, thank you,' she insisted.

He chose to ignore her words and was already taking the silver coffee jug from her. His cool slender fingers brushed her own warm hands as he did so and the brief contact caused her to shy away from him nervously. He smiled down at her then, as though to disarm her, as silently she poured it for him, silently handed him sugar and cream before filling her father's cup but leaving her own empty. She sat tensely then, listening to the two men discussing the problems that came from running a large estate with a limited work force as though they were already firm friends. Then, when her father was leading his guest to the drawing room with the offer of a dram or two of the fine malt whisky from the nearby distillery she saw her opportunity to escape. It came with the appearance of her father's retriever, who wagged his tail and looked hopefully in the direction of the front door.

'Later, Argyll,' Malcolm Kerr promised. 'Lie down now!'

With a sigh the big pale golden dog flopped down on the tiled floor of the hall, eyes reproachful but body obedient to his master's command.

'I'll take him, Dad,' Katrina offered, her heart lifting at the thought of getting away from Dr Dunbar.

Her father looked doubtful. 'Will you be able to manage with your bad arm? He's not fully trained yet. I don't seem to have had the patience with him that I've had with my other dogs.'

'Why don't I go with your daughter, Malcolm? I haven't had a good walk since the last time I was up here.'

Malcolm Kerr looked pleased at the idea. 'I'll certainly feel happier if you are going with Katrina,' he told his guest, to Katrina's dismay.

'I can manage.'

'I'm sure you don't want your father worrying about you while you are out,' the American put in. 'So why not give in and put up with my company for a little while? I promise I won't talk to you if you prefer it that way.'

She gave in then and turned her back on the two men while she collected an old jacket from the cloakroom at the rear of the hall. When she had slipped this on she saw that Matthew Dunbar was waiting for her by the back door. She frowned. He interpreted this correctly.

'I might as well get used to using the back door, ready for when I come to live here,' he told her with a wry grin.

'Nothing is settled about that yet,' she reminded him curtly.

'It's as good as. Your father has made his mind up to sell this place to me and if you really care about him enough to want what is best for him you are going to have to accept that.'

'We'll see,' she muttered. 'You haven't won yet, Dr Dunbar,' she threw over her shoulder as they left the house.

# TWO

Determinedly, Katrina tramped on, struggling to keep ahead of Matthew Dunbar as they left the formal gardens of Castle House behind and allowed Argyll to lead them into a copse of silver birches carpeted with bluebells. The dog knew that here he would be given his freedom. As Katrina straightened up from unclipping his lead she became aware that Matthew Dunbar had caught up with her and was leaning against the trunk of one of the trees.

All about them the air was soft and damp with the mist that rose from the loch on the other side of the wood, and full of the scent of bluebells. She had always loved this place with its wild flowers, its grazing pheasants and its herd of fallow deer. The sight of the American leaning so nonchalantly there on the tree as though he already owned it brought a lump to her throat. It was to Kerr's Wood that she had come as a child to pick flowers for her mother, as a young girl to dream of becoming an artist, as a young woman to mourn the fact that Daig Hamilton had not waited for her but married Helga instead. Now she was here grieving because soon this man would own her home.

'Do you want me to keep my promise and not talk to you?' he asked quietly. 'Or are you willing to declare a truce so that we may both enjoy this place as it was surely meant to be enjoyed?'

'I don't know what you are talking about,' she began.

'I think you do,' he interrupted. 'You've been treating me like an enemy ever since your father introduced us.'

Since she could not deny that she remained silent and stared past him at the place where the shining water of the loch could be glimpsed as the trees thinned out.

'I'm not going to plead with you to accept my presence here, even though I would much rather you did so, but I am going to remind you that if I don't buy this estate and the house someone else will, sooner or later. If it is very much later it could be too late for your father, since he's no longer well enough to cope with the stress of trying to carry on at Castle House,' Matthew Dunbar went on, quietly.

'How do you know?' she burst out. 'You are not his doctor, Daig Hamilton is.'

'I've been in medicine for long enough to be able to recognize the signs of acute stress and hypertension when I see them.'

'My father hasn't said anything to me about not feeling well.' That was not quite true, was it?

'He probably didn't want to worry you. To bring you rushing up here to take care of him.'

'You mean – he needs to be taken care of?' Alarm flared inside her as she searched his face for the truth.

'He will do, if he continues with his present life-style.'

'He seemed well enough when I was last home,' she said, trying to convince herself.

'Was that before he had the bad bout of influenza?'

She bit her lip. 'I didn't know about that. Why didn't Daig tell me about it?'

'Because you were a long way from home and busy with your job, I suppose.'

'I would have come home, if he had asked me to.' Guilt stirred inside her at the thought that her father had been ill, needed her perhaps, and she had not come to him. A new thought came to her then and was voiced at once.

'If my father is so unwell, won't the upset of leaving here make him worse?'

'He won't be leaving the estate, only the house that is too big for him now. The one he'll be moving into will be much better for him because it will be specially adapted for his needs.'

Because she did not want to believe that, she refused to do so. 'You are only trying to convince me of that so I won't influence my father against you. So you can go ahead and make our family home into your expensive private nursing home,' she accused.

Matthew Dunbar straightened up. He took a couple of swift strides towards her. The leaves above his head quivered as though the wrath that was about to explode inside him had reached up to disturb them.

'Obviously I have been wasting my time, and yours, in trying to reason with you Miss Kerr,' he said crisply. 'Unfortunately you are one of those people who will only see what they want to see, and in your case this does not include the truth. So, while I am a guest in your home, we must try to talk of other, less important, things.'

'I wouldn't think we have anything in common to talk about, Dr Dunbar.' She knew her voice was trembling so she turned aside from him and called to Argyll.

The dog did not return until her third call to him. To her chagrin he did not present himself to her but to Matthew Dunbar, whom he greeted with pleased barks and wildly waving tail. For Katrina this was the last straw.

'Come here Argyll! At once!' she snapped, so that the dog gave her a reproachful look before obeying her reluctantly and allowing her to fasten on his lead.

In silence they made their way back through the wood and from there through the heather and rose gardens to the front of the house because Katrina intended it to be quite plain to Matthew Dunbar that he was a stranger in her family home and that the back door was reserved for friends.

Her father had been watching out for them from the drawing room and came to meet them in the hall. She found herself scanning his face with anxious eyes, looking for the signs that would surely be there if he were really ill. Certainly there were new and deeper lines about his mouth and forehead that even his smile could not completely banish.

'I asked you if you would be joining us for a drink, my dear?' Malcolm Kerr repeated as she did not seem to have heard him the first time. 'Or are you too tired after your long journey?'

Gratefully she seized the excuse he had provided

for her. 'Yes, I am rather tired. I haven't slept properly since I had the accident because of the pain in my arm.'

'Didn't they give you painkillers at the hospital where they treated you?' That was Matthew Dunbar butting in.

'Of course, but they don't seem to be working,' she replied without looking at him.

'Perhaps I could help –'

'If I need anything stronger I'll ask Daig Hamilton. He's our doctor. All I really need is to be left alone.'

Her father gave her a reproving glance that brought instant shame to her for her rudeness.

'In that case, I'll say goodnight to you, Miss Kerr, and hope that you sleep well,' the American said formally as she moved past him to the stairs.

'Goodnight, Dr Dunbar.' Impulsively she turned back to her father, reaching out to kiss his cheek. To assure him that her quarrel was not with him but only with this stranger he had invited into their home. 'Goodnight, Dad.'

'Goodnight, my dear. I hope you feel better in the morning.' He gave her a troubled glance along with the words. He found her attitude bewildering, and hurtful.

Wearily Katrina began to mount the beautiful staircase, hanging on to the banister for support as her injured arm throbbed painfully. Half way up, where the staircase turned beneath a tall arched window, she looked back and saw that the two men were watching her progress from the open door of the drawing room. She was unable to read the expression on Matthew Dunbar's face, but she thought that her father looked distressed. Forcing a smile, she threw him a kiss as she had done as a child when being sent up to the nursery at bedtime with her older brother, who had been killed in a climbing accident while a student.

Now her room overlooked the lawn where Matthew Dunbar's helicopter had come to rest. As she went to draw her curtains she stared down at it resentfully. How was it a doctor could afford to own a helicopter, even an American doctor in private practice? How come he could afford to even consider buying Castle House and the part of the estate that had not already been sold in recent years? She was still pondering on this when Mrs Muir tapped on her door and entered the room.

'I thought a wee milky drink might help you to sleep, Katrina, and maybe you'll have a tablet to take with it,' her old nanny said in a soothing tone. 'You look as if you've been missing some sleep.'

Katrina felt warmed by her concern. 'How kind you are, Mrs Muir.' She took the mug and began to sip from it. Then as the older woman was preparing to leave the room she put a question.

'Why didn't you let me know when Dad had flu, a while back?'

Mrs Muir's face took on a closed look. 'I don't think Mr Kerr would want me to discuss that with you.'

'Don't give me that, Mrs Muir! We know each other too well. If he was ill I should have been told.'

The housekeeper sighed. 'He just didn't want you worried enough to come rushing up here to nurse him. He knows how important your job is to you.'

'Not so important as my father!'

'Well, you are here now when he needs you.'

'Yes, just in time to stop Dr Dunbar from taking our home from him.'

Mrs Muir looked worriedly at her. 'If it's not him it might be someone who wouldn't make such a good offer.'

'Is it such a good deal? If you are forced to stand by and see your family home turned into a refuge for hypochondriacs.'

'That's not fair to Dr Dunbar or his patients, Katrina. They are people who need help badly. My husband had such an illness, and he took his own life while I was still a young woman. If there had been someone to help him it might not have happened.'

It was rarely that Mrs Muir talked about the tragedy of her brief marriage. Katrina thought it was time to change the subject.

'Practising that sort of medicine has certainly helped Dr Dunbar to become rich. I mean, can you imagine Daig Hamilton ever being able to afford a helicopter? Or to buy a place like this?'

The housekeeper shook her head. 'No, the poor man must find it hard going having to pay others to do most of the things a doctor's wife usually does.'

Katrina's frown deepened. 'It doesn't seem fair, does it Mrs Muir? I mean, they are both doctors yet one has money to burn and the other must have a struggle to manage.'

Mrs Muir shrugged. 'The world has always been like that, and always will be. You can't get away from the fact that one young doctor was the son of a tenant farmer, while the other is the son of a pharmaceutical tycoon in America.'

'No wonder he can afford the helicopter!' There

was contempt in Katrina's voice. 'No wonder he thinks he already owns us! Well, if he's going to be here long I certainly am not.'

'Then your father will be very disappointed in you. Please don't make any decision in a hurry, Katrina.'

Katrina sighed. 'I don't know that I can bear to stay on. Things are so different, and I'm afraid of what's going to happen in the future. So afraid.'

The older woman who had known her for so long tried to comfort her.

'You are very tired now after your long journey so things are bound to look black to you. Everything will seem better in the morning when you've had a good sleep.'

Katrina touched the lined cheek that was nearest to her with a light kiss. 'You are so good to us, Mrs Muir. What would we do without you?'

'Away with you now to your bed and stop worrying,' came the answer.

Amazingly, since she had so much on her mind, Katrina slept well and did not wake until far into the morning. Then, yawning and stretching, she staggered to her window to look out at the beauty of the sun-drenched landscape. The sight of the helicopter beneath her window gave her a jolt and the feeling of well being which had filled her on waking in the familiar room evaporated rapidly. She turned her back on the view and went to shower before going downstairs to the kitchen in search of tea.

'I was about to bring some up for you,' the housekeeper told her.

'It's nearly lunchtime. I ought to have been up before now.'

'Och no! Not on your first morning home. I looked in on you a couple of times but you were sound asleep. You must have needed the extra rest.'

Katrina drained the china mug of tea then rose from her seat at the kitchen table. 'Do you know where my father is, Mrs Muir?' she asked.

'He went off with Dr Dunbar to look at the West Row cottages.'

Katrina sucked in her breath. 'The American doesn't believe in wasting time, does he?'

'To a busy man, time is money,' came the house-keeper's response. Her closed expression warned Katrina that she was not in the mood to listen to any more critical remarks about Dr Dunbar so Katrina decided to take Argyll for the sort of long walk that she missed while living in London.

Soon she found herself on the shore of the loch with the shingle crunching beneath her feet and the big golden dog racing in and out of the water to retrieve the sticks she threw for him. She spent a happy hour there enjoying the increasing warmth of the sun and listening to the gentle swish of the water lapping the shore. It was only when she became aware that she was feeling hungry that she headed back to the house. Her footsteps quickened as she recognized Daig Hamilton's car coming to a halt in front of the building.

She watched as he ran up the steps and entered the house. A small knot of anxiety gathered inside her and added speed to her feet so that she was breathless by the time she reached the hall to find Daig listening to Mrs Muir.

'I expected Mr Kerr back before now. It's not like him to be late for an appointment.'

Daig was glancing at his watch. 'I'm maybe a little

early. I said I'd drop by at the end of my round.'

'Here's Katrina now, she'll talk to you while I see to the meal. I wouldn't want it to spoil when we've a guest staying.' Mrs Muir hurried back to her kitchen and left Katrina alone with Daig.

'I see the helicopter's here again, which means the American is visiting.' Daig frowned as he made the observation.

'Yes. I was worried when I saw your car come tearing up the drive.'

He smiled at her. 'Just a routine visit Katrina. Nothing to get worried about.'

'Does he need routine visits, Daig? Is he really ill?'

'I think he does, since his illness early in the year.'

'Which no-one told me about.'

'On his instructions. Otherwise I'd have let you know. He's been through a lot in the last few years, first losing Robert then your mother. The worry about the house hasn't helped,' Daig added.

'Do you think it would be best for him to sell, Daig?'

He was slow about answering that. 'It's not really for me to say what he should do, other than he should take life easier. Which means, I suppose, getting rid of the stress that trying to keep Castle House in good repair puts on him.'

'That's what Matthew Dunbar said.'

'Well of course he would, if his visits mean what I think they mean. What village gossip says they mean, that he's after buying this house to convert to a convalescent home for his wealthy patients.'

'It doesn't seem fair,' Katrina began, then broke off as she heard the sound of her father's car stopping in front of the house. 'I'll see you later, Daig,' she threw over her shoulder as she made a dash for the stairs to make herself tidy for lunch with her father and his guest.

Brushing her hair before the dressing table in her room, she wondered if her father would ask Daig to join them for lunch, but before she was ready to go down again she heard the gravel flying from beneath the wheels of the estate car Daig used to cover the many miles of his sparsely populated rural practice. That meant there would only be herself, her father and the American doctor to eat lunch in the shabby but elegant dining room. Her heart sank at the idea of having to sit for an hour or more in Matthew Dunbar's company. She waited as long as she dared before going downstairs as Mrs Muir carried in the soup tureen.

Her father and his guest were already deep in conversation when she joined them. Both rose to their feet at her entry. It was Matthew Dunbar who spoke first to her.

'Good morning, Miss Kerr. Or ought I to say good afternoon?'

She shrugged. 'It really doesn't matter.'

'You look better today, Katrina,' her father remarked. 'Mrs Muir tells me you slept well.'

'Yes. Then I took Argyll for a long walk. Daig was here when I got back. I thought you might have asked him to stay to lunch.'

'Not today. There are things to be discussed today which only concern Matthew and me, and you of course,' her father added.

That sounded ominous to her, as if he had already made up his mind about the sale of the house to Dr Dunbar. She soon discovered that her

fears were justified as the meal came to an end and
Mrs Muir brought coffee.

'Matthew and I have been over to the West Row
Cottages this morning for discussions with the
architect about the conversion of them into one
dwelling,' Malcolm Kerr told his daughter.

'So it's all settled?'

'It's almost settled. I'd like to know what you think
about the cottages, or West Lodge as it is to be
called.' His eyes pleaded with her to see things his
way.

'Does it matter what I think?'

'Of course it does, my dear.'

She knew he was embarrassed by her attitude but
she seemed unable to help herself.

'Why, when I won't be here for most of the time?'

'Because the new home we are planning there will
be yours one day, so I want it to be to your liking.
Matthew suggests that we add a separate self-
contained wing for your use when you are here.'

'He seems to have thought of everything,' she
remarked with such irony that her father frowned
at her while Matthew Dunbar watched her with a
glint of amusement in his eyes.

'I have tried to think of everything,' the American
said, 'even though I realize that whatever I offer will
not compensate for the loss of a cherished home.'

Suddenly Katrina had heard enough. All the
anxiety about her father's health, all the dismay she
felt at the thought of no longer being able to call
Castle House home, began to overwhelm her and
caused her to lose control of herself. She poured out
her distress in an avalanche of ill-considered words.

'How can you expect me to believe that when you
are bulldozing my father into this deal? How can

you be so certain that your money will buy you anything and everything that you want? Even the place that has been our family home for generations –'

Hot-eyed and with her throat swelling unbearably, she faced Dr Dunbar for a long, tension-filled moment before stumbling out of the room and out of the house. Of their own volition her legs carried her into the little wood, where she flung herself down on the carpet of bluebells and wept out her frustration. Once, she thought she heard someone coming in search of her, but a startled upward glance showed only a pair of deer in flight from some unseen terror.

Later, she walked to the edge of the loch and bathed her face in the icy water. She felt quite calm now and able to make a decision. She would not stay here where there was the constant temptation to be rude to Matthew Dunbar. Her father would be upset by her abrupt departure, she knew, but to stay would only be to put more stress on him. So she would return to London, and the sooner the better.

# THREE

When Katrina told her father of her decision to go back to London the next day he was both hurt and bewildered. She felt guilty then.

'I don't understand, Trina. You've only been here for twenty four hours. I was hoping you'd be staying for at least a couple of weeks. After all, you can't be fit for work yet,' he protested.

'I have an appointment at the hospital on Friday,' she lied, and hated herself for doing so. 'I'll have to get back to my job as soon as possible too, even if I can't use my arm properly, because I'm planning to put on an exhibition of my students' work at the end of term.'

Malcolm Kerr looked at his daughter with sorrow. He was not fooled by her excuses; he knew perfectly well that she would not have made such a long journey to spend such a short time with him. He was certain she was rushing back to London to get away from Matthew Dunbar. Yet he did not attempt to change her mind for her.

'You must do what you think is best,' was all he said to her once he knew her mind was made up.

Late that evening, as she was walking on the shore of the loch with Argyll she met Daig Hamilton, who was fishing there. He looked up when he heard the crunch of her feet on the shingle and she saw his rugged, freckled features light up with pleasure.

'Hello, Daig,' she said quietly, noticing now that there was a button missing from his shabby tweed jacket and that he was thinner than she remembered.

'It's good to see you, Katrina. I was hoping we'd have some time alone together to talk while you are here.' He left his fishing gear and came to stand closer to her.

'I won't be here for much longer,' she told him. 'I'm going back to London tomorrow.'

Her words shocked him. 'Why? You've only just arrived. What does your father have to say about it? Or haven't you told him yet?'

'Dad said I must do what I think best, though I know he is disappointed.' Her eyes were troubled as she admitted that.

'Do you have to go? Couldn't you try and stay a little longer, for his sake?'

'I can't Daig! I can't! Not while Matthew Dunbar is staying at Castle House.'

She found herself pouring out all her hatred of Matthew Dunbar, all her pain and grief at the prospect of losing her family home to the American doctor. Daig listened with growing dismay, wondering if it would be possible to make her see reason but at the same time feeling deep compassion for her.

'I can't stay on, Daig, because I keep losing my temper and being rude to Dr Dunbar, which upsets Dad. That can't be good for him, can it?'

'No, certainly not.'

She sighed. 'So you do understand why I can't stay any longer, don't you?'

Now it was his turn to sigh. 'Yes, but I wish you weren't going so soon. You haven't been up for ages, and I've missed you terribly.'

'Have you?' she asked softly.

'Why haven't you been home for so long? Is there someone down there in London you'd rather be with?'

He waited a long moment for her answer, and in that time a great wave of sadness washed over her because it was too late now for Daig to realize that he cared for her.

'There was someone, a few months ago, but not any more.'

'What happened? Or would you rather not talk about it?'

She shrugged. 'What happened was that he found someone he liked better than me.' As Daig himself had done a few years ago when he married Helga.

'I'm sorry. You must have been hurt.'

Katrina smiled faintly. Not as much as she had been hurt by Daig a few years ago. 'Not that much. My job still comes first with me. My job, and Dad, and this place.'

'So maybe he wasn't the one for you?'

'Maybe. What about you, Daig? How are things with you?'

He looked away from her to where a few houses were visible on the other side of the loch. One of those dwellings belonged to him, and to Helga when she was at home. Which was not often these days. His loneliness threatened to overwhelm him at times. Especially just now.

'Not good,' he admitted. 'Helga seems to be away more than ever, and when she's home she doesn't seem to be happy.'

'I'm sorry. It must make life very hard for you.'

His mouth set in a grim line. 'I dread having her home now because of the way she drinks, yet her mother tells me she hardly drinks at all when she's staying with her. I don't know what to think or what to do.'

'Perhaps she needs medical help?'

'I've suggested it, but she won't listen. Says she doesn't need help and that it's just me who doesn't understand.'

'It doesn't seem fair that this should happen to you.' There was a great lump in her throat that she swallowed with difficulty.

'I suppose I only have myself to blame,' he said bitterly.

'What do you mean?'

'Well, you know what they say "Marry in haste, repent at leisure". Fortunately I don't have much time for repenting at leisure. At least I have my work to keep my mind occupied. It helps me to keep a sense of proportion.'

There was no comment she dare make on that statement. All she could do was reach out to him, instinctively, offering comfort in the meeting of her hands with his.

'Oh, Trina,' he murmured, with his lips in her hair, 'if only I'd waited for you to finish growing up. You were too young when I went away to medical school, but I should have waited for you.'

He drew her close, so close that she could feel the fast beating of his heart through the thin blouse she wore. For a long, long moment she allowed herself to rest in his arms; gave herself up to the surge of feeling that seemed to be drawing them together like a magnet. There had always been

something between them, something unacknow-
ledged until now. Something that went far beyond
friendship.

Something that was dangerous, she told herself
in the second before his mouth engulfed her own.
His desire for her made him careless so that he
caught her injured arm too roughly and brought
an exclamation of pain from her. Her cry brought
them both back to earth, and reminded them that
kissing was not for them; making love was not for
them.

'I'm sorry, darling,' he said tenderly.

'I must go, I have my packing to do,' she told him
breathlessly as she struggled out of his arms.
'Please let me go, Daig.'

He did so, reluctantly, and put a hand up to
touch her cheek. 'You are right, of course. I have to
let you go, but oh God I can hardly bear to do so.'

'Goodbye, Daig,' she whispered. 'I don't suppose
I'll see you again before I leave, but you will let me
know if Dad needs me, won't you? If he's ill, I
mean. Promise?'

'I promise, darling.'

She left him then and stumbled back along the
shore towards her home, with Argyll trotting
happily beside her. Her heart was still hammering
when she reached the back garden of Castle
House, where she decided to get into the house
unseen if possible because she did not want to meet
either her father or his guest. At dinner she had
managed to evade Matthew Dunbar by asking Mrs
Muir to let her have a small meal in her room as the
pain in her arm was making her feel unwell. Later
she had slipped out of the house with the dog while
her father and his guest were having coffee and

brandy in the drawing room. Now Argyll was rushing, barking wildly, into the house as Matthew Dunbar emerged from the drawing room and met her face to face at the foot of the stairs. She stared at him in dismay, all too conscious of her dishevelled appearance.

'Are you feeling better now?' he asked courteously.

'A little, thank you.' She made an effort to get past him and on to the lowest step, but he was standing in her way. Deliberately, she thought.

'Your father tells me you are going back to London tomorrow. I must confess I was surprised to hear that because I had gained the impression that you were intending to stay for some time.' He eyed her gravely as he waited for her response.

'I was, but I changed my mind.'

'I'm disappointed to hear that. I was hoping you would be here to help with the planning of the new house, as it is to be your home as well as your father's.'

'This is our home, Dr Dunbar!' Anger was beginning to boil up inside her again. He always seemed to have that effect on her. It was as if his presence close to her set alight a torch of fury within her.

'Yes, for the present time, but you have to accept that your father is going to sell it to me. In fact our lawyers are already drawing up the contract for the sale of Castle House and part of the estate to me. So it would be much wiser if instead of opposing me you would co-operate in the planning of your new home,' he said smoothly.

'It won't be my new home,' she flared. 'I've no intention of living in that place, and my father will hate it.'

Matthew Dunbar seemed quite unperturbed by her anger. There was even a trace of a smile on his firm-lipped mouth. 'We shall see,' was his comment. Which left her feeling uneasily that he held all of her future, as well as her father's, in his ruthless hands.

He stepped aside at last to allow her to go up the stairs, which she did with as much dignity as she could muster. When she was close to the top of the first flight he called after her.

'I hope you have a good journey. I'll be seeing you later.'

'Oh no, you won't,' she muttered under her breath as she gave him a final cold glance.

Katrina slept very badly that night, waking continually to try and sort out her muddled thoughts, weeping sometimes for the sadness of Daig and his disintegrating marriage as well as for her own bleak future. Fighting the dull, nagging pain in her arm with bouts of resentment against Matthew Dunbar for threatening to take possession of the only home she had ever known. Because the flat she shared in London was not really a home but merely a base from which she and her flatmates went out each day to their work and their pleasures. She was angrier about the loss of Castle House than her father was, she acknowledged in her calmer moments. He appeared to have accepted this as inevitable. She said as much to him when he drove her to the station the next morning.

'You are going to accept Matthew Dunbar's offer, aren't you, Dad?'

He faced her sadly. 'Yes. I know the idea of my doing so distresses you but there really is no alternative. Even to delay my decision would not help, because the agent tells me that there is a slump in the property market which would affect the price I could expect to get from anyone else. He advises me to take advantage of what is after all a very good offer.'

'There must be something we could do –' she began.

'I've explored what possibilities there were, and now I'm just too tired to go on fighting to keep the place. So I've given in, for the sake of my health. Dr Dunbar is a dedicated doctor and a good man, if someone else is to have Castle House I'd rather it were him than anyone.'

So there was nothing more to be said. They awaited the arrival of the train at the little station in silence. As it came round a bend beneath the towering mountains a lump swelled in Katrina's throat. She did not want to leave those mountains, or her father, but it was too late now because the train was sliding to a halt and her father was lifting her travel bag on board and taking her shoulders in his hands to give her a hug.

'Don't be too long before you come to see me again, Trina, will you?' he called as the train began to move again.

Tears misted her last view of him, but she remained there staring out of the window at that solitary figure which grew smaller and smaller while the train gathered speed. How would she be able to face coming back when the man she hated was living in her home, she wondered with an ache in her heart. It would be impossible.

When she arrived in London her flatmates expressed their surprise at her speedy return. She explained why she had felt compelled to rush back so soon, and found them full of sympathy for her but not really able to understand her feelings since both of them came from such different backgrounds than her own. Both of them were fond of their parents but had no particular affection for the modern homes which they had quite happily left to make new lives in London.

'Maybe you won't mind so much when you get used to the idea,' the older of the two suggested.

'I'll always mind,' Katrina said passionately. 'So would you, if you knew Castle House. It's like a very small castle and it's built from stone that came from the ruins of Kerrbridge Castle, which is on the edge of the estate. Our garden ends on the shore of the loch.'

'It sounds wonderful,' her younger flatmate put in, then added. 'I suppose you'll still be able to see it all if your father is going to have a smaller house on the estate?'

'No! I shan't ever go there again once that man has taken over,' she told them vehemently.

They eyed her with concern, thinking privately that she was making too much of an issue out of something that was more her father's business than hers. Because she was by nature reserved she had never shared with them her dream of one day living in Castle House with her own husband and children. Or allowed them to know of the devastation she had experienced when Daig, whom she had loved since her school days and hoped to make her home with in Castle House, had married someone else.

In the days that followed Katrina tried not to think of Castle House, but, shut in the flat on her own for hours on end while her friends were both at work, it was hard to think of anything else. As she became more depressed by her thoughts she forced herself to go out and visit the art galleries in between the routine visits to her doctor, until at last she persuaded the doctor that her injured arm was healing well enough for her to return to her teaching job.

At the end of her first week back at the huge comprehensive school she felt exhausted and was still suffering at times from nagging pain in her elbow, but her mind was now looking ahead to the exhibition of her students' work which she was planning to stage at the end of term. She had a number of pupils who were really interested in the art classes, and a couple who showed promise in the work they did, so she was happy to give extra time to these at the end of the day.

The exhibition was going to be well worth being looked at by those parents who were interested enough to come along on the open evening, she decided as she slowly leafed through a batch of drawings. So absorbed was she in these that she was startled when the headmaster spoke to her as he came slowly into the art room.

'You've done some very good work here, Miss Kerr,' he told her.

She looked up, her cheeks going warm with pleasure. 'Thank you, Mr Whiteley.' Then she saw the frown that creased his brow.

'That's why I find it so grieving to bring you the news that we won't be able to retain your valuable services to the school next term,' he said awkwardly.

Appalled, she stared at him. 'Why?' she whispered.

He sighed. 'Because of cutbacks in our funding, we are compelled to dispense with two full-time members of staff. Reluctantly we have decided, in view of the area our pupils are drawn from, that it will be best for the school if we make the cuts in the music and art departments. I can't tell you how sorry I am to be losing both you and David Bell.'

A rush of sympathy for David Bell, who had two small children and a large mortgage, washed over Katrina. Then she was back to considering her own position again, and finding it bleak because she had been lucky to get her job at this school with so little teaching experience behind her. Of course it had helped that she was at the lower end of the pay scale, but that fact had not helped her to keep the job when cuts in funding came. What was she going to do now, she wondered as the headmaster left her? The flat she shared with Tessa and Lyn, though spacious and comfortable, was also very expensive so she would not be able to remain there for long if she did not get another reasonably paid job soon. Feeling thoroughly miserable, and with her arm aching in sympathy, she went to break the news to her flatmates.

'Poor you!' Lyn said softly.

'It won't be so easy to get another teaching job if everyone is cutting back,' said the more practical Tessa, who worked in banking.

'I know. That's what worries me.' By now Katrina's head ached with worrying about her situation.

'Do you have to teach? Couldn't you use your art in another way? Say in advertising or publishing?' Tessa suggested hopefully.

'I suppose I could, but I do enjoy teaching. I like

working in a school, belonging to a community of mostly young people. It's really marvellous when you find sometimes that you've got a student who shows promise and who wants to learn from you. I may not have the right sort of experience to get into commercial art,' Katrina ended gloomily.

'Something's bound to turn up,' they tried to comfort her. 'You'll see.'

Something did turn up to take the place of her teaching job, but it was not what any of them had had in mind. It came at the end of the long, hectic day when Katrina had finally finished preparing the exhibition of her students' work. As she pushed open the door of the flat, feeling weary but exhilarated because the other teachers had been so complimentary, she heard the telephone ringing.

It would probably be another call from the boyfriend Lyn was trying to get rid of, she decided, not hurrying to answer it because he had wearied them all with his constant calls during the last few days. If she did not pick the phone up he would perhaps get discouraged, she hoped. When the ringing went on and on she gave a cross exclamation and snatched up the receiver, snapping out the number impatiently. The voice that replied was not the one she expected to hear.

'Daig! This is a surprise! I didn't mean to snap at you, I thought it was someone else.'

'I've been trying to get in touch with you for the last hour or so, Trina. I tried your school but they said you had gone.'

The breath caught in her throat. 'Was it so urgent, Daig? Is it about Dad?' She waited for him to answer while fear grew inside her.

'Yes. Your father is in hospital.'

'Since when?'

'Since early this afternoon. I've just come from there.'

'How bad is he?'

'Quite bad, I think you ought to come as soon as possible.'

Anguish gripped her. 'Oh, Daig, is he going to –?' She could not complete the sentence

He hesitated. 'I don't know. Honestly, Katrina.'

'I'll see if I can get a flight to Glasgow.'

'I'll check on arrivals from here, and get someone to meet you.'

'Thanks, Daig. I'll be there as soon as I can.'

Her fingers were shaking as she dialled the number of the airport and obtained the information that there was a seat on a flight leaving at eight-twenty if she could get there in time. She could, she told herself as she telephoned for a taxi and flung a few clothes into a bag while waiting for it to arrive, then scribbled a note to Tessa and Lyn.

Tessa arrived just before the taxi and listened to her hurried explanation. 'I'm so sorry! We'll ring you in a day or two and hope you'll have better news by then, and we'll send on any letters to you that look as if they might be important. You know, answers to your job applications,' her friend promised.

'The job applications don't seem all that important now,' Katrina said sadly.

'They will be when your father is better.'

'If he gets better, Tess. My taxi is here now. I'll see you sometime.'

The next few hours had a nightmare quality about them for Katrina as she journeyed through the end of the rush hour traffic to the station and

from there to the airport, all the time saying
snatches of prayers in her mind that her father
should get better; that his heart attack should not
prove to be fatal. By the time she reached Glasgow
she was on edge with weariness and anxiety. So
much so that when she scanned the faces of the
people who were waiting to meet the flight in and
could not immediately see the face of Daig panic
set in.

Daig had said he would meet her, hadn't he? So
where was he? She was gnawing her lip with
anxiety when she felt a light touch on her shoulder.
At once she spun round, expecting to see Daig.
Then she froze.

'What are you doing here?' Even as she put the
question she knew what the answer would be.

'I've come to take you to the hospital,' Matthew
Dunbar said.

'I'm expecting Daig, Dr Hamilton, to come for
me.'

'He can't make it. So I said I would come in his
place.'

She was too tired to argue. 'Thank you,' she said
stiffly. 'It was kind of you.'

Matthew Dunbar picked up her bag and tucked a
hand under her elbow as he steered her out of the
building and into the chill wind that blew across the
car park. She felt lonely and afraid as he directed
her towards his car. Afraid of what news awaited
her at the hospital, and lonely because it was the
American who had come to meet her and not Daig.

# *FOUR*

Was that really her father, Katrina thought as she stared at the still, grey-faced man who was lying in the narrow hospital bed amid a welter of electronic monitoring equipment. He looked so lifeless, as though already he had gone to some place beyond her reach.

What would she do if he did not pull through? Who then would be left that she could call her family? A couple of ancient maiden aunts who lived in the Western Isles and kept in touch only at Christmas. She shuddered, then turned her head to see who was standing close behind her. With an uplift of her heart she saw that it was Daig. In a second she was on her feet.

'Oh, Daig, I'm so glad to see you.' She buried her face in his tweed-clad shoulder and felt his arms reach out to enfold her. She seemed to have been waiting hours for him to come, though it was in reality no more than an hour and a half.

'Sorry I couldn't get here sooner. I was on call and there was an accident out beyond Balinluig so I had to go out with the emergency unit.'

His face looked strained, his eyes were dull with fatigue.

'Was it very bad?' She touched his face with

gentle fingers.

'Bad enough. They had to be cut free. Both are in here now, and one is critical.'

Katrina bit her lip as she listened. Poor Daig, he had shed the emergency garments he had worn at the scene of the crash but his mind had not yet managed to distance itself from the horror he had just witnessed. Yet she knew that he loved his chosen work and would not wish to do anything else. All he had ever wanted was to be a doctor, right from the days when as a boy he had found and tended injured wild creatures.

'He's still very ill, isn't he?' She indicated the motionless figure in the bed behind them.

Daig moved away from her to take a closer look at the monitor. 'Yes, but he's holding on to life. So we must hope for the best.'

He urged her away from the bed and towards the door of the small intensive care unit.

'Where are you taking me?' she whispered. 'I want to stay with him.'

'You can come back in the morning. It's best that you go home now and get some rest.'

'I won't be able to sleep,' she argued.

He smiled wearily. 'I still think you should go to bed. You've had a bad shock, and a long journey.'

Already he had managed to steer her away from the ITU and along a corridor which led to the reception area which was empty except for the lone figure of a man who sat in a low chair reading a newspaper.

'Is he waiting for me?' she murmured to Daig.

'Yes.'

'But I –'

'You need someone to drive you home, Trina. I

can't go yet or I would take you myself.'

Matthew Dunbar stood up as he heard their footsteps echoing on the tiled floor.

'How is he?' The question was put to Daig.

'Holding on, just.'

Katrina stared at Matthew Dunbar. Her eyes were hostile. Acute anxiety and utter weariness had taken her over completely, pushing aside common sense and reason. All she could think of at that moment was that ever since the American doctor had entered her life things had gone terribly wrong for her. It had been disaster after disaster. Now she put her thoughts into unwise words.

'It's no thanks to you, Dr Dunbar, that he's holding on! In fact I'd say it's the pressure you've been putting on my father to sell Castle House to you that is responsible for him being so ill!'

'Katrina!' It was Daig who uttered the rebuke. Daig who laid a restraining hand on her arm. 'You don't know what you are saying.'

'I do! I'm saying that we've had nothing but trouble, Dad and me, since Dr Dunbar came to Kerrbridge.'

'Katrina,' Daig begged. 'Please don't go on. You are saying things you are going to regret later.'

She turned reproachful eyes on him. 'I thought you, at least, would have understood how I feel, Daig.'

As yet Matthew Dunbar had not uttered a word in his own defence. He just stood there, staring at Katrina with an inscrutable expression on his face.

Daig looked acutely uncomfortable. 'If you knew the truth, Katrina, you would be bitterly regretting what you have just said. I can tell you that if it were not for Matthew —'

The American doctor silenced him with an angry gesture. 'You are wasting your breath, Daig. Miss Kerr is quite incapable at the moment of rational thought. She is acting like a bewildered child, and should be treated as such. So I'll say goodnight to you, and take her home.'

With that, he grasped Katrina's arm quite firmly and propelled her away from both Daig and the young man who was on duty behind the reception desk. Outside, the night air made her shiver after the over-warm atmosphere of the hospital.

'You'd better put this round your shoulders,' Matthew Dunbar told her as he reached into the back of his car to bring out a thick Aran sweater.

'No thank you! I don't need it.'

He sighed, as though exasperated beyond endurance by the behaviour of a truculent child. 'Do as you are told, for once, and try not to be so darned difficult,' he drawled as he slid into the driving seat, after opening the front passenger door for her.

To her chagrin he left the sweater where it had fallen when she refused to accept it, so close to the front seat that she could not get into the car without stepping on to it. After a moment of hesitation she bent and picked it up, finally slipping it over her shoulders.

'Thank you,' she muttered as he switched on the ignition and prepared to set the car in motion.

'You are welcome,' came his response.

After that there was not a word spoken between them as he drove the few miles from the hospital to Castle House. Katrina sat in numb misery, unaware of anything but the fact that her beloved father was hovering between life and death, until exhaustion set in and sent her into sleep. She awoke with a start when the car came to a halt on the gravelled drive of her home.

She wondered, in those first few seconds when she was mid-way between sleeping and waking, what she was doing in the front seat of this unfamiliar vehicle while the place next to her was empty. Then Matthew Dunbar was opening the door on her side and waiting for her to get out. A moment later Mrs Muir was there, putting a comforting arm about her and asking for the latest news of her father.

'He's still critically ill, but holding on. I wanted to stay with him, but Daig wouldn't let me,' Katrina told her through chattering teeth.

'You were right to come home. I'm sure Dr Daig knows what's best for you. Now come away in and have something warm to drink. You too, Dr Dunbar,' the housekeeper urged.

Feeling light-headed and unsteady on her feet, Katrina stumbled up the short flight of stone steps and into the house, hardly aware of the man who walked a step or two behind her ready to catch her if she should fall because of her exhaustion. Inside the house her father's dog came to welcome her with a warm tongue and a wagging tail, though he left her soon to make his way to Matthew Dunbar, and then to sit by the front door, where he uttered a melancholy whine. This brought Matthew to stroke his head and utter soothing words.

For Katrina this sight of the hated American so obviously on good terms with her father's dog was the last straw. The dog's howl expressed all her own loneliness and despair. With a strangled sob she bent her head and stumbled up the stairs, desperate to be alone with her misery. Mrs Muir made a move to go after her but the American doctor intervened with a few quietly spoken words.

'I'd wait a few minutes, Mrs Muir. Give her time to pull herself together a bit. Then she'll be ready for some food and drink, and perhaps an aspirin or two.'

'I'll bring some coffee and sandwiches to the drawing room for you, doctor, and take some for Katrina later,' she told him.

'Thank you, but I'll come and have them in the kitchen with you if you don't mind?'

'Of course I don't mind. I'll be glad of a wee chat. It's seemed a long time since you left to pick up Katrina from the airport, and I've been so worried about poor Mr Kerr. Will he recover, do you think?'

'It's not possible for me to say, right now, but everything that can be done for him is being done,' was all he could give her in the way of assurance.

While he ate the sandwiches she had prepared, sitting in one of the kitchen rocking chairs beside the solid fuel cooker, she took up a tray to Katrina.

'I was too late, the poor wee lamb is already sound asleep. I expect she'll be feeling better in the morning,' she said as she brought the tray back a few minutes later.

He gave a rueful grin. 'I certainly hope so. Unfortunately at the moment she sees me as the cause of all her troubles, Mrs Muir.'

The housekeeper sighed. 'Katrina was always a bit on the hasty side. Too impulsive by nature for her own good at times, and she hasn't been able to come to terms with the fact that her father has had to part with this house. It's nothing personal to you, Dr Dunbar, I'm sure.'

'I wish I could be as certain of that, but only time will tell.'

'Things will sort themselves out, you'll see, once Mr Kerr is better,' she tried to comfort him as he left to go to his room.

Katrina slept soundly until well into the morning, and woke to find Mrs Muir at her side with a large cup of tea. Instantly she put the question that was uppermost in her mind.

'Is there any news from the hospital?'

Mrs Muir smiled, and Katrina knew then that there was news and that it was good, or at least not bad.

'Dr Daig telephoned just before he left the hospital and said that your father had shown a slight improvement.'

'Oh!' Katrina let go of a long sigh of relief, then said she would get up at once.

'There's no hurry, my dear. Dr Dunbar had his breakfast an hour ago, so you are not keeping him waiting.'

'Has he been here all the time, ever since I went back to London?' Katrina frowned as she asked that question.

'Och, no! The doctor has had his patients to see, down in the south of England. He's been coming and going between there and here. He's a very busy young man. It's a good thing he was here yesterday, though,' the older woman told her.

'You mean so he could collect me from the airport and take me to the hospital?'

'Och, no! Any one of your friends could have done that, but I doubt if any of them could have saved your father's life as Dr Dunbar did.'

That gave Katrina a jolt. 'Do you mean he was

actually with Dad when he had the heart attack?'

'Yes. Didn't Dr Daig tell you?' Mrs Muir looked surprised.

'No.' Vaguely then from her jumbled memories of the night before Katrina brought to mind how Daig had tried to tell her something when she accused Matthew Dunbar of being responsible for her father's collapse, and how the American had stopped him. 'At least, he tried to tell me, I think, only Dr Dunbar stopped him. Exactly what did happen, Mrs Muir?'

The housekeeper gave her the truth then, and in doing so brought a flood of shame to her for the accusations she had made the night before.

'They were down at the cottages looking at the work that had been done there since Dr Dunbar's last visit when your father collapsed. Of course, there's no telephone installed there yet so one of the workmen came running here to phone for an ambulance. Later another man came to tell me that the doctor had got Mr Kerr's heart beating again.'

Katrina listened in stunned silence to more about the life and death drama that had taken place in the cottages which could be glimpsed from her bedroom window. Her mouth went dry as she realized what could have happened if Matthew Dunbar had not been there to give her father prompt medical attention. She shuddered as Mrs Muir came to the end of her story.

'I don't like to speculate on what might have happened if the doctor had not been there with him; if he had just been alone somewhere on the estate walking Argyll,' Mrs Muir finished with a worried shake of her head.

'Where is Dr Dunbar now? I must speak to him,'

Katrina broke in.

'Not until you've got some clothes on, I hope,' came the housekeeper's cheerful response, although Katrina was already out of bed and heading for her dressing gown.

'Do you know where he's gone this morning?' she called over her shoulder from the door of her bathroom.

'I'm not sure. He just said he would be back for lunch, but not to go to too much trouble over that as some bread and cheese would do fine for him. He went on foot, and took Argyll with him.'

She ought to have been up hours ago herself, and giving her father's dog his walk, Katrina knew then. Why was she always getting it wrong with Matthew Dunbar? There was last night's outburst, and all those times when she had last been at home, and now she owed him an apology. It was going to be hard for her to say she was sorry for her hasty words, and to admit that she was grateful to him for saving her father's life.

With this in mind she chose her outfit carefully when she had showered and brushed her hair. Not that he would care what she was wearing. It was simply to boost her own confidence that she donned her newest suit of soft amethyst wool which matched the colour of her eyes, and put on a blouse of toning silk stripes.

Mrs Muir's eyes showed her approval when they met in the hall.

'You'll be going to the hospital I expect, but you should have something to eat before you go.'

'No thanks, Mrs Muir. I couldn't eat anything yet. Not until I've made my peace with Dr Dunbar.'

The housekeeper shook her head. 'He won't bite

you, and it's you who'll be collapsing next after all those hours with nothing to eat.'

Katrina laughed and told her not to fuss. Then hesitated, wondering which of the paths through the estate Matthew Dunbar was most likely to have taken for his walk with Argyll. If she waited here he would come back, sooner or later, but she could not bear to wait while those words which must be spoken were burning so fiercely inside her. Even as she hesitated, she heard the dog bark from some distance away and decided that he was somewhere in the copse, with Dr Dunbar near at hand. The sound of another bark acted as a spur to her feet and sent her hurrying through the garden and from there into the wood.

'Argyll!' she called when she was beneath the canopy of trees. 'Argyll!' If the dog came to her the man was sure to follow, she reasoned. Soon she knew she had been right about that because as her father's dog bounded up to her Matthew Dunbar also appeared.

'Good morning,' he said quietly. 'I thought you would still have been sleeping after your bad day yesterday.'

Katrina moved swiftly over the uneven surface of the bridle path to confront him before she lost her courage. She could hear her own heart thumping madly as she stared at him. Then words came tumbling out of her trembling lips.

'Good morning, Dr Dunbar. It seems I have to thank you for saving my father's life, and to apologize to you for my unforgivable rudeness last night.'

'I accept your apology, but I hardly think any thanks are due to me just because I happened to be there when your father needed help. I only did what any other doctor would have done.'

'All the same, I'm more grateful than I can tell you.'

His face was enigmatic; she was unable to tell whether or not he was pleased that she had made her peace with him.

'I didn't know, when I lost my temper at the hospital last night, what had happened at the cottages.'

'I was only doing my job. Now, shall we talk about something else?'

She managed a smile. 'Yes, I'd like to thank you for walking Argyll.'

'No thanks are needed for that either, since I'm a dog lover and I miss my own dog still.'

'Did you have to leave your dog behind in America?'

'In a way. She died while I was making plans to come here and wondering how she would stand up to being in quarantine, since she was an old dog.'

'I'm sorry,' she whispered. 'You ought to get another one.'

'I will, once I'm settled here.' He picked up a stick and threw it for Argyll to retrieve before asking, 'Have you been in touch with the hospital this morning?'

'Yes. At least, Daig telephoned before he left there to say that Dad had made a slight improvement.'

'Good! You'll feel a lot happier now about him.'

'Yes.' Suddenly then the tension which had filled her ever since she had heard that it was Matthew Dunbar who had saved her father's life evaporated and she felt light-headed. The slender figure of the doctor grew indistinct, the sky seemed to darken and close in on her, and there was a roaring in her ears. She experienced a moment of blind panic, before she became aware that she was now sitting on the ground with her head between her knees.

'Keep your head down, you'll feel better in a minute,' she heard a voice say from a great distance away, then mercifully the darkness receded and her spell of faintness passed.

'I'll be all right now,' she tried to protest, but Matthew kept his fingers on her pulse.

'When did you last eat?' he was asking as she attempted to struggle to her feet.

'I don't remember exactly. I think it was at lunch-time yesterday, when I had a sandwich.'

'I'm not surprised you are feeling faint. That's far too long to go without food.'

'I intended to have a meal when I got back to the flat after school, only Daig rang then to tell me about Dad.'

'Why haven't you had any breakfast?'

'Because I couldn't eat until I'd found you and said I was sorry.'

Quite unexpectedly, he grinned at her. 'Was it such an ordeal for you?'

'Yes.'

'Well, it's over now, so shall we go back to the house and have some of Mrs Muir's good broth?'

Without waiting for her to answer, he took a firm hold on her forearm and turned her in the direction of Castle House. She was very conscious of the hold he kept on her as they moved together along the bridle path and glad of the support he gave because her legs still felt unsteady and her whole inside seemed to be trembling. It must, as he had said, be hunger.

As soon as they reached the hall he called to Mrs Muir and asked her to heat up some of her home made broth right away. He then gently urged Katrina into one of the chairs which were grouped about the kitchen table so that immediately the delicious aroma of the thick vegetable soup penetrated her nostrils and made her feel ravenously hungry.

'I'll set up the table in the dining room for you,' Mrs Muir told them as she bustled about collecting silver and linen.

'There's no need to do that, we'll be perfectly comfortable in here, won't we Katrina?' the doctor insisted.

'I warned her she ought not to go out without food,' the housekeeper worried. 'Now she doesn't look at all well. I don't think those girls bother to feed themselves properly down in London. I expect it's all snack meals and those things they call take-aways, don't you, doctor?'

That made Katrina smile, and Matthew chuckle. 'One of my flatmates is a great cook, Mrs Muir. She makes marvellous meals.'

'She doesn't seem to be feeding you very well. You are thinner than ever, but you are going to be fed well while you are at home this time,' the housekeeper declared.

'I don't suppose I'll be here that long, once Dad is on the mend.' Matthew Dunbar would not want her here any longer than he was forced to have her, after some of the things she had said to him.

'It could be some time before your father is really well again,' he warned her now. 'He'll need to take things very quietly for some months, but I suppose

you will be anxious to get back to your job as soon
as possible, Katrina?'

She noted his use of her first name and knew
that he was eager to establish a less formal
relationship between them. All at once she felt
quite pleased about that, but she decided against
telling him that by the end of the week she would
have no job to go back to. Instead she said 'There's
no great hurry, they can manage without me as
they had to do when I hurt my arm.'

Surprise was mirrored on his face when he heard
that, but he made no comment. Instead he sat
down opposite her and began to enjoy the soup
and the warm crusty bread roll which Mrs Muir
had served for both of them. When the soup was
finished there was a fruit flan and the cheese board
to take its place, and at this stage Matthew began to
outline his plans for the West Row Cottages which
would soon be her father's home.

'I'd like you to go over there with me as soon as
possible to see the work that has been done already.
I'd like your approval of the annexe which will
form a self-contained unit for you to use when you
are visiting your father,' she heard him say then.

'There was no need to go to those lengths. I
mean, I won't be here all that often,' she began.
Then it occurred to her that if she did not manage
to get another job fairly soon she would not be able
to go on living in the flat with Tessa and Lyn, and
then she would perhaps be glad to join her father
in West Lodge.

'All the same, it was your father's wish that you
should have a small place of your own in the West
Lodge. Somewhere you could shut yourself in with
your painting, if you wished.'

Katrina was touched by this evidence of her father's thoughtfulness, and excited at the idea of having somewhere to paint until she managed to find another teaching job. While she was still smiling at the thought of this, a hefty crash sounded from the floor above her head.

'What on earth's going on up there? Is there someone staying that I don't know about? Or are there workmen in repairing something?'

Matthew Dunbar exchanged glances with Mrs Muir, then the housekeeper hurried to explain. 'It's the plumbers who are putting in new bathrooms on the top floors.'

Katrina's eyebrows rose. 'New bathrooms?'

It was Matthew who answered the question in her voice. 'As the two top floors are not in use I decided to get work on them started at once.'

'You mean – before my father had even moved out? Before Castle House was legally yours?' Her temper was at flash point again.

He met her hot gaze with steady grey eyes in which lurked a hint of amusement. He helped himself to a substantial wedge of Orkney cheese before correcting her.

'Not before Castle House was legally mine. The house and the parkland, except for the farms, has belonged to me officially since the end of last month.'

'Then why was my father still living here? Why is Mrs Muir still here? Why am I here?'

Her anger smouldered on. Matthew was aware of it as he laid aside his cheese knife and gave all his attention to enlightening her.

'Firstly, your father was living here until he went into hospital because West Lodge was not yet ready for him to move into and I did not want to put him to the inconvenience of making two moves within a short time. Mrs Muir is here because she has decided not to retire yet from housekeeping for your father because his new home will be so much easier to run.' Matthew paused, then went on. 'As for you, Katrina, you are here as my guest for as long as you feel able to stay. Does that answer your questions?'

She sighed. 'Yes.' Her mind was full of shock and bewilderment. She simply did not know how to cope with the situation she now found herself in. It would have been easier for her if she had still hated him, but at some time during the last hour or so she had stopped hating him. Where did she go from there?

# FIVE

'Why didn't Dad tell me that everything had been signed away?' Katrina looked to the housekeeper for an explanation.

Mrs Muir looked troubled. 'I can't really say, my dear. He hasn't been well, and maybe he thought it best not to mention it, as you were so against the whole thing.'

Katrina turned her attention to Dr Dunbar, who was watching her intently.

'Couldn't you have postponed the completion date and given my father more time to move out, instead of bringing in hordes of workmen while he was still here?'

'Unfortunately, no. Because you see my existing nursing home is to be demolished due to a road widening scheme at the end of September. As I didn't want to subject some of my older patients to two moves in quick succession, I've been compelled to move with all possible speed on this house.'

Katrina rose to her feet. Once again he was coming up with a good reason for his actions and making her see that she had spoken too hastily. She must get away from him before she made a fool of herself again.

'I'll go and look at the West Row cottages

immediately, Dr Dunbar, and arrange to move in there as soon as I possibly can. I wouldn't want to be responsible for holding up your plans,' she said hurriedly.

With that she marched out of the kitchen, leaving both Matthew Dunbar and Mrs Muir staring after her in astonishment. Matthew made a move to go after her but Mrs Muir put a restraining hand on his arm and gave a few words of advice based on the years she had known Katrina. 'I'd let her be for a wee while, doctor. She'll simmer down if she's left to herself. She was always a bit hasty, but a good girl for all that.'

Katrina raced down the front steps and along the drive at such speed that her feet sent the gravel flying beneath them. She did not stop until she reached the row of grey stone cottages set close to the perimeter of the estate. A couple of vans stood beside the buildings and she could hear sounds of work going on inside one of them. Her feet came to a halt then and she stopped to get her breath back and at the same time take a look at what was being done.

The exterior of the three early Victorian dwellings had been left almost untouched. In the centre a small door had been removed and a larger and more ornate one with brass fittings installed. Where the other two small doors had been, patio windows now opened off the front rooms into the garden. She entered through the main door and looked about her at the square hall, then a spacious drawing room to one side of the hall and a dining room to the other. Both of these were full of light, due to the new windows, and gave views of the copse and the loch. Behind the main rooms she found a large, well fitted kitchen, a small utility room, a study, and a cloakroom.

Katrina said good morning to a young man who was fitting a radiator in the study before making her way up the staircase to explore the rooms on the upper floor. Four double rooms, two bathrooms and an immense linen cupboard awaited her inspection before she went downstairs again.

It was then that she saw the door she had not noticed before because it was tucked away in a corner of the hall, almost as a cupboard might have been. Full of curiosity, she tried the handle and found it locked. The sound of a workman crossing the hall brought her head round as she asked her question.

'What's behind this door?'

'The annexe, miss.'

'Where's the key?'

'I can't say for sure. It was handed over to the doctor as soon as work on that section was completed.'

'You mean – that part of the house is finished?'

'Yes. It was finished yesterday. Mr Kerr was here looking at it when he was taken ill.'

'Is that the only door, or is there another?'

'There's one on the outside of the house, but it will be locked as well. The doctor said it was to be kept locked, once work on it was completed.'

'I see. Thank you.'

She waited until the workman had disappeared into one of the rooms before going outside in search of the other door. This she discovered at the left hand side of the house, where former outbuildings had been attached to the main building as a single storey unit. Close to the door a neat brass plate bore her name Miss K.M. Kerr. Her lips tightened as she looked at this. He had thought of everything, it seemed to her, so determined had he been to gain possession of her home in record time. Now he actually owned Castle House and there was nothing she could do about that, but she would not remain there as his guest. Not for another single night, she vowed.

With this thought uppermost in her mind she rested her hands on the nearest broad window ledge and peered through the glass to see if it would be possible for her to move into the annexe immediately. The room revealed to her was large and full of light, it would be perfect for a studio, she decided before moving on to the next window ledge and her first glimpse of a small but well fitted kitchen. She was startled then when Matthew Dunbar spoke from only a few feet away from her.

'You'll get a much better view from inside. I've brought the keys for you.'

She spun round to face him as he thrust a hand into the pocket of his cords and brought out a bunch of keys, which he held out to her.

'Thank you,' she muttered, taking the keys from him with fingers which were still gritty from their contact with the stone.

He seemed in no hurry to go away and leave her to take her first look at the property on her own, so she turned her back on him and inserted the largest key into lock and opened the door, stepping inside the largest room and finding herself looking down through a huge double-glazed window at the end of the loch and the corner of the village which was nearest to the estate. To her relief, Matthew Dunbar did not follow her. She was able to go alone into the tiny kitchen, to the beautifully fitted bathroom, and to the spacious bedroom at the back of the annexe which looked up into the tree clad hill behind.

The accommodation in the annexe was far superior to her share of the flat in Streatham, she had to admit to herself as she locked the door again and went out to face the man who was waiting for her verdict.

'Will it do for you? As a holiday home I mean. A place where you can paint, or just be on your own.'

'Yes, it will do well enough.' She would not allow him to see how delighted she was with the annexe, with the simple, plain design of it and the well-loved views to be enjoyed from its windows. 'It's finished, isn't it? So I can move in right away?'

He seemed taken aback by her suggestion. 'There's no need for you to do that. I can't see any reason why you shouldn't stay on at Castle House for the time being and furnish this place at your leisure.'

'I'd rather be here, out of the way!'

He frowned at that. 'I don't want you to feel compelled to move out of your home immediately. The painters and plumbers and joiners can get on with their work in the other rooms and leave yours until last.'

She faced him with a sombre gaze. 'It isn't my home any more, is it Dr Dunbar?'

Matthew's mouth tightened. 'So you haven't forgiven me yet? Well, I suppose it was too much to expect at this stage. Shall we at least declare a truce for the time being so that I can drive you to the hospital to see your father? I imagine you'll want to see him as soon as possible?'

'Haven't you got things to do, since you are in such a hurry to open your nursing home?'

'Of course, but they can wait for a couple of hours. They'll have to wait, because Mrs Muir tells me your father was having trouble with his car, so you won't be able to use that.'

Her heart sank. 'What sort of trouble?'

'The starting motor keeps jamming, I believe.'

'It would! Everything that can go wrong has gone wrong, lately.' She could feel tears of frustration beginning to prick behind her eyes and was terrified that they might escape, so she went to stand beneath the shade of the rowan tree that grew on the far side of the annexe. Putting distance between them so he should not see her distress.

'Not quite,' he reminded her very quietly. 'Your father is still alive, and he'll be waiting to see you. So shall we go now?'

A little later, sitting beside him in the front of the powerful car as they left Kerrbridge behind, Katrina struggled with her emotions. She knew she had been unfair to Matthew Dunbar. Some people would say she had been downright rude. Yet she seemed unable to help herself. There was something in his personality that struck sparks from her own volatile nature.

Would it have been like this if they had met in some other way, she found herself wondering. Was the friction between them due solely to the fact that Matthew had persuaded her father to sell him their home? Or would it have been the same no matter where or how she and Matthew Dunbar had met?

Her thoughts kept her so deeply engrossed that she made no attempt to converse with him, and he, sensing her mood, respected her silence until they reached the hospital car park.

'Thank you,' she said as he came round to open the door of the car for her. She was prepared for him to go back to the driving seat then but he did not do so. Instead he walked beside her to the entrance, and from there to the Intensive Care Unit.

Once there, he made for the young woman doctor who was just leaving a patient. She appeared to recognize him at once, and be delighted to see him.

'Matthew! I'm so glad you dropped in. Your friend Mr Kerr is still very poorly but his condition is stable now. I'll come with you to have a word with him.'

Katrina felt shut out as the vivacious dark haired woman who could be only a few years older thàn herself began to move away with him. He seemed to have forgotten that she was there. She hesitated, trying to cope with the surge of feeling that caught her so unexpectedly, then saw that he was turning back to her.

'Come along, Katrina! Alexa, this is Malcolm Kerr's daughter. You haven't met her before because she only arrived from London late last night. Katrina, this is Dr Alexa Dale, who is helping to look after your father.'

She felt her hand being gripped briefly in the cool fingers of a tall, slender girl whose black hair was cut short to curl about a heart shaped face in which a pair of vividly blue eyes looked frankly at her. The starched white coat worn open over a plain deep blue cotton sweater and with a stethoscope topping the whole ensemble made a picture so immaculate that she immediately felt conscious of her own windblown hair tumbling about her shoulders, and the faint film of perspiration that the heat of the unit was bringing to her upper lip.

'Hello, Miss Kerr.' The blue eyed woman had taken in every detail of her appearance and was now giving Matthew a long and beautiful regard. 'I'd like a word with you in private, Matthew, if you can spare the time.' The voice was low pitched and attractive. Little wonder that Matthew responded to it with a wide smile which illuminated his normally rather serious features.

'Of course, Alexa. I'm free until Katrina is ready to leave again. Shall we go to your office?'

It sounded to Katrina as though the two doctors were on very friendly terms, which surprised her. How could such a busy man spare the time to make friends? Maybe it was worth while making the effort for a woman as beautiful as Alexa Dale?

'Shall we go and find your father? He'll be pleased to see you, and you'll feel happier about him today.'

With a brilliant smile over her shoulder at Matthew, Alexa led Katrina to her father.

He was where she had left him the night before, opposite to the central nursing station. Dr Dale approached him cheerfully with the words 'I've brought your daughter to see you, Mr Kerr,' as though she had been personally responsible for her being here, Katrina thought, and knew a niggle of irritation as Alexa Dale flashed her father another of those brilliant smiles of hers before leaving them alone.

'Hello, Dad. How are you feeling today?' she asked softly and was rewarded by the way his eyes filled with joy at the sight of her.

'Better than I was yesterday, so they tell me,' he said in a weak voice.

'You certainly look better than you did when I saw you last night.'

He did, but not very much. There was still a greyness about his face, a look of utter exhaustion. He had worn himself out with the fight to keep Castle House, and lost in the end, she thought with a pang.

'I'm sorry you had to come chasing up here like this,' he began.

'I came because I wanted to come. Because I wanted to see you.' She picked up one of his bony hands and gave it a squeeze.

'What about your job?' he worried. 'Won't it make things difficult for you at your school?'

She shrugged that off. 'They managed without me when I hurt my arm.'

'That's only a few weeks ago. You ought to go back....' He broke off, visibly distressed.

Because of that she found herself blurting out the news she had not intended to share with him yet. 'They'll be doing without me altogether next term, Dad, because the recent cut-backs in spending on education mean two of us have to be made redundant. The music teacher, and me.'

His face relaxed when he heard that. 'So you'll be here to help me move into West Lodge?'

'Yes. I've been to look at it this morning. I thought I might be able to get on with the moving for you. Save you from some of the hassle.'

'There hasn't been much hassle as yet. Matthew has done everything possible to make it easy for me. Even to allowing me to stay on in Castle House. He insists I'm to stay on until I feel able to cope with moving.'

'That won't be necessary now that I'm here to help,' she was quick to point out. 'I'll get everything ready at West Lodge while you are in here and then you can come straight from the hospital to West Lodge as soon as you are well enough.'

Her father frowned. 'I suppose I could do that, but I don't want to give Matthew the impression that we are not grateful for all he has done to help us.'

'It's been in his own interest to help, hasn't it?'

As soon as she had uttered the words she regretted them, but they could not be recalled now.

'It's time for you to accept what has happened, my dear, as I have done. Since the workmen have been working on the upper floor of the house they've found more work that needs to be done. Work I could never have managed to pay for.'

Suddenly then she knew that he was right, and acknowledging that came as a great relief to her. She felt the weight of the animosity she had been nurturing for so long slip away from her as easily as her father was now slipping into sleep. For a long time she sat there holding his hand, wrapped in a strange sort of peace, until Matthew Dunbar and Alexa Dale came back to her.

'I think I'd better take you home now, Katrina,' Matthew said.

'Yes,' Dr Dale broke in. 'Too much talk will only weary your father, and you must keep off any subject that might put stress on him. Any anxiety would be very bad for him in his present condition. Do I make myself quite clear?'

Katrina bit her lip. It sounded, from the woman doctor's warning to her, as if Matthew Dunbar had been briefing her on the background of her patient, maybe on her own opposition to his purchase of the family home. She did not like the idea of him doing that.

'Do you understand what I'm trying to say?' Alexa Dale was asking now.

'Yes. I understand you perfectly, Dr Dale. I can promise you I'll do nothing to hinder my father's recovery. After all, he's the only close relative I have left.'

There was an exchange of glances between the two doctors that did nothing to dispel her uneasiness. Then she turned her back on both of them and made her way out of the Intensive Care Unit. As she was walking across the reception area on her way out to the car park Matthew Dunbar caught up with her and held open the heavy swing door for her.

'Did you have to tell Dr Dale that I was so against my father selling our home to you, Dr Dunbar?' she asked as she took her seat beside him in the front of his car.

His hands fell away from the steering wheel. 'What on earth are you talking about?' he asked crisply.

'You know what I'm talking about. If you had not been discussing our affairs with her she would not have given me such a warning, would she?'

Now his anger escaped and filled the air about them. 'She should not have needed to warn you against upsetting your father. Your own common sense should have been sufficient to do that.'

Her cheeks burned. 'Surely you don't think I would risk jeopardizing my father's health?'

'Isn't that exactly what you have been doing by

constantly voicing your opposition to what your father saw as the only course open to him when he sold Castle House to me?'

Katrina knew that she deserved the rebuke, but it seemed unfair of him to deliver it now when she had accepted defeat.

'You are quite wrong about that Dr Dunbar,' she said coldly. 'I've already told my father that I'll be happy to move into West Lodge as soon as possible. So if you'll drive me back to Castle House I'll move my things out of your house and into my new home immediately.'

# SIX

As soon as the silent journey back to Castle House was over Katrina went in search of Mrs Muir to tell her of her intention to move at once into the annexe of West Lodge. The housekeeper stared at her in disbelief.

'You don't mean today? Not after the day you had yesterday!'

'I do mean today Mrs Muir. I mean to make a start right now, but I'll need some help with getting my bed and one or two other things over there.'

'You know I'll do all I can to help, Katrina, but I'm not much good at moving anything heavy these days, and I'm not so sure your father would approve of all this haste to move while he is still in hospital.'

'He won't know about it, will he, until he comes home? I can move into my own rooms at West Lodge and be so much nearer while I get his rooms ready,' Katrina explained.

'What does Dr Dunbar have to say about your plans?' Mrs Muir was plainly uneasy about the way things were going. 'Or haven't you told him yet?'

'I don't see that it's anything to do with him.'

'He's been very kind to your father, and to you since you came home. I'm sure you wouldn't want to be discourteous to him.'

Katrina chose to ignore that remark. Already she
was on her way up the stairs to change from her
new suit to a pair of jeans and an old shirt. Soon
she was hauling suitcases from a boxroom so she
could pack clothes and bedlinen. Then she left that
task to telephone Mrs Mackay at Home Farm, who
had two strong young sons.

'Of course Ian and Neil will give you a hand with
your moving, if you can manage to wait until after
the evening milking is done. That big van they use
for the farm shop should do fine if they make a
couple of trips with it. You did say you wanted to
move to the West Lodge tonight?' Mrs Mackay
could not hide her surprise.

'Yes, if I possibly can. There are lots of workmen
in Castle House taking the place apart, so I'd much
rather be out of the way,' Katrina said by way of
explanation for her hasty departure.

'I'm sure you would. It must be very difficult for
you, my dear, having to leave the place where
you've spent most of your life, and for your father
too. No wonder he's ended up in hospital, poor
man. Is there any better news of him today?'

'Yes, he's still very ill but his condition is stable
now.'

'I'm glad to hear it. We've all been very
concerned about him, he's been looking so ill. He'll
be better now you are here.'

'I hope so, and thanks, Mrs Mackay, for saying
you'll help.'

'It's a pleasure. Ian and Neil will give you a ring
about times when they get back from market.'

With her spirits beginning to rise at the prospect
of being able to put some distance between herself

and Matthew Dunbar, Katrina went back to her packing. The time seemed to fly as she filled case after case with the things she intended to keep, and crammed the rest into huge plastic bags to be sent to the next jumble sale held at the village hall. What a lot of stuff she had accumulated during her twenty two years, she thought as she stared at the pile of suitcases and the heap of bags, and there were still all her books and ornaments, lamps and clocks to be packed. She was interrupted then by Mrs Muir, who came to tell her that Daig wanted to speak to her on the telephone.

Daig told her that he had the evening off, and would drive her to the hospital to see her father as he knew her father's car was out of action. She hesitated about accepting his offer.

'I'll need to go very early, Daig,' she explained. 'Because I'm going to move into the annexe at West Lodge tonight.'

'So soon? Are you sure –'

'I can't wait to get away from here, Daig. I can't bear to go on living here now that it all belongs to – someone else.'

'I'll help you with the move then, when we get back from the hospital,' he told her.

'Won't Helga want your company, if it's your night off?' She had to ask that, even though she hated doing so.

There was a perceptible pause before he replied. 'She's not here to mind. She's away again.'

That meant Daig would be coming home from his rounds of visits, or his spells of duty in the village Health Centre, to an empty house and the indifferent cooking of Maggie MacTosh, who acted as general help when his wife was at home and cook-housekeeper when she was not. Poor Daig! On the spur of the moment she found herself issuing an invitation to him.

'If you like, I'll ask Mrs Muir to pack us a picnic and we'll eat it on our way back from the hospital. What do you think, Daig?'

'Yes, please! I'll bring a bottle of wine to go with it.'

'What time will you be here?'

'I'll call for you at six.'

With that settled, Katrina went to find Mrs Muir. As soon as she had asked for the picnic food to be prepared she sensed that the housekeeper was not pleased.

'You'd be best to have the dinner I've prepared for you. I told you I'd have it ready early so you could go to the hospital afterwards,' the house-keeper said with the candour that came from her long association with the family at Castle House.

Katrina smiled at her. 'I'm sorry if I've made you extra work Mrs Muir, but I promised Daig that we'd have a picnic on the way home from the hospital as Helga is away again. I can make up the picnic myself if you are too busy,' she added.

Mrs Muir was not won round by her offer. 'I'd have thought you had enough to do with packing your things for the move to West Lodge. Besides, Dr Daig needs to be careful about not stirring up any more gossip if his wife's away from her home again.'

'Gossip? About Daig?' Katrina could not believe it.

'It isn't a good idea to be seen out on a picnic alone with a young woman when your wife is away. Not in a place as small as Kerrbridge, where everyone knows everyone else.'

'But we've been friends since our school days, and he's taking me to the hospital to see Dad.'

'It's because you used to spend so much time together that you need to be so careful about not setting tongues wagging, my dear. Dr Daig needs to be more careful than most folk, since he's left on his own so often.'

Katrina tried to laugh that off. 'Who's to know about the picnic, except Daig and me?'

Mrs Muir tightened her lips. 'You never know where folks get to these days. Or what they see, now that they all have cars,' she warned. 'A man on his own, and especially a young doctor, is more vulnerable than most people.'

Katrina laughed again. 'What an imagination you've got, Mrs Muir!'

'Well you can't say I didn't warn you,' came the housekeeper's reply.

Although she had laughed at them, Mrs Muir's words troubled Katrina for a few minutes, until she became immersed again in her packing. At five-thirty she abandoned this and took a shower before putting on a cool cotton dress. When she went downstairs she found that in spite of her disapproval Mrs Muir had prepared a picnic hamper for two, with cold chicken and ham pie and a container of salad, with fruit and cheese to follow.

'You're a darling!' Katrina told her, giving her a quick hug just as Matthew Dunbar entered the kitchen.

'I just came to say that I can drive you to the hospital after dinner tonight, if you would like to visit your father again, Miss Kerr?' he began as she moved towards the door.

'Thank you, Dr Dunbar, but there's no need for you to go to the trouble.'

'It's no trouble. I'm going there anyway.'

'I've arranged for Dr Hamilton to take me. That sounds like his car now.'

As she spoke Katrina picked up the picnic basket from the worktop. Inside her she could feel the now familiar tension building up that the close proximity of Matthew Dunbar always seemed to induce in her. Why did he always seem to assume that she would fall in with any plans he made? Did he think she was incapable of making her own arrangements? As she hurried to open the door to Daig her colour was high and her hands were shaking a little.

Daig noticed her edgy state at once. 'What's wrong, Trina? Not news from the hospital, I hope?'

She shook her head. 'No, it's nothing like that.'

'What is it then?'

'It's that man, Matthew Dunbar! He really puts my back up.'

'Why? What's he been doing now?' There was a trace of laughter in Daig's voice that irritated her.

'Saying he would take me to the hospital. As though I'm not capable of making my own arrangements!'

'Surely that's not so terrible? Though of course I'd much rather you went with me.'

'So would I,' she said, loudly enough for Matthew Dunbar to be able to hear through the open door.

Daig took the picnic basket and stowed it on the back seat of his car while she took her place in the front passenger seat. Soon they were traversing the winding road that ran alongside the loch and talking easily together about things that had happened in the area since her last visit to

Kerrbridge. She noticed that Daig talked much about his work but little about any social life he might find time for, and said nothing at all about his wife.

When they reached the hospital she found her father awake and very glad to see her. Though he was startled when she told him she was moving at once into the annexe at West Lodge.

'Why all the rush? Surely there's no need for that?' he protested.

'There is, Dad, as far as I'm concerned. I want to be out of Castle House as soon as possible. So I've arranged for Ian and Neil to come over from Home Farm when they've done the evening milking. They are going to bring the farm shop van, which will be quite big enough to carry the things from my room.'

Malcolm Kerr frowned. 'I don't understand you, Katrina. Your attitude has me bewildered. First you were absolutely opposed to us leaving Castle House, and now you can't get out of it quick enough. I think you are in too much of a hurry.'

'It will be so much easier for me to get your rooms at West Lodge all ready for when you come out of here if I'm already on the spot there. Also it will free my room and bathroom immediately so that Dr Dunbar's workmen can start refurbishing them, since he's in such a hurry to get his nursing home moved up here.'

'The hurry isn't of his choosing. I'm sure he would have liked more time to get things exactly as he wanted them before moving any patients into Castle House Clinic.'

Katrina drew in her breath. 'You seem to be on his side always.'

'I do see yours as well, my dear, but as Matthew has told me more about his work and the problems that go with it I do feel sympathy for him, as I'm sure Daig does?'

Daig, sitting further back from the bed, nodded his agreement then changed the subject for a less emotive one. It was not until they were leaving that Malcolm Kerr referred again to the move.

'Take anything you need to make yourself comfortable in your annexe, my dear. There's far more stuff still left in Castle House than either of us will need for West Lodge.'

'Thanks, Dad. That means I won't need to send for any of my stuff from the flat in London. I can leave it for Tessa and Lyn. I do like the annexe, you know. It will be a great place to use for my painting.'

With that she and Daig left him and began to walk down the long corridor to the exit. As they did so Daig put the question she had been waiting for.

'Am I to take it that you are not going back to London, Trina?'

'Yes. I haven't got round to telling you yet, but the cut-backs in education have made me redundant from the end of this term. So I've no job to go back to. I'll be able to stay on up here until Dad is really well again.'

Daig caught her by her shoulders and turned her round to face him.

'That's wonderful news for me. The best I've had for ages.'

Her heart began to thump madly as he drew her close. Surely he was not going to kiss her here and now in the hospital where he was so well known? She tensed her body, half afraid, half eager, then

heard with overwhelming relief rapid footsteps
approaching from the other end of the corridor.
Her swift attempt to put distance between herself
and Daig was not made soon enough to stop
Matthew Dunbar from glimpsing their moment of
intimacy. Mrs Muir's blunt warning flashed into her
mind then and brought with it a flood of embarrassment.

'Good evening, Daig,' the American doctor
drawled. Then nodded to Katrina.

'Hello, Matthew,' Daig responded, looking him
straight in the eye and not appearing in the least
abashed.

Katrina looked away from them both. Why did
the American always have to come on the scene at
the wrong moment? Matthew did not seem inclined
to linger. Already he was striding towards the
Intensive Care Unit.

'He'll be looking for Alexa, I suppose,' Daig
commented as they moved on. 'They seem to be
rather friendly.'

Katrina felt her inside give a jolt. So her guess of
that morning was correct. There was something
going between Matthew and the beautiful Dr Dale.
With an immense effort she pushed the thought
away from her and quickened her pace so that Daig
had to hurry to catch up with her.

As they drove back alongside the loch from the
small town where the hospital was situated she
began again to think of Matthew and his
relationship with Alexa Dale and became so
immersed in this speculation that she was taken by
surprise when Daig pulled the car off the road and
into a tree-sheltered parking space beside the loch.

'Why are we stopping here?' she asked as the

engine became silent.

Daig laughed. 'Because we've brought a picnic with us. Remember?'

She felt rather foolish then. 'Yes, of course. I thought we might be waiting until we got to West Lodge to eat?'

'No. This will be much nicer. We won't be interrupted here.' He left the driving seat and brought a rug from the back of the car to spread beneath the shade of a rowan tree.

Katrina opened the hamper and spread out the food while Daig produced the bottle of wine he had promised. It was an ideal place for a picnic, only just off the road yet quite private, and with only the bird song to disturb them.

At first she felt completely at her ease with Daig. He was the same good companion that she had known as a child and as a young girl growing up and falling in love with him. They talked about some of the people from those days, mostly long since departed from the area in pursuit of career or marriage, and they talked about her job teaching at the big London comprehensive school and the difficulty she would have in finding another job where she could teach art. Then they spoke about what she would do in the immediate future, and it was then that things changed; changed with such suddenness that she was unprepared for what followed.

'You don't know how much it means to me, Trina, to have you back here where I can see you often. It's like the sun coming out after a long grey winter. Is it the same for you? It must be!'

These last words were uttered as he reached for her lips and caught them in a long and demanding kiss. Her own response to that kiss was at first one of blazing excitement because it was so long since Daig had kissed her and it was something she had longed for, and known was out of reach of her, since he was married. When the first kiss became another and then another, when his mouth had begun to move from her lips to her throat and then into the depths of her neck, and when his hands had begun to search for the softness of the flesh within her blouse, panic stirred inside her.

'No, Daig,' she muttered as she struggled to free herself from a hold that she could no longer control.

'Why not? I love you, Trina. I've always loved you, I know that now.'

He had possession of her lips again while he held her so close that the heat of his body threatened to set alight her own. Yet there were those words that had to be spoken by her because they would not be dismissed even by her own longing.

'There's Helga, Daig, isn't there? You have to remember her.'

His body tensed at the mention of his wife. Then he gave a sigh that was half way to being a groan before he began to talk about Helga, the hopelessness of his position, and the rapid disintegration of his marriage.

'I can forget her for days on end when she's away, but there is always something waiting to remind me that she's still my wife, and yet not my wife in any sense that really matters. She's never there when I need her. Never there when I come in at the end of the day tired and discouraged, or when I'm just plain out of my mind because everything I did for a patient was just not enough to save them. She's never there when I need

someone to share a problem with, or to laugh with.
She's never there when I want someone to share
my love with and my bed with. You don't know
what it's like, Trina. The utter loneliness and
emptiness of my life. If it were not for my work I'd
have nothing.'

Anguish was written on his features, and
underlined by the intensity with which his hands
gripped her shoulders. A great wave of pity for
him washed over Katrina, followed by a surge of
exaltation. Daig needed her at last! This was the
moment she had longed for since she had realized
when she was barely seventeen that she loved him.
She relaxed against him.

'I hate even talking about my marriage, and the
mess I've made of my life,' he said on another long
drawn out sigh.

'Can't you – shouldn't you be trying to get a
divorce if things are as bad as that?' The words
hung between them, a question she had wanted to
ask on other occasions but always been afraid to.
Afraid, perhaps, of the answer Daig would give
her.

'Of course I should get a divorce! I want to be
free, but Helga won't agree. She just keeps
repeating that things will come right for us if we
give them a chance. Only then she goes away again,
or starts drinking again. I don't know which is
worse.'

His pent-up anger communicated itself to her
through the pressure of his fingers on her flesh. She
winced, and a small exclamation of pain escaped
her. This brought instant remorse from him.

'I'm sorry, Trina, I didn't intend to hurt you.' He
relaxed his hold on her. 'I didn't mean to allow my

feelings to run away with me, but being here alone
with you has made me realize how much I love you.
How much I need you.'

The last few words were whispered into her hair
with such tenderness that Katrina felt her whole
being reach out to him. It would be so easy for her
to let herself love Daig.

'Do you remember when we used to come here
as kids on our bikes, Trina?' he was murmuring
now. 'To our special place, our secret place?'

'Yes.' He had promised there, the night before
he went away to medical school, to wait for her to
grow up, but he had not waited. Instead he had
met Helga and married her while Katrina was
finishing her last year at boarding school.

'I must have been mad, not to wait for you Trina,
but you were so young,' he said as though able to
read her thoughts.

'I waited for you.' She bit her lip as she recalled
the intensity of the pain she had suffered when she
heard about his marriage. That pain had lasted
until long after she had gone to work in London
because she could not bear to see Daig with Helga.

'You are still waiting, aren't you? Only now we
both know we are meant to be together. I can't
offer you anything right now except my love. Will
that be enough, Trina?'

She opened her mouth to tell him that his love
was all she wanted, knowing where her words and
his desire would lead them both. Then the words
of warning uttered by Mrs Muir only a few hours
ago came rushing back into her mind. Words she
had not wanted to hear. Words that spelled out
danger for Daig if there was gossip about him. For
a few seconds she fought with her conscience,

asking who was to know if she and Daig became lovers.

'Will my love be enough for you, darling, since I can't offer you anything else yet? Can you manage without the home and marriage I'd like to have been able to give you?'

It should have been so easy for her to answer that, since she had loved him for so long, but she found to her dismay that it was not. Startled by that realization, she drew back from him.

'I don't know if it would be enough for me, Daig. I just don't know! Don't rush me, please!'

# SEVEN

'Sorry, Trina darling! I didn't mean to rush.you. My feelings just ran away with me. Forgive me, please?'

Katrina swallowed. 'Of course. It was as much my fault as yours. I'd forgotten Helga, for a while. Perhaps we ought to be moving Daig?'

'Yes. Just one kiss, before we go, so I know you really have forgiven me.'

There was no passion in the kiss this time, just Daig's lips firm and tender on her own warm mouth then the raising of her hand to be kissed before they began to stow the picnic basket and the travel rug in his car. Katrina could not speak for the sadness that filled her. Maybe tomorrow she would regret being so strong minded and wish she had given Daig all the love and comfort she had to offer, but for now she just wanted to be away from the picnic place and the temptation it presented.

Daig was also quiet as they drove beside the shining water of the loch until Kerrbridge came in sight. When they reached Castle House it was to find the two muscular MacKay sons awaiting them with the van they normally used for their mother's farm shop. It was a relief then for Katrina to give all her thoughts to the moving of her possessions into the annexe at West Lodge, and to supervise the loading of her bed, her dressing-table. her bureau and her small armchair, followed by a shabby chintz covered sofa, a gate-legged table and some dining chairs which she found in the old nursery suite. A couple of bookcases and an antique chest of drawers also came from there before she decided that she had all she needed in the way of furniture.

'You've no carpets down yet, have you?' Mrs Muir pointed out when Katrina went to the kitchen in search of a few necessary items for use in the kitchen of her annexe.

'Oh, no! I forgot about carpets, but I can manage without any for a few days. I don't suppose I'll have much time to spend in the annexe if I'm going to the hospital to see Dad a couple of times a day.'

'There are plenty of old rugs stored in the sewing room, and all the curtains and cushions we moved from the top floor rooms when the workmen moved in.'

'Oh, good. I'd forgotten about needing curtains, too.' Katrina laughed.

'That's because you are in too much of a hurry my dear, as usual,' the housekeeper reproved her. 'I still don't see the need for all this haste. You won't be at all comfortable in the annexe with no carpets on the floors and no cooker in yet.'

The cooker was something else Katrina had forgotten, and she would need a fridge too, but she dismissed Mrs Muir's warning with the remark that she would picnic, or eat at the village inn for the time being.

'There will be food here for you, as usual, since I'll be cooking for Dr Dunbar.'

Katrina had no intention of sharing meals with Matthew Dunbar, but she did not think it wise to say as much to Mrs Muir since it was quite obvious that Mrs Muir was already devoted to him. Instead she changed the subject and asked Mrs Muir if she had time to help her choose some curtains for the annexe from the ones in the sewing room.

'Of course I'll help you,' came the reply. 'Though I'll have to see about taking a pot of coffee to Dr Dunbar and his young lady first.'

'His young lady?' Katrina was unable to keep the astonishment out of her voice.

'The young lady he brought to look over the house with him. I think he said she was a doctor from the hospital.' As she finished speaking, Mrs Muir took the coffee percolator from the top of the Rayburn, set it on the tray alongside china cups, sugar and cream, and departed from the kitchen.

So he had brought Alexa Dale to look over Castle House! He might at least have waited until she had moved out. Or was Matthew Dunbar deliberately underlining the fact that he could now do as he pleased with her former home? Resentment burned inside her as she made her way to the sewing room on the first floor. The sooner she was out of Castle House for good, the better, she told herself. That way she would no longer be in danger of coming into contact with the pushy American doctor.

Soon she was immersed, with the help of Mrs Muir, in sorting out rugs, cushions and curtains and carrying them out to Daig's car ready to be taken to her new home. With so many rooms in the house now emptied and undergoing renovation there were plenty of soft furnishings for her to choose from. Most were old and some were faded, but all were of good quality. She was carrying the last great pile of velvet curtains down the front staircase when the door of the drawing room opened and Matthew Dunbar came out, preceded by Alexa Dale.

'Hello there! You look very busy, Miss Kerr.' There was a hint of amusement in Alexa Dale's voice. Her vivid blue eyes appraised Katrina from her decidedly untidy hair to what could be seen of her crumpled blouse, so that at once Katrina was conscious of the contrast she made to the woman doctor in her elegant tailored suit of creamy silk, her glossy newly styled black hair and her high heeled court shoes.

'Yes, I am very busy. Too busy to stand and talk,' she heard herself reply brusquely. A hot tide of shame washed over her then as she realized how rude she had sounded.

'Then we must not detain you, must we Matthew?' the other woman replied coolly, turning her beautiful eyes to Matthew for his assent.

Matthew was already making his own comment. 'As you see, Alexa, Miss Kerr has had all she can take of my company. She would far rather rough it in an empty house than put up with sharing this one with me for a few more days.'

His words spiked Katrina with a fierce and totally unexpected pain. A pain which brought such confusion to her that she attempted to move on too quickly, caught her foot in a fold of heavy velvet which had escaped from the bundle she carried, and pitched forward to land in a heap at the foot of the stairs.

For a long breathless moment she lay there

feeling utterly mortified, hiding her face in the crumpled dusty velvet and wishing with all her heart that Matthew and Alexa would just go away and let her suffer her indignity in private.

'Are you hurt?' Matthew asked as he put a hand on her wrist.

'No,' she wheezed as she began to free herself from the folds of material.

'Let me help you get to your feet.' His hand moved to take a firm hold on her elbow as she staggered to her feet.

'I can manage,' she insisted when he seemed inclined to hang on to her longer than she considered necessary.

'You should have known better than to carry such a heavy load on a flight of stairs. You could have been seriously injured,' he told her before he bent and gathered in one effortless movement the pile of curtains.

'I'll take them now,' she snapped.

'No, I'll take them. We don't want you ending up as a patient alongside your father.'

It was useless for her to offer any further protest since he was already going across the hall with his burden and out to where Daig's estate car waited. All she could do was stumble after him and watch as he stowed them into the back. He turned to her then, his mouth twitching upwards at the corners.

'Isn't there an old English saying that warns "Most haste, less speed" Katrina? You might do well to be guided by that in future.'

'But I'm not hurt,' she protested.

'You are not hurt this time,' he said fiercely as his glance left her and took in Daig, who was taking his place behind the steering wheel.

She knew then that the warning he gave her had nothing to do with the carrying of heavy loads of curtains and everything to do with her friendship with Daig. It called for a swift response from her.

'I can look after myself, Dr Dunbar.'

An even swifter reply came from him. 'Can you? I wonder about that, sometimes.'

This sparked fresh anger in her. 'Shouldn't you be looking after Dr Dale, not me?'

A slow smile relaxed his firm mouth. 'Dr Dale is perfectly capable of looking after herself, I can assure you. Which is something I can't say with any truth about you, Katrina.'

She gave him a scornful glance. 'You worry too much, Dr Dunbar, and it's not as if I were one of your patients, is it?'

Without waiting for him to answer she slipped into the front seat of Daig's car, slammed the door and fastened her safety belt as Daig switched on the ignition.

'What was all that about?' Daig wanted to know as they moved off.

She shrugged off his question with an edited version of the truth. 'I tripped over one of the curtains. He said I was in too much of a rush to get down the stairs with them.'

'Did I see Alexa Dale in the hall?'

'Yes. It seems he brought her to look over Castle House.'

Daig chuckled. 'So she's winning!'

'What do you mean?'

'Only that she set her sights on our American friend from the moment I introduced them.'

'She's welcome to him,' Katrina said shortly as they drew up outside West Lodge.

It was easy enough after that for her to dismiss both Matthew and Alexa Dale from her mind as she and Daig set to work placing furniture in the rooms of the annexe. The final effect, when the two hefty sons of Home Farm had departed, was not quite what she had expected. Because of the lack of carpets, and because the curtains did not fit properly, there was an unfinished and rather bare look about the studio-lounge and her bedroom. She stared about her with puzzled eyes, and knew by Daig's silence that he shared her opinion.

'It's not quite like home yet, is it Daig?'

'Perhaps you were in rather too much of a hurry to move in. It would certainly have been easier if you had put the carpets down first and got the curtains altered so they fit properly. I don't quite understand what all the rush was about.'

'I didn't want to stay in Castle House with him there all the time.'

'It's a big enough house. You wouldn't be under one another's feet all the time.' Daig was puzzled by her attitude, she knew.

'You don't know how much he tries to interfere in my life.'

'I think you are imagining that, just because he's going ahead so fast with the alterations at Castle House.'

'I'm not!' she interrupted. 'If you'd heard what he said to me when he carried out that last pile of curtains –'

'What did he say?'

'He said I was –' Katrina came to a stop there. How could she go on without telling Daig that Matthew had tried to warn her that she could be hurt by her friendship with him?

'Go on,' Daig prompted.

She moved away from him and went to stand by the window, from where she could look down on the mist-shrouded loch. When she did not speak, Daig followed her. His hands came to rest on her shoulders first, then slid down to her waist. He drew her back so that she was leaning against the firmness and warmth of his body.

'You haven't answered me, Trina,' he whispered with his lips on her forehead.

How could she answer him truthfully? 'I can't remember exactly what he said. It was just something I didn't like. I suppose I'm just angry with him still for taking Castle House away from us,' she hedged.

'Forget him now, darling, and let's just enjoy one another's company,' Daig urged.

That was not something she could do to order, she had already discovered. Forgetting Matthew was not easy. Just enjoying Daig's company was not easy either, because his very nearness reminded her of those moments by the loch when she had almost forgotten that Daig was married to someone else. Forgetting that Daig was married to Helga could be dangerous for her, and for him. She had told Matthew Dunbar that she could look after herself, now she must prove it, to herself, if not to Matthew.

'You must go, Daig,' she whispered as his lips moved down so that they were too close to her own. 'You know you must. I care far too much for you to risk us getting involved while Helga is away.'

'Who's to know what happens when Helga is away? If she cared for me as you do she wouldn't leave me alone so often. There's no-one to know if I don't go home. I'm not on duty...'

Katrina stared down at the smooth bare floor boards beneath her feet while doubts crowded into her mind. Doubts she was unable to still.

'Matthew Dunbar will know,' she said at last in a low voice. 'Mrs Muir will know too. They've both already hinted as much...'

'It's not their business!'

'They meant it for the best. At least, Mrs Muir did. She said there could be gossip if we were seen together having a picnic, as Helga is away, and that it could harm your practice.'

'We were not seen –'

'Matthew was afraid I would be hurt. He said – he hinted –'

'Don't go on.' Daig's hands fell from her. 'It matters too much to you what people think. I couldn't care less. I'm past caring about that.'

'Then you shouldn't be!' she hit back. 'You've worked hard and people round here look up to you because they know it hasn't been easy for you. Not like Matthew Dunbar, with all the family money to help him through his training. You can't risk losing your patients' respect, Daig, because of me. I won't let you!'

Daig sighed. 'All right, Trina, you win. For tonight, at least, until I can think of somewhere we can meet right away from Kerrbridge.'

Katrina kissed him, thanked him for helping her, then watched him drive away into the dusk. Yet for long after he had gone that final remark of his stayed with her and deepened her feeling of uneasiness because she did not want secret meetings with Daig in places where they had to be careful not to be seen by any of their neighbours or his patients. Nor did she want to deceive Helga.

Did she even want this new relationship with Daig that he seemed to want so much? She could find no answer to that question as she lay that first night in her new home waiting vainly for sleep to come to her.

The days that followed passed very quickly for her as she set about bringing comfort and order to her rooms in the annexe of West Lodge. There were curtains to alter, a laborious task for her since she had never undertaken such work before; there were cupboards to dust out and fill with the contents of her room at Castle House. A rather elderly carpet rescued from that room needed to be cut to fit the new and smaller bedroom at West Lodge, and there was the floor of her studio-living room to be sanded, stained and polished. This last task she almost gave up on until she recalled what the estimated cost of carpeting the room had been quoted as. Since she was no longer a salary earner she was forced to keep a tight hold on her money, because pride would not allow her to ask her father for any help. Already her bank balance was much depleted after the purchase of an electric cooker and a fridge, while there was still a telephone to be paid for when it arrived.

In between her spells of hard work at West Lodge there were visits to be made to her father, who continued to make steady but very slow progress towards recovery. These twice daily visits to the hospital she was able to make in her father's car now that it had been repaired by the garage in the village. This was a great relief to her because it meant she need not accept lifts from Matthew Dunbar. She saw little of Daig at that time since he was under pressure in the practice with one doctor on holiday while the other attempted to cope with the effects of a particularly nasty virus which was sweeping that area of Scotland. It was as well they did not see each other, she thought, because they both needed time to think seriously before rushing into a relationship that could affect other people's lives. Her father, for instance, would be very upset if she became involved with Daig, even though he had always liked and admired Daig. He had very strict and rather old fashioned ideas about such things, and there was always the risk of causing a setback to his health if she brought anxiety to him.

So far, although he was so much better in health, Malcolm Kerr showed little interest in her plans to have the main part of West Lodge ready to welcome him when he left the hospital. Mrs Muir was of no help to her since all she could repeat every time the subject came up was 'I think we'll be best to wait until Mr Kerr comes home before we see about moving him to West Lodge.'

'Won't Dr Dunbar be wanting to get Dad's room ready for one of his patients?' Katrina asked that afternoon when both she and the housekeeper were visiting him.

'He says there's no hurry, that they can leave that room until last.'

'I'm very glad you don't have to hurry back to London, my dear,' Malcolm Kerr said when his housekeeper had departed to do some shopping.

'I'll need to find some sort of a job fairly soon,' she told him, thinking of how rapidly her bank account was diminishing.

'Surely there's no hurry for you to do that?'

'I can't just go on being on holiday, now that I've done about everything I can to my rooms in the annexe.'

'Something will turn up for you,' he assured her with an optimism she was unable to share.

There had been nothing in the letters sent on to her from the flat in London. No-one, it seemed, was interested in giving a job to a young art teacher.

When visiting time was over and she went out to the car park she found Daig waiting beside her father's car. She had not expected to see him there, but the sight of him lifted her spirits.

'Daig! How are you?' She smiled her delight at seeing him.

'Better for seeing you,' he told her with a grin.

She frowned. 'Does that mean you've not been feeling well, or are you joking?'

'Both. I am feeling slightly under the weather because of too many disturbed nights and too many people down with this damned virus.'

'I'm sorry. Poor Daig!' Impulsively, she put out her hands and he took them in his. He seemed about to kiss her, which stirred panic inside her because they were in such a public place. Then abruptly he released her hands as they both became aware of approaching footsteps.

'Can you spare me a few moments, Daig?' Matthew Dunbar asked from a few feet away.

'Yes, of course. I'll see you in reception in a moment or so.'

'What is he doing here? Has he come to see my father?' More likely Matthew had come to see Alexa Dale, Katrina thought, and wished she had not asked the question.

'Matthew is helping out at the hospital for the time being, while so many of the staff are down with this virus that is causing us so many problems. Alexa Dale is one of the latest casualties, which is why Matthew is here.'

'I'd better go, then you can see what he wants. I have to pick Mrs Muir up at the supermarket, she'll be waiting for me.'

'I'll see you as soon as I can. As soon as I get an evening off. Will I be able to give you a ring, have you got your phone in yet?'

'No. I'll let you know when it arrives.'

Daig left her then, striding swiftly across the car park with his hands thrust deep into his pockets and his shoulders slightly hunched. Helga must be away again, as he had spoken of taking her out one evening. Why didn't she stay at home and look after him? Katrina thrust the thought away from her and drove into the town to pick up the housekeeper and her shopping.

Back at Castle House, she lingered over a cup of coffee in the kitchen with Mrs Muir since she knew Matthew was not likely to walk in on them. The house was alive with the sounds of men at work and every corner of it bore traces of the scent of fresh paint and wallpaper. Mrs Muir insisted on showing her the rooms which were finished, and she was forced to admit that she had never seen them looking so lovely. It was amazing, the difference an abundant supply of money could make, she thought wistfully as she left Castle House behind and went back to her annexe at West Lodge.

She had persuaded Mrs Muir to let her have Argyll with her at West Lodge. In fact the housekeeper had thought it a good idea that she should look after her father's dog while he was in hospital.

'He'll be company for you, and protection too in that lonely place,' she had said.

Katrina was glad of the dog's company because West Lodge was some distance from Castle House, part way up a lane on the edge of the estate. She was glad of his company on her walks through the woods or down to the loch, especially so on this evening when low clouds and mist were bringing an early dusk. Her heart began to thud with alarm when as West Lodge came in sight Argyll raced ahead of her and began to bark madly. Was there someone prowling about, she wondered. It struck her suddenly how vulnerable she was, living alone in the house while her father was still in hospital and Mrs Muir still at Castle House. Then she let out a long breath of relief as she heard a familiar voice speaking to the dog.

'Sit down now! Good boy!'

It was Matthew, clad she could now see as she drew nearer, in off duty clothes of shorts and open-necked cotton shirt. Then alarm flared again inside her.

'What are you doing here?' she whispered with her mouth going dry. Had he brought news about her father from the hospital? Bad news? She began to feel rather sick.

'Waiting for you. I wanted to have a word with you.'

Her legs began to shake. 'It's not – not about my father? He was all right when I saw him early this evening.'

'Yes, he was certainly in good spirits when I saw him. He's making good progress now and should be home before long.'

'Oh! I was so afraid, when I saw you waiting for

me...' The shaking had spread to her whole body now and she was unable to control it. She shivered violently.

'I'm so sorry, Katrina. I guess I gave you a bad fright.'

'Yes,' she whispered. 'I couldn't think why you would come here, if not to bring me bad news.'

'That doesn't say much for our relationship, does it Katrina?'

She shook her head, took a deep breath and gained control of herself. 'Then why are you here?'

'Because this is the only free time I have, while I'm standing in at the hospital for Alexa, and I can't talk to you on the phone, as you haven't got one yet.'

A different suspicion began to grow inside her then. A near certainty that he had come to warn her again about her friendship with Daig, after seeing them close together in the hospital car park that day.

'If you've come here to give me advice about my private life you are wasting your time,' she began. 'My private life is nothing to do with you.'

He seemed startled by that. So much so that he took a step back, putting more distance between them, before answering her accusation. 'If you imagine I have either the time or the energy, after the sort of day I've just had, to come here and give you advice you'll ignore anyway then you are very much mistaken, Katrina.'

Now it was her turn to be startled by his bluntness. 'Then why are you here?'

'Because, as I said earlier, I've been talking to your father and he tells me that as your job in London no longer exists you will be staying on here.'

'Yes. He seemed to be pleased about that.'

'I'm pleased too,' he told her quietly.

She was mystified. 'You are? Why?'

'Because having you here will help Malcolm to recover.'

'I won't be able to stay for ever. I need to get a job as soon as I can.'

'That's what I wanted to talk to you about. You see I am able to offer you a job, if you feel able to accept it.'

Katrina was more mystified than ever. 'What sort of job? I'm an art teacher, you know.'

'Yes, I'm aware of that, and it's because of that I think you could be very useful to me in my clinic.'

'How? What would I do in a private clinic?'

'Your father tells me that as well as your painting and drawing you have had training in calligraphy and other crafts too. The sort of things I'd like to get my patients interested in.'

'Yes, although I've been teaching mainly drawing and painting, as well as the history of art, I've taught some craft work too. But do you think you could bear to have me working in your clinic? I mean, just because you've become friendly with my father it doesn't mean you have to try and take on all his responsibilities. It's not as if you approve of me as a person, is it Dr Dunbar?' she ended all in a rush.

He was silent for a long moment while the dusk thickened about them and the last of the birdsong died away.

'What do you mean?' he asked then, very slowly.

'You know what I mean. You've already hinted at your disapproval of my friendship with Daig, haven't you?'

'I shouldn't need to point out to you how vulnerable to gossip a young doctor is in a place like this. Especially if his wife is constantly away from home.'

'Daig and I have always been friends, ever since our childhood.'

'You are not a child now, and neither is he. You are a woman, and beautiful enough to tempt any man. I do not blame him for finding you attractive.'

Hot colour flooded her cheeks and tension began to build up inside her again. With a great effort she controlled her temper. It would not do to let him see the effect he was having on her.

'I thought you came here to offer me a job?' she said.

'I did, and I have done so. There isn't much point in saying any more about it, other than that I can afford to pay you the sort of salary you were earning in London, until I know whether you are interested in the idea or not.'

'I need time to think about it.'

'I'll need to know your answer fairly soon because the first patients will be here in less than a fortnight.'

'I'm surprised you haven't got someone already, in that case.'

'I had, but she has just found she has to have a major operation and won't be fit for work for some months.'

'I see. I'll let you know tomorrow, if that is soon enough?'

'Yes, I can wait until then. I'll say goodnight to you now.'

'Goodnight, Dr Dunbar.'

Why hadn't she asked him in, she wondered as she inserted her key into the lock and listened to him striding away towards Castle House. As she pushed open the door she saw an envelope lying on the mat behind it. She bent and picked it up. It was unstamped, so must have been delivered by hand, and bore her name. There was a single sheet of paper inside on which a few words were printed. Words that stunned her.

'Leave Dr Hamilton alone. Or you'll be sorry.'

# EIGHT

Horrified, Katrina read those few words again and again. Those words of warning which held such a hint of menace. Who knew her well enough, and knew Daig well enough, to pen that stark warning? She could not begin to guess at the identity of the anonymous letter writer. All she could do was stand there, feeling sick inside with shock and shame.

What Mrs Muir had been so afraid of must have happened; someone who knew both her and Daig had seen them together on the day they shared a picnic in the secluded parking place close to the loch while returning from the hospital. Who? Who was close enough to Daig to be jealous of their friendship? It could not be Helga, because Helga was away again staying with her mother. Daig had told her so.

Her first instinct was to pack her bags and run away from the threat implied in the note, but that would require an explanation to her father. Her second, arrived at while she made herself strong coffee in the kitchen of her new home, was to stay and show the anonymous letter writer that she was not afraid because she was not guilty of what she had been accused of. Her third decision, made

111

during a long and sleepless night, was to accept the job Matthew Dunbar had offered her.

Early the next morning she hurried to Castle House, intent on telling Matthew of her decision. She arrived there so early that Mrs Muir informed her that Dr Dunbar was still in bed.

She was taken aback. 'Oh, I thought he always had his breakfast very early. I wanted to catch him before he left for the hospital.'

'He put in a very long day there yesterday, so he said he would have his breakfast an hour later this morning. I don't suppose he was expecting you to call on him at this hour. Have you had your own breakfast yet, my dear?' the older woman asked.

Katrina shook her head. 'I had a cup of tea, then decided to walk Argyll over here and catch Dr Dunbar before he went to the hospital.'

'Why don't you have some breakfast with him, then?' the housekeeper suggested.

Katrina thought about that while Argyll went to take the biscuit Mrs Muir was offering him. She did not know what to say. Matthew might not be too pleased at the idea of sharing his breakfast with her. He might be one of those men who preferred to have only his morning newspaper for company.

'Good morning, Katrina!'

The man himself was standing in the open doorway of the kitchen. At once Argyll bounded across the room to welcome him, barking madly.

'I'm sorry if we woke you. I expect you heard Argyll barking when we first arrived?'

'You didn't wake me, it was the sun that woke me.'

Matthew looked alert and immaculate in his open-necked shirt and smoky blue cashmere sweater worn with casual cords. She felt suddenly shy and could think of nothing to say that would explain her appearance this early in the day.

'Have you come to join me for breakfast?' Matthew asked now.

'I – I just came to tell you that I've thought over what you said to me last night and –'

'Then why not tell me over breakfast? I don't suppose you've had yours yet, as you are here so early?'

'No,' she admitted. 'I wanted to catch you before you left to go to the hospital.'

'Then come and sit down. I'm sure Mrs Muir can find enough food for us both.'

Mrs Muir beamed. 'Och, certainly I can Dr Matthew.'

Matthew led Katrina into the breakfast room next to the kitchen, which had been newly decorated and furnished with a lovely pale oak table, dresser and chairs which she recognized as being the work of a local craftsman.

'Do you like it?' he asked when her glance had admired the room and its contents.

'Yes, very much. The furniture must have come from Robbie Macrae?'

He nodded. 'I wanted to use as many local people as possible in the refurbishing of the house. Now, shall we talk first before our breakfast comes in?'

As she took her seat at the table he poured fresh orange juice for her from the jug which was already waiting. She drank deeply of this before telling him why she had come.

'I've decided to take the job you offered me last night. That is, if you haven't changed your mind?'

He smiled at her. 'I'm not a man to change my

mind, once it is made up. I expect you would like to hear more about the job now?'

'Yes, please.'

'First I must warn you that some of my patients will be difficult because they have lost all interest in life, for one reason or another. You'll find them apathetic, lethargic, hard to stimulate into any sort of enthusiasm for the work I want you to do with them. Others will be keen enough but will lack concentration.'

'Some of my pupils at the comprehensive school where I taught were apathetic and downright disinterested,' she told him.

'You might find it helpful to spend a couple of days with some of the O.T. people at the nearest psychiatric hospital before my patients arrive. I could make arrangements for you to do that if you are willing?'

'The nearest place would be Rowanburn.'

'Are you willing to go there?'

'Yes. I did some voluntary work there when I was a student at art school. I quite enjoyed it, but I hadn't realized that your patients came into that category. I had imagined they were –' She broke off, too embarrassed to go on and tell him exactly what she had thought his patients would be like.

Matthew laughed. 'I can guess what you thought, Katrina. You were fairly certain that I spent my working life making a lot of money out of rich hypochondriacs, I suppose?'

He was so close to the truth, but she could not say so. Instead she remained silent.

'Well, am I right? I can see by your expression that I am.' He chuckled at her discomfiture, yet she found it hard to be angry about that because she had deserved it. His face sobered and he spoke to her gravely then. 'I wish they were like that, Katrina. It would make it so much easier for me then to leave the caring for them to someone else, as my father wants me to do so that I can take his place as head of the family drugs company in America. I only came here for a few months, to work with a man who was trying out some of our company's new drugs on the patients in his private clinic, but I became so involved with that sort of medicine that when he died quite suddenly I couldn't bring myself to allow his good work to be wasted. You see by then I had got to know some of his patients very well and to have great sympathy for their problems. So I decided to stay on, and continue with the work he had begun. To go on treating people like old Mrs Whitaker, who still waits for her husband to come home from the office even though he left her years ago, and Annabel, who is afraid to go out since a plane crashed in her garden and killed her child. Or Tim Brownlow, who can't come to terms with the fact that a mistake he made caused the death of one of his employees. My patients are certainly not idle hypochondriacs, Katrina, they are simply people who have lost their way in life through no fault of their own.'

She felt humbled by the truth he had revealed to her, and appalled by her own misjudgement of him. What could she say that would not sound totally inadequate to express her regret? Words milled around in her brain, but before she could utter them Mrs Muir was bustling into the room with a dish of eggs and bacon.

At Matthew's suggestion then they postponed

the rest of their discussion until later and gave all
their attention to the food, which she found to her
astonishment she enjoyed.

'Shall we continue our conversation while we
walk?' Matthew suggested when they had finished
their meal with oat cakes and marmalade.

'Walk?' She was not certain what he was
intending.

'Yes, by the loch. With Argyll, perhaps?

'Do you have time for that? I mean, aren't you
spending most of your time at the hospital just
now? At least that's what Daig said.'

'I am, but I'm not due there until this afternoon.
So shall we have that walk?'

She got to her feet, calling to Argyll, who had
been keeping Mrs Muir company in the kitchen.
Her interest in Matthew's patients and the work
she would do with them was thoroughly aroused
now and she found herself eager to hear more
about the role she would play in helping them to
recover.

At first as they left Castle House behind Matthew
was, it appeared, lost in his own thoughts. Then, as
the noise made by men at work in her old home
died away and there was only the sound of the
breeze stirring the trees and the singing of many
birds, he began to talk to her again.

'You must be prepared to be discouraged at
times in your work with the patients,' he warned
her. 'Disappointed too when someone you've
helped a great deal suddenly loses all interest. I
wish you could talk to Julia Jones, who has worked
in the clinic ever since it opened. She could tell you
more about that than I can, but unfortunately she
was not able to move up here with me because her

husband's job made that impossible. So I engaged someone else, and then she had to give backword because of needing an operation. I hope you won't change your mind now that I've told you more about what is expected of you, Katrina?'

'How can you be so certain I'm what you are looking for?' She had halted at the place where the woods gave way to the stony shore of the loch, and now faced him with her doubts. 'You don't know all that much about me, do you?'

'I know enough,' he said, after a pause that seemed to her to be interminable. 'In fact you would be surprised, I think, at how much I have learned about you from your father, from Mrs Muir, and from Daig Hamilton.' He smiled as he told her that, his grey eyes full of warmth.

Her doubts had not quite disappeared. 'Well, I suppose they've all known me for long enough. Does Daig know you have offered me this job?' she added.

'Not as yet. Is it important to you that he should know?' There was challenge in his steady regard. She could feel the tension in the air between them strengthening and she was half afraid of it, half excited by it. Aware again of the way he seemed to make her feel more alive every time they met. He was, she knew in that moment, a man like none she had ever known before...

'You haven't answered my question,' he was reminding her harshly.

'I can't remember what it was you wanted to know,' she confessed after racking her brains for a moment or so.

A great burst of laughter escaped him then. It rose up into the air about them, and lightened his face so that he looked momentarily boyish and carefree.

'Have I said something funny? Something to amuse you. I can't think what it was.'

'No, honey. Not really. It was just that you made me happy by giving me exactly the answer I wanted.'

'Now I'm more puzzled than ever. What was it you asked me?'

He considered that, then said 'I asked you if it was important to you that Daig should know I had offered you this job. As you couldn't remember me asking you that it can't have been important to you, can it?'

'No, I make my own decisions about such things. I have something to say that is important to me though.'

'Then say it!' he challenged.

'I'm very sorry I misunderstood about the sort of patients you care for in your clinic.'

He smiled. 'Shall we forget about that now and begin again as we mean to go on when we are working together for the good of those people?'

'Yes.' She smiled back at him, full of relief that he had accepted her apology.

'Shall we shake hands on it?'

For answer she held out her right hand and he took it in his to hold it fast. As the hand clasp went on it took on a profound significance, as though it were a vow, a promise or a long embrace. This last thought, when it struck her, shocked her into trying hastily to withdraw her fingers from his firm grasp.

'A new beginning, Katrina, and a most important moment for us both. Agreed?'

Wordlessly, she nodded. It seemed to her for one breathlessly exciting moment that he was about to kiss her. Her heart gave a tremendous jolt, then simmered down as he drew back again.

'You were going to tell me more about your patients, Matthew,' she reminded him hurriedly, because she knew she must not get ideas about him being attracted to her. It was Alexa Dale he was falling in love with, and there had never been anyone for her but Daig, had there?

'Oh yes, my patients. They are usually in the forefront of my mind, but not always since I came to live here. That's another story though, and one to be saved for a later date.'

After that he began to talk about what he wanted her to do when his patients began to arrive at Castle House, while she listened with deep interest and found herself eager to be a part of the work of Castle House Clinic. The time seemed to fly past, so that she was amazed when he glanced at his watch and said that he would have to be getting ready for his spell of duty at the hospital.

'Perhaps I'll see you there later, if you are going in to see your father?'

'Yes, I'm going in tonight. He seems to prefer me to go in the evenings because he has plenty of visits from his friends in the afternoons now.'

'He'll be home quite soon, I hope.'

'Then I'd better hurry up and get the rooms at West Lodge ready for him.'

'There's no need for that. Malcolm can come home to Castle House if he would rather.'

'He doesn't seem terribly interested yet in moving into West Lodge,' she confessed.

'Then don't put any pressure on him to do so.

He'll make the move in his own good time I can promise you.'

'Thank you for being so good to him.'

He brushed her thanks aside as though they embarrassed him.

'It's the least I can do, in the circumstances,' he told her.

Then, when her face expressed her surprise, he gave her a hasty word of farewell and strode rapidly in the direction of Castle House.

As she neared her own new home in the annexe of West Lodge, Katrina found herself wondering what Matthew would have had to say if she had told him about the note which had been waiting for her there last night. That anonymous letter with its menacing words. When she entered the annexe she looked at once on the mat, dreading the appearance of another poison pen letter. The mat was empty of anything except the stick Argyll had carried back from the shore.

'Time to do some chores, Argyll,' she told the dog. 'While you catch up on your sleep.'

Even though she kept herself busy for the next couple of hours she could not quite put that letter out of her mind. It was probably the work of a crank, she told herself. All doctors were at risk from such people, she had heard, and Daig was no exception. All the same, she would have to make sure she was not seen alone with him. So she was dismayed when his car drew up in front of West Lodge later in the afternoon. She went out to meet him, full of uneasiness as she wondered if he too had received one of those horrible letters.

'Daig, I didn't expect to see you here today!' She knew her voice sounded forced, her welcome less warm than once it would have been.

'I was so near, coming back from some calls at Strathkerr, that I couldn't resist dropping in for a few minutes.'

He looked very tired. There were dark shadows beneath his eyes and his shoulders sagged wearily as he leaned against his car.

'I was just going out,' she told him, feeling pity for him yet also a sense of constraint which had not been there a few days ago.

'Can't I come in for a moment?' he pleaded. 'Are you in such a hurry to be off?'

'It's not just that –' Once the words were out she wished them unsaid, because now she would have to explain them.

'Have you gone off me all of a sudden? Or found someone else?' he teased, but his eyes were hurt.

'No, of course not.' Ought she to tell him about that letter which had as soon as she read it spoiled their long years of friendship?

'What is it then?'

'I just think it's best if you don't come in. We ought to be careful. We have to be careful.'

His frown deepened. 'What do you mean? Perhaps you ought to explain.'

'We have to be careful because someone is out to cause trouble for us Daig.'

'What sort of trouble?'

'I got an anonymous letter last night warning me to leave you alone, or else!'

He drew in his breath sharply. 'Oh, God! Who would send such a thing? Let me see it.'

'I can't. I burnt it, I was so angry. But I can't forget it. We have to stay away from one another, Daig. You must see that.'

'Who would do such a thing?' he said again. 'Have you any idea?'

'No. Obviously it was someone who saw us together on the day we had the picnic.'

'You must have been frightened by it?'

'Not for myself. For you, Daig.'

'Have you any ideas about who could have sent it?'

Katrina hesitated. She had given a lot of thought to the subject, yet she did not like any of the suspicions that had entered her mind in the process. So she shook her head.

'Was there a postmark on the envelope?'

'No.'

'So it obviously came by hand. Did you recognize the handwriting?'

'No. The words were block printed.'

'What exactly did they say?'

She told him, and saw the disgust on his face. 'I don't like it,' he said then. 'Someone trying to harm you.'

'Or to drive me away from here.'

'What are you going to do? Tell the police?'

'Oh no! I don't want anyone to know about it, except you.'

'You are not leaving, either, I hope?'

'No, I'm staying. I'm going to work for Matthew when he opens his clinic.'

Daig was startled to hear that. 'Doing what?'

'Occupational therapy, mostly. Trying to get his patients involved with painting or drawing or other crafts.'

It was impossible to tell from his expression whether or not he was pleased that she was going to work in Matthew's clinic. All he said was 'So I'm not to be invited in?'

'I'm sorry, Daig. I think it's best not. If someone is watching us and trying to cause trouble we'll need to be very careful. Especially while Helga is away, that's if she is still away?'

'She is,' he said curtly. 'She's with her mother again. It seems she's got involved with some local drama group and they are rehearsing for a play.'

'Perhaps it will help her, doing something like that?'

'Help her to stay off the drink? Who knows? My hopes have been raised before. So many times.' His tired face was full of pain as he told her that.

'Poor Daig!' she said, reaching out to touch his arm in a gesture of sympathy then drawing back again when he seemed about to gather her into his embrace. 'I must go. I promised Mrs Muir I would call in and have a cup of tea with her this afternoon. She'll be wondering where I am. I'll be seeing you, Daig.'

She knew she had hurt him with her refusal to ask him in, but it was safer that way for both of them she argued to herself as she walked briskly through the landscaped gardens of her former home. Once at Castle House she gave her mind to Mrs Muir and the local gossip, all the time wondering which, if any, of the people they talked about would stoop to the penning of a malicious anonymous letter. A deep and private sadness filled her at the idea of someone who had known her and Daig for a long time setting out to destroy their friendship. Because that was what the poison pen letter had done.

After an hour or so with Mrs Muir, she walked back to West Lodge with Argyll, and again found herself opening the door into her annexe with dread in her heart until she saw that there was no suspicious letter awaiting her. She must stop herself from expecting there to be another letter, she told herself firmly, because probably there would never be another. It could be that the person who had sent the first one was already regretting having done so.

When Katrina arrived at the hospital that evening to visit her father she found him very pleased when she said she was going to work for Matthew at Castle House Clinic.

'I know. It was all my idea,' he boasted.

'What do you mean, Dad?'

He grinned. 'When he told me the occupational therapist he had engaged for Castle House couldn't start work there after all I suggested that you might be able to help him.'

She was appalled. 'Oh, Dad, you didn't!'

'Why not, my dear? You said you wanted to get a job as soon as possible, and having you working at Castle House will suit me very well.'

'You shouldn't have! I don't suppose he really wanted me, but he wouldn't want to hurt your feelings.'

'It wasn't that at all. He said he had been thinking of suggesting it himself.'

How could she believe that? It was very naughty of her father to persuade Matthew that he ought to take her on, and maybe she would not have accepted the job if she had known.

These thoughts were still rankling in her mind as she walked out to the hospital car park when visiting was over. She felt tired and dispirited and wanted only to get back to West Lodge and go to bed, but to her dismay she could not get her father's car to start. In the next few minutes she tried everything she could think of, to no avail. Then, admitting herself defeated, she got out of the driving seat and uttered an explosive 'Damn! Damn! Damn!' as she slammed the door and prepared to lock it. There was nothing for it but to ring the National Breakdown Service and ask for help.

'It sounds like you've got problems, Katrina,' a familiar voice commented from just behind her.

She swung round to face Matthew. 'Yes. I can't get her started.'

'Let me see what I can do.'

He took her place, but failed to start the engine. So he lifted the bonnet and began to poke about underneath it while Katrina shivered as the chill evening air began to penetrate her thin blouse.

'I'm sorry, Katrina,' he said as he pulled himself upright. 'I can't help you. You need to get someone from the garage.'

'They'll be closed by now. I suppose I'd better find a phone and ring National Breakdown.'

'Why not leave it until morning as it's so late and you are obviously tired? I'll drive you home.'

She was too tired and too depressed to argue with him. Instead she thanked him and slipped into the front passenger seat of his car, which was parked quite close to her own.

'I suppose you'll be very pleased with your father tonight? He's in excellent spirits just now,' Matthew began as they left the hospital behind.

'Yes. I'm very glad to see him getting on so well.' She hesitated, then went on. 'I'm not too pleased with him for begging you to give me a job, though.'

He laughed. 'It wasn't quite like that, Katrina.'

'He seemed to think it was.'

'You are uptight about it, aren't you?' He seemed to find that amusing, which made her quite cross.

'Of course I am! He shouldn't have done it.'

Matthew chuckled again. 'He didn't beg me to give you a job, Katrina, as a matter of fact the idea came from me when your father happened to mention that your teaching job in London had come to an end. Do you really think I would have been persuaded by him to do something I didn't want to do? You should know me better than that by now.'

Katrina relaxed then as he went on to discuss which room in Castle House she was to have as her O.T. room.

'You can start to get it ready as soon as you like now that the painters have finished work on it,' he told her. 'My first two patients, Mrs Whitaker and Annabel Robinson are due to arrive at the end of next week.'

'Will you have time to help at the hospital once they get here?'

'I probably won't be needed then. Alexa will be back on duty and Daig's partner will be back from his holiday.'

Matthew gave all his concentration then to negotiating a tricky part of the winding road that led to the outskirts of Kerrbridge leaving Katrina to speculate, and not for the first time, about his relationship with the glamorous woman doctor. Alexa Dale MD was not only beautiful she was also determined. If she had set her sights on Matthew he had better watch out for himself. Unless, of course he was only too willing to be caught.

They were entering the Castle House grounds

now and running into a rain mist that made the atmosphere gloomy enough for headlights to be needed. A couple of deer sped away gracefully as they reached West Lodge.

'Lovely creatures,' Matthew remarked.

'Yes. They come down from the hill to my garden late every evening,' she told him.

Matthew pulled up and switched off the engine. 'This is an isolated spot for a woman to live alone. That's why I wanted you to stay at Castle House until your father and Mrs Muir were ready to move in with you.'

'It doesn't bother me. I'm used to it, and I have Argyll for company.'

'All the same, it's a bit spooky on an evening like this. I think I'd better see you safely indoors.'

'There's no need to worry,' she assured him, but he appeared not to have heard her because he was getting out of the driving seat and marching up to the door of her annexe. He waited while she found her key and inserted it in the lock.

She was turning the handle when it occurred to her that he had just put in many hours of work at the hospital, and that Mrs Muir would by now have gone to bed. There would be no-one at Castle House to make him a hot drink because as yet the local domestic staff he had recruited for the clinic had not started work.

'Would you like some coffee, Matthew?' she asked, half hoping, half fearing that he would decline her offer.

'I sure would, if you are not too tired to make it. If you are, I guess I can make it,' he told her with a smile.

'I'll make it right away.'

She left him to close the door while she hurried to the kitchen, where she set the kettle to boil and placed china mugs, sugar and cream on a tray. A moment or so later he startled her by calling her name harshly from the hall.

'What is it, Matthew?'

Yet even as she put the question, she knew. Knew that the piece of wet paper he held in his hand had to be another of those disgusting letters.

Her whole body began to shake as she held out her hand to take it from him. Coldness invaded her and nausea stirred within her as she stared at Matthew speechlessly.

'I'm sorry. I couldn't help seeing what it said. How long has this sort of thing been going on?' Matthew's voice was crisp, authoritative. She knew she must answer him truthfully.

'I've had one before. A few days ago.'

The words printed on the wet paper in large letters danced before her eyes, sinister, revolting, obscene. The message was the same as before, only there was more of it and it ended with the words 'Go back to London. Stay there, or else!' Her mind recoiled from those words and the threat they represented.

'Have you any idea who sent this?' Matthew asked sternly.

She shook her head. 'It could be anyone, I suppose, who knows Daig and me.'

'Could it be his wife?'

Again she shook her head. 'I doubt it. Helga is staying with her mother in Aberdeen, and this has been delivered tonight since it started to rain. Perhaps just before we got back from the hospital. In any case, I don't think she cares enough about him to threaten me.'

'Someone cares enough to threaten you.'

'It can't be her. If she cared so much she would stay with him, and stay off the drink for his sake.'

Matthew's face was stern. 'The fact that she drinks too much doesn't prove she no longer cares for him. It could be the reverse; that she loves him too much and knows he doesn't love her any more. Have you thought of that, Katrina?'

She shook her head. 'No. I only know that Daig is very lonely and unhappy.'

'And very glad to have you back in Kerrbridge.'

She flinched. 'I haven't encouraged him, if that's what you think! I'm just sorry for him.'

'You should spare some pity for her too. I guess she could be just as lonely and unhappy.'

'Then why won't she accept some help? Get some advice? Try to save her marriage.'

'That is exactly what she is trying to do. Her doctor in Aberdeen has referred her to my clinic because he knows I've had some success in treating people like Helga Hamilton. She'll be one of our first new patients when we open next week, Katrina.'

# NINE

Shock kept Katrina silent for a long moment after Matthew had told her that Daig's wife was to be one of the first patients at Castle House Clinic. Why hadn't Daig told her that when he called to see her this afternoon? She was conscious of feeling disappointed in him for not sharing the news with her. With an effort she brought her mind back to what Matthew was saying.

'You can't possibly stay here alone after this sort of threat,' he was repeating with his eyes still on the letter which lay on her hall table.

'I'll make the coffee,' she told him, as if she had not heard his earlier remark, and went back into the tiny kitchen.

Her hands were still trembling as she poured boiling water into the two mugs before she had remembered to put in the coffee. Anger and confusion caused her to splash her fingers with the boiling water as she attempted to pour it back into the kettle. She gave a smothered exclamation as Matthew took her by the shoulders and spoke to her urgently.

'I said you can't stay here alone! You must not stay here alone! Didn't you hear me?'

'Yes, but I don't agree with you. I have to stay

here, or the writer of that letter will think she has won, and driven me out.' She did not look round at him but went on stirring the coffee until his fingers digging into her flesh made her protest.

'Don't be such a fool, Katrina! If you are not concerned about your own safety then at least try to consider the feelings of those who care about you.'

'But Dad won't know, will he, about the letters?'

'I'm not talking about your father. I'm talking about me. I know about the letters, and I care about your safety and I certainly have no intention of letting you spend the night here on your own. So what I propose to do is have that coffee you've just made then settle down on your sofa for the night.'

Katrina gasped at his audacity. 'You can't!'

He smiled, but there was a steely glint in his grey eyes now that gave her a warning she could not ignore.

'I don't see how you can stop me, Katrina, and if you are wise you won't even try.'

Matthew seemed to tower above her in the confined space of her little kitchen. Yet she was not afraid of him. In fact there was a sense of exhilaration in accepting that he would do as he thought best, and not as she wanted him to do. She looked him up and down, and felt her heart race at what she saw.

'Aren't you afraid for your reputation, Dr Dunbar?' she asked as coolly as she could manage.

That made him laugh heartily. 'Why should I be? I'm not married, and neither are you, so even in Kerrbridge I might be expected to enjoy the company of my beautiful young lady neighbour until the wee small hours of the morning, don't you think?'

'I doubt if Alexa Dale will be so tolerant about your spending the night here,' Katrina said crisply.

That brought another smile to his features. 'Why would I be so concerned about what Alexa thinks?'

'Daig told me you and she —'

'Daig wants you to think that way. He wants to keep you for himself; to keep you standing by in case he's ever free to marry you. You've waited too long already for Daig, Katrina, and if he had really wanted to be free to marry you he would have found a way. You know he would, don't you?'

Katrina swallowed. Matthew had just put into words a thought she had not allowed herself to dwell on before.

'How can you be so sure about that? Why are you so eager that I should realize it?'

His answer came at once, and without hesitation. 'Because I've got to know Daig quite well, and you even better these last few weeks. So well that I know it is me you should be marrying, Katrina, and I expect you to realize that quite soon.'

The breath caught in Katrina's throat as she heard him utter those last few words. He could not possibly mean them, could he? She gave a nervous laugh and dropped her gaze from his.

'You don't believe me, do you?'

'No,' she whispered. 'I think you are joking with me, for some reason best known to yourself.'

'Perhaps this will convince you.' In one swift stride he had closed the space between them and pulled her into his arms.

Her mouth was lost in that first kiss. Her whole being was out of her control as she responded as naturally as if this was what she had been waiting for all her life. Responded with a fire and passion that left her breathless. Then she pulled away from him and gained control of herself as doubts began to crowd into her mind.

Matthew laughed softly. 'Well, are you convinced yet? Or do I have to give you another demonstration of how right we are for one another?'

'No!' she said sharply. 'Keep away from me! I may have waited too long for one man, but I'm not ready yet to rush into a new relationship with you, Matthew, even if you do intend to spend the night here.'

That made him laugh again. 'So now you've cast me as the villain, honey! The sex-mad doctor intent on seducing his new occupational therapist.'

It sounded so ludicrous that her own lips began to twitch. 'You know I didn't mean it like that!' she protested.

'Then drink your coffee and let's go to bed. and don't misunderstand me honey. I mean you to your single bed and me to your couch.'

All her suspicions about his motives seemed absurd now that she was fully in control of herself again, so much so that she even managed to remember her duties as a hostess.

'You won't have had any supper, will you Matthew?'

'Mrs Muir will have left something cold for me. Probably there will be more than enough for two, so why don't you come to Castle House and eat with me?'

She shook her head. 'No, thanks, Matthew. You go to Castle House. I'll be fine here on my own.'

'As I said before, I've no intention of leaving you here on your own tonight.'

'Then you'll have to share my cheese and salad.'

'And your company! Yes, I'd like that.'

As she prepared the simple meal for them she admitted to herself that she was glad she would not be alone here in the isolated house on the edge of the estate with the knowledge that somewhere out in the rainy darkness was an evil person who was trying to harm her. It was comforting to share her supper with Matthew in her studio-living room with the lamps lit and a fire glowing in the stone hearth.

Matthew did not refer again to the anonymous letter, or to the fact that he proposed to marry her. At first he spoke of the opening of Castle House Clinic, and went into some detail about the way it was to be run. She soon found herself utterly absorbed in this and intensely interested in his plans for the future.

'I hope to create the atmosphere of a country home in Castle House rather than that of a hospital. A place where disturbed people can find peace and relaxation as well as treatment. That's where I think you will be able to help, honey. If you can persuade some of the patients that there's pleasure, and forgetfulness of problems, in sitting down to draw or paint you'll be a tremendous help to me. In a place like this there are so many beautiful places to provide inspiration, aren't there?'

'Oh yes! I can't wait to get on with some painting myself, now that Dad is so much better and doesn't need visiting so often,' Katrina confessed.

'I'm hoping that when your father is fully recovered he might help to interest some of the patients in fishing. I found him rather good at passing on his own enthusiasm for fishing when I first came to stay at Castle House. At that time I was the one who needed help.'

'You were? Do you mean that you had been ill?' Astonishment filled her voice. Matthew looked so fit even after his long day at the hospital that she could not imagine him being ill enough to need help.

'Not ill,' he answered quietly. 'Just very unhappy.'

Katrina waited for him to go on. She wanted desperately to know what had caused his unhappiness, yet hesitated to ask lest she intrude in an area that was too personal for him to wish to discuss.

'I'd like to tell you about it, if you are not by now tired of hearing me talk about myself. It's something I want you to know.'

'Then go on, Matthew.'

'I was engaged to be married, when I first came to England. I wanted Dawn to marry me and come to England with me only she was very much involved with her employment agency business, which she was just building up. She said she would marry me when I came back, but I postponed my return because of Dr Clifton's death. That upset her because she thought it meant I put my work first rather than her, which was true, I suppose. I tried to explain, but it's not easy by letter and phone. Before I could explain in person and put things right she was killed in a car crash. I found it hard to come to terms with that, and the fact that Dawn had thought I didn't care for her. I found it difficult to concentrate on my work for a time, until a colleague who had been on one of your parents' sporting holidays at Castle House suggested I do the same. I took some persuading, but that first week I spent here helped me to get everything into perspective again. I came back, because something here seemed to draw me back, maybe a kind of longing to spend all my days here. By then I was wondering where I could move my clinic to, because the new premises I was considering proved to be not very suitable. Your father talked about having to sell because he could no longer carry on with the sporting houseparties, and I knew at once that Castle House would make an ideal clinic.'

As Matthew finished speaking Katrina felt she knew at last so much more about the private man inside the doctor. Knew and understood so many things which had puzzled her before. The remoteness that was at times a part of his personality, and the determination to go ahead and open his clinic in Castle House in spite of her opposition.

'I'm glad you've told me, Matthew,' she said. Then she turned her head to give a startled glance at the clock on her bookcase, which had just chimed.

'Was that two o'clock or three?'

'Does it matter?' he asked. 'Does anything matter, except that we should learn about each other's past?'

'You must be very tired, Matthew. You've been working all day.' She got to her feet, realizing that he could not get any sleep until she vacated the sofa.

Matthew's smile illuminated his features. 'You sounded just like a wife, Katrina.'

She bit her lip. 'I didn't mean to –'

'I'm glad you did. It showed me that you cared a

little.' He touched her chin lightly with one long slender finger.

She turned away from him, confused, and said 'I'll make us another cup of coffee.'

That made him chuckle again. 'You sounded more like a wife than ever then.'

Katrina stared at him. 'How do you know about wives, if you haven't been married?'

'I do have a mother, and a married sister, and I also have my dreams about how a wife should be.'

They were nearing dangerous ground again. She had to escape, so she ignored that last remark and hurried to her kitchen. Matthew followed, bringing the remains of their supper and setting about the washing of dishes as though this were something he did often. When she had made the fresh coffee she looked at him with a question in her eyes.

'Shall I get you some blankets, Matthew?'

He gave her a slow smile that aroused strange emotions inside her.

'If you insist. Though I'm not in the least tired. In fact I'd far rather stay awake and go on talking to you, if you can stay awake.'

'You will be tired, in the morning,' she warned.

'So will you, but it could be worth it, I think, for us to take this chance of being alone together away from everything and everyone who has caused tension and misunderstanding between us. Do you agree?'

'Yes,' she heard herself reply.

Matthew took the tray on which she had placed the coffee mugs and carried it back into her living room. There he placed it on a low table in front of the sofa before putting out a hand to draw her down to the place beside him. She found herself relaxing into the familiar comfort of the piece of nursery furniture which was older than she was, and knowing a feeling of intense happiness.

'You've forgiven me at last, haven't you honey, for taking your beloved home?' Matthew murmured.

She nodded, unable to speak for the emotion that filled her.

'Forgiven me, too, for interfering in your private life and warning you to be careful of your friendships?' He was less certain that she had forgiven him for that, as yet.

'Yes,' she said on a long sigh. 'Though I thought you were making too much out of my friendship with Daig. I never dreamed anyone would go so far as to make threats against me because of that.' She shivered, in spite of the warmth of the room. 'It's such a terrifying feeling, Matthew, to know that someone is spying on you and trying to make trouble just because you spend a bit of time with an old friend whose wife is away from home.'

'He should have known there would be gossip,' Matthew broke in. 'If he was seen with his old love.'

'I was never his old love,' she said sadly. 'He was mine, when I was very young, but he went away to medical school and met Helga. He didn't wait for me to grow up.'

'Did it hurt so much?'

'It did at the time, then I went away and made a new life for myself.'

'What happened when you came back and found his marriage was falling apart?'

'I felt sorry for him.'

'Was that enough to bring the anonymous letters?'

She winced at his candour. 'No. I think we were seen having a picnic on the way back from the hospital one night. Seen kissing, perhaps, but there was nothing more than that, I promise you.'

Suddenly it was vitally important that he should believe her. She clenched her hands to stop herself from beating them on his breast to convince him, because she was sure she saw doubt in his eyes.

'Don't you believe me, Matthew?'

He sighed. 'I find it hard to believe only because I know that in his shoes I would never be able to rest until you belonged to me.'

Now she was angry. A torrent of passionate words escaped her. Words she had not intended to utter because they revealed too much of that inner self that she had never yet exposed to anyone.

'I used to believe that I loved Daig, wanted Daig, more than anything in the world. That I wanted to comfort him and care for him in every way. Only when my chance came and he told me he loved me I could never make myself forget that Daig had married Helga, and was still married to her. That I had no right to love him. Or him to love me. That's why there were only kisses, and nothing more. Though I don't suppose you'll believe me any more than the person who wrote the letter would believe me. I suppose you think I lacked the courage to refuse what I wanted when it was offered to me. Or what I thought I wanted,' she added in a whisper.

Matthew took her hands in his and raised them to his lips.

'I suppose I asked for that,' he said with a wry grin. 'With my darned jealousy every time I saw you with him.'

She began to smile. 'So it was jealousy on your

part, and not concern for Daig's reputation or my own that made you warn me off him?'

'A bit of both. A lot of both. I am concerned about both of you, but mostly about you, Katrina. I couldn't bear to see the way he looked at you. Or you at him. I had to try and stop it, if I could.'

Suspicion entered her mind then. A suspicion that she wanted to reject, but dare not. She had to voice it, before she lost her courage.

'You didn't – you wouldn't – I have to know – was it you who wrote those notes?'

The minute the words were out she wanted to recall them; to run away from them and from the man she had addressed them to. She was already on her feet, ready for flight. Matthew was also on his feet, his whole being vibrant with his anger.

'Even after all these hours alone together you don't trust me, do you? You are still looking for an excuse to quarrel with me so that you don't have to admit yet that you are as much in love with me as I am with you. Yet you must know that I am not capable of writing such vile letters or acting in such a way. You must know that I have no need to act in such an underhand way when I can fight for you openly, and win you openly.'

'Win me?' She stared at him, not understanding.

'Yes, win you.'

Her eyes widened as he seized her and imprisoned her mouth with a kiss that took all the breath from her body. A kiss that went on until it became another, and another. There was no room in her mind for doubts now. No room for anything except the surging joy of loving Matthew and being loved by him. Of belonging to him in a way she had never belonged to anyone else.

The belonging was full of tenderness at first, then it was a shared passionate delight and a shared fulfilment that left them sleeping at last in one another's arms as daylight strengthened in the sky above the mountains. Katrina was not aware at first of the daylight as she came to slow life from her deep and satisfying sleep.

'Matthew,' she murmured, tucking her head more firmly into his shoulder.

'Good morning, honey.' His lips lingered over her hair before coming to rest on her mouth.

From a long way off then she heard a fist hammering on the door of her annexe while a voice shouted her name.

Matthew was on his feet and pulling on his clothes before the fist hammered on her door again and the same voice shouted her name again. The voice belonged to Daig. Dread filled her mind as she realized that. Shivering, she dragged herself upright and grabbed her dressing gown.

'I'll go,' Matthew said in a voice that warned he would take no argument from her.

She waited, tense with apprehension, while he made his way to the front door and unlocked it. She listened then, with her hands clenched, while Daig told why he was there. His message brought a fresh chill to her heart, even though it was not the news she had feared.

'They need you at the hospital, Matthew. Need every trained person they can get hold of. There's been a bad train crash. Get there as soon as you can!'

That was all Daig said, and Matthew wasted no time at all in asking questions. The still, early morning air that hung over the estate was

shattered by the roaring of first one car engine and
then another as Daig drove away, followed swiftly
by Matthew, who said only a few words to her
before he went.

'Wait for me, beloved.'

By now, Katrina was too fully awake to be able to
finish her sleep, so she took a hot shower and
dressed then made herself tea and toast. While she
was sipping the tea she reflected sadly that on this,
their first ever morning together, Matthew had
been forced to leave without her being able to
make his breakfast. It would not happen again, she
vowed. In future she would make certain he had
the sort of good Scots breakfast she knew he
enjoyed.

This thought brought a smile to her face, but the
smile vanished when she switched on her radio and
heard the early morning news bulletin. She learned
then that a train had collided with an Army bus on
a level crossing not far from Kerrbridge, that the
wreckage had caught fire, and that medical staff
from all over the area were being called to the
scene to give aid to the many casualties. There was,
she heard last of all, the danger of an explosion.

Her mind recoiled with horror from this last
piece of information. Maybe, even now, Matthew
was at the scene of the crash giving treatment to
those who had been injured. If so, he could be in
acute danger. Yet he would not flinch from doing
his duty as a doctor, she knew with a mixture of
pride and fear.

As she moved restlessly about her home she
caught sight of the note Matthew had found on her
doormat last night. It lay, crumpled but quite dry,
where she had dropped it last night before that

terrible suspicion had entered her mind that Matthew himself could have been responsible for writing it and the one she had received earlier. It had not taken Matthew long, once she had voiced her suspicion, to prove that he had no need of such tactics. That he could win her openly and without deceit. Warmth invaded her as she recalled how thoroughly Matthew had proved that to her. Her thoughts moved on then to how pleased her father would be about her and Matthew. Right from the start her father had liked Matthew, even when she herself had been full of resentment towards him for buying Castle House.

Quite suddenly then she longed to be at Castle House instead of alone here at West Lodge. At Castle House she would have Mrs Muir for company, and also Argyll, whom she had left with the housekeeper while she visited her father last night. She would have the use of a telephone too. The phone was to be installed at West Lodge next week, but she wanted to get news of Matthew this morning.

Acting on the impulse, she slipped a jacket over her slacks and jacket then set off at a brisk pace for her old home. Once there, her father's dog gave her a boisterous welcome while Mrs Muir's face showed her relief.

'I was just setting off to come to you, Katrina dear, to bring you a message from the hospital,' she began.

The blood drained from Katrina's face. Her hands began to shake.

'Is it Matthew? Has something happened to him?' she whispered.

Mrs Muir put an arm about her and hastened to put her mind at rest.

'Och no! It's nothing like that. Dr Dunbar will be fine I'm sure. The message is about your father. This train crash has put a strain on the hospital. They need all the beds they can get, so as your father is so much better they are letting him come home today.'

'Oh!' Katrina let out her breath on a long sigh of relief. Her father was coming home at last. That was marvellous! Then she remembered that her father's car was still on the hospital car park where she had left it last night when it would not start.

'I'll have to ask someone to give me a lift to the hospital. Dad's car seized up again last night and I had to leave it there,' she told the housekeeper.

'So Dr Dunbar drove you home,' Mrs Muir finished for her, with an affectionate, probing glance.

'Yes. It was quite late and I thought you might have gone to bed, so I gave him some supper. I hope you weren't worried about him not coming back?' She bent over to stroke Argyll as she said that in order to hide her face from Mrs Muir.

'Och, no! I knew where Dr Dunbar was. Maggie MacTosh told me he was with you at West Lodge.'

'Maggie MacTosh told you? How did she know where Matthew was?'

'She saw him driving you there as she passed on her motor scooter when she was coming to drop in a knitting pattern she borrowed from me.'

'What was she doing near West Lodge? She didn't need to come that way to see you, in fact it would have been a long way round for her. Especially on such a wet night,' Katrina added thoughtfully.

Mrs Muir was puzzled too. 'I don't know why she

came that way. She didn't say, but then you know
Maggie was always a bit secretive.'

Katrina's frown deepened as she considered
Maggie MacTosh, who cooked and cleaned, after a
fashion, for Daig. It was easy then to put together a
picture of Maggie penning the sort of note she had
found at West Lodge last night, and driving up to
deliver it on her ancient scooter in the pouring
rain. Maggie appeared to be devoted to Daig's wife,
but only, Katrina suspected, because Helga did not
interfere with her slapdash housekeeping methods
and was so often away. Perhaps Maggie MacTosh
saw her own return to Kerrbridge as a threat to her
easy-going existence as Daig's housekeeper, especially if it appeared that she and Daig were becoming
involved. The more Katrina thought about it, the
more possible it seemed that the woman was afraid
that one day she would replace Helga in Daig's
home. She must have seen them together when
they were sharing their picnic supper in the
parking place beside the loch...

'I said, what are you going to do about getting
your father home?' Mrs Muir's voice broke into her
chaotic thoughts and reminded her that there had
been the accident and her father's bed was needed
for one of the casualties. Reminded her, too, that
Matthew had gone to help with the injured.

What did anything matter, except that Matthew
could be in danger if he had gone to the scene of
the accident and there was an explosion? She must
get to the hospital at once and see if there was any
news of him.

# *TEN*

Having decided to get to the hospital with all possible speed, Katrina was faced with the problem of having no car. A call to the Home Farm at once brought the offer of the little vehicle used by the farmer's wife, and Katrina was on her way.

It was difficult, as she drove alongside the loch, not to let her thoughts dwell anxiously on Matthew. She must think only about how good it was to be bringing her father home at last. Thoughts about Matthew and the danger he could be in would keep until later. He might not even be at the scene of the accident. It was just as likely that he would be at the hospital when she arrived, busy treating the injured there.

When she arrived she found the car park crammed with vehicles belonging to the emergency services and also to medical staff who had set aside whatever they had been going to do that day and gone to help with the treatment of casualties. A hasty word with the desk clerk brought the information that Dr Dunbar was one of those at present at the scene of the accident, along with Dr Dale and old Dr Collier from whom Daig had taken over the practice. Her heart gave a great lurch when she heard this, but she told herself not to

panic, that everything would be all right, that
Matthew would come safely back to her. Then she
went to collect her father and drove him back
through the dripping, mist enshrouded landscape
to Castle House.

That day proved to be one of the longest and
most awful that she had ever experienced. It was
like some nightmare from which she would surely
soon wake up as she tried to behave normally in
front of her father and Mrs Muir, and the people
who were at work in Castle House, while from time
to time listening to the news bulletins on the radio
which could only tell her that medical staff were
still treating casualties at the scene of the accident
and that the danger of an explosion had not yet
passed.

She ate what lunch she could manage to swallow
with her father, then settled down in the drawing
room to help him with his crossword puzzle, and all
the time her ears were alert for the sound of the
telephone ringing to bring her news of Matthew.
Perhaps Daig would let her know the moment
there was any news, since he must have guessed
how she felt about Matthew after discovering that
they had spent the night together at West Lodge?

It seemed a million years since Daig's hammering on the door of her annexe had brought to an
abrupt end those unforgettable first hours of
belonging to Matthew. At least she had those hours
to look back on and to treasure for the rest of her
life if Matthew did not come back to her. Nothing
could take the joy of them away from her.

Her only regret was that Matthew had waited for
so long before telling her that he loved her. Yet
would she have listened to him, or believed him, if

he had told her earlier? No, she admitted to herself as she stared out of the window with unseeing eyes, because she had made up her mind to hate Matthew even before she got to know him properly. She had put all the blame on him for something which had been by then inevitable, the handing over of her family home to someone who could afford to put it to good and valuable use, as Matthew would do when he opened his clinic. That is if he were still able to do that...

'You must be miles away, my dear. That's the third time I've asked you what you think 21 across could be, and I don't think you've even heard what I've said.'

Katrina swallowed. 'I'm sorry, Dad. I was just trying to imagine what it would be like here when Castle House is full of Matthew's patients.

Malcolm Kerr laid down his pen and gave her his opinion, slowly and thoughtfully. 'It will be a place of hope again, a place with a future, and you will be a part of that future.'

'Will I?'

'Yes, you'll be working here every day even if you are living in the annexe at West Lodge, and I'll be coming here sometimes to play bridge or scrabble with the patients. Matthew has asked me if I'll help him by doing that.' Obviously her father was pleased to be asked to help Matthew.

'If he's here to be helped,' she whispered.

'Why shouldn't he be here?' Malcolm Kerr asked quietly.

Suddenly her control went and she began to sob helplessly. 'Don't you understand! He might not even be alive! He's still at the accident, and there's a fire, and there might be an explosion. Why did

Matthew have to be there, instead of here getting ready for his own patients moving in. Why, Dad? Why?' She put her head down on the newspaper and let her tears soak into it while her father watched her with pity in his eyes.

'You know why he has to be at the accident, Trina. Matthew is a doctor and must go where he is needed most. By the end of the week he'll be needed most here, and that's where he'll be, but for now he is most needed by those poor young soldiers and the train driver who is still trapped. That's something you have to learn to accept if you are in love with Matthew. It's something I know you can accept, and he knows it too.'

'Does he?' She raised her burning eyes and stared at him.

'Of course. That's one of the reasons why he wants you, because he knows you will help him through the bad times, as you've helped me. He needs someone like you, not like that poor girl Daig chose. So have courage, my dear. Your waiting will soon be over now and Matthew will be back.'

She managed a shaky smile as she dabbed at her eyes. 'You seem to know all about Matthew and me, Dad.'

'Of course. It's been obvious to me for a long time that you were meant for each other.'

'Has it?'

'Yes. Matthew was frank with me about why he wanted you to stay here and work in his clinic. He wanted you to see, before you married him, what sort of life you would be in for.'

'I didn't realize that.'

'Perhaps you were still too busy worrying about Daig?' her father suggested.

She nodded. 'I was so sorry for him, and we have been friends for a long time.'

'It wouldn't be wise of you to be too friendly with him now, but I'm sure you realize that?'

She dropped her gaze, and wondered what he would think if he knew about those two anonymous letters. Ought she to tell him about them? No, she decided at once, because there would probably be no more of them once the news got around that she was engaged to Matthew.

'Talking of Daig's wife,' she heard her father say as he got to his feet and moved towards the window. 'I believe she's just coming to the house.'

Katrina sprung to her feet and went to stand beside him. Yes, that was certainly Helga coming up the front steps.

'I'll go and see what she wants,' she told him.

As soon as she opened the front door, before Helga could ring the bell, Katrina was struck by the extreme fragility of Daig's wife, by her frightened eyes and her ashen face.

'Hello, Helga. I wasn't expecting to see you here today,' she greeted her as calmly as she could.

Helga began to talk quickly, nervously. 'I wasn't due to come until next week, but I came today because Maggie MacTosh rang my mother and told her I ought to be coming back because Daig needed me. Only last time I spoke to Daig he said he wouldn't live with me again unless I got myself sorted out. So I came to find Dr Dunbar, because he's going to help me do that; to stop relying on a drink to give me courage, I mean. Where is Dr Dunbar? I need to see him –'

'He's not here, Helga. He hasn't been here at all today because there was a bad rail crash just a few miles away early this morning and all medical personnel were called out to help. Matthew went to the scene of the crash hours ago and I don't know when he'll be back.'

Helga clutched at her arm. 'Does that mean Daig will be there too?'

'No. He's still at the hospital I think.'

'Are you sure? I couldn't bear it if anything happened to Daig! I do care about him, you know!'

Katrina gave her a long, searching look. 'If you care about him, why don't you stay at home and look after him? Be there when he needs you. At times like this, when he's under stress and tired out, he ought not to be going home to the sort of rubbish Maggie MacTosh will cook for him.'

Maybe she had spoken out of turn! She took a pace back and waited for Helga to flare up and tell her to mind her own business. That it was nothing to do with her. Helga, though, was agreeing with her.

'I know Maggie isn't much of a cook or a housekeeper, Katrina, but I'm afraid to say anything to her in case I upset her. She's known Daig since he was a boy and she says she knows what he likes better than I do. I feel so inadequate when I have to deal with her. I'd really like to tell her to go because I don't really like her all that much. She's so possessive about Daig and the house that sometimes I feel it's more her house than mine. When she knows she is getting on my nerves and I can't cope with her she suggests that I have a little drink to calm me, or says that a few days with my mother will do me good. I know I ought to stand up to her, but you've no idea what she can be like when we are in the house alone together and

Daig is out for hours. In the end I just have to get away. I have to!'

Daig's wife looked so young and so defeated that Katrina felt a wave of sympathy for her. Maggie MacTosh had a lot to answer for, she knew then. How much damage had she done to the marriage of Daig and Helga? Was it beyond repair, or was there still hope for them?

'Haven't you ever tried to talk to Daig about it? To tell him what's going on,' she asked.

'I tried to talk to him about it at first, but he just laughed and said it was all in my imagination; that Maggie was a bit slapdash in her ways but she meant well. Later, when I mentioned it he thought I was just looking for another excuse to go and stay with my mother.' She sighed. 'Later still he didn't care whether I stayed at home or not, because by then he knew he wished he had married you instead of me.'

Katrina bit her lip as guilt stirred inside her. She had been so sorry for Daig that she had never taken the trouble to look at the marriage from Helga's point of view.

'I don't know what to say, Helga,' she began when the silence between them had grown oppressive. 'I'm sure I wouldn't have coped with Maggie MacTosh any better than you have done because she is a rather overbearing woman, and I don't really think Daig wishes he had married me. He may have given you that impression just because he was fed up of being left on his own so often.'

Helga faced her bravely and told her the rest.

'Maggie says Daig has been seeing you recently. That's why she said I should come back.'

Anger exploded inside Katrina then so that the words she voiced reverberated around the lofty hall of Castle House and brought curious stares from some of the workmen who were painting the upper landing.

'Maggie MacTosh is a malicious old busybody who is out to cause trouble! Of course I've seen Daig sometimes. We've been friends since we were children and I thought I was in love with him when I was very young, but he chose you instead. Daig was kind enough to drive me to the hospital once or twice to see my father when he was very ill and our car was out of action, but it's Matthew Dunbar I'm in love with, Helga, and it's him I'm going to marry as soon as I can.'

'So it's not too late for me and Daig?'

'Of course not, but you must get rid of Maggie MacTosh if you want to save your marriage.'

Helga's face filled with dread. 'How can I do that? She won't take any notice if I tell her to go. I know, because I tried it once and she just laughed at me and said I'd had a drink too many again.'

Suddenly then Katrina knew what she had to do. She had to confront Maggie MacTosh, for the sake of Helga and Daig.

'Maggie MacTosh will take notice of me,' she said confidently. 'I know she will!'

She went at once to find her father. 'I'm just going to take Helga home,' she told him. 'If there's any message from Matthew, tell him I'll soon be back.'

'Why, isn't she well enough to drive? If so she ought not to have driven here in the first place –'

'She's perfectly sober, Dad, but she needs help with something she has to do when she gets home. I'll tell you more about that later.'

'As long as you know what you are doing. It isn't always wise to meddle in other people's affairs, you know.'

'Yes, I do know, but this is something I have to do.'

She left him then and joined Helga in the front seat of the other girl's car, asking her to call at West Lodge on the way so she could collect something she needed. Then with the crumpled note, which she was now certain had been pushed through her door by Maggie MacTosh, clutched in her hand she sat in silence as Helga drove them to the house on the outskirts of the village which was known locally as The Doctor's House. As the car came to a standstill Helga turned to face her with frightened eyes.

'I don't know if I can –' she whispered.

Katrina opened the door, then turned to squeeze her hand. 'Come on, it'll soon be over and everything will begin to come right for you and Daig.'

'Will it?'

'Yes, I promise you.'

They went into the house together and they found Maggie MacTosh asleep in a rocking chair at the heart of an untidy musty smelling kitchen.

'I wasn't expecting you back just yet,' she blustered as she struggled reluctantly to her feet. Her mean little eyes darted from the doctor's wife to Katrina, then moved hastily away from what she saw there.

'But you rang my mother's house and said I ought to be coming home because I was needed here,' Helga pointed out.

'I meant to have a bit of a tidy up before you got here.'

'The place certainly needs it. The cooker is filthy, and so is this floor,' Helga said bravely, to Katrina's satisfaction.

'Dr Daig hasn't complained!' Maggie MacTosh hit back.

'I expect he's been too busy.'

As Helga said that the older woman's malevolent gaze turned on Katrina. 'Oh yes, he's certainly been too busy to notice a bit of dust, hasn't he Miss Kerr?'

It was then that Katrina pulled the crumpled anonymous letter from her pocket and held it very close to Maggie MacTosh's face. So close that the woman could not fail to recognize it. Her mouth gaped.

'Someone else has been busy too, haven't they Mrs MacTosh? Busy trying to cause trouble, and not for the first time,' she said coolly.

'I don't know what you mean!' The dark red flush in the flabby cheeks gave Maggie MacTosh away.

'I think you do, but I'm sure you wouldn't want Dr Hamilton to know about this. Or my fiance, Dr Dunbar,' Katrina added sternly.

'I'm not staying here to be accused! I've always done my best,' the woman began belligerently.

'Done your best to cause trouble for Dr Hamilton and his wife, and for me, but Mrs Hamilton is home to stay this time,' Katrina broke in. 'She'll have friends to help her with her problems, so I don't think she'll miss you, Mrs MacTosh.'

'We'll see what Dr Daig has to say about this,' came the spiteful retort.

Katrina laughed. 'I doubt he'll have anything to say to you that you'll want to hear, once he knows what has been going on here. I should go at once and be out of the way when he comes back from the hospital. Unless you want me to show him this note and tell him who wrote it, and who put it through my door last night?'

With that Katrina turned and walked out of the kitchen, taking Helga with her into the sitting room. From that dusty room they watched through grimy windows as Maggie MacTosh left The Doctor's House for the last time on her motor scooter.

'I wonder what sort of state her own home is in?' Katrina said as she disappeared from their view.

'I dread to think,' Helga shuddered.

'Are you going to let Daig know that you are here?' Katrina asked then.

Helga shook her head. 'No. He'll be too busy to be interested if they are still coping with the accident victims at the hospital. I think I'll set about doing some cleaning up while I wait for him to come home, and see what there is in the deep freeze that I can cook for supper. I hope when he does come that he will be just a little bit pleased to see me,' she added in a whisper.

'He will be,' Katrina assured her, sending up a silent prayer that this would be so.

'Thanks, Katrina, for everything,' the other girl said. 'I'm glad about you and Dr Dunbar. I've only met him twice, but I like him and I feel he'll be able to help me once I start attending his clinic.'

Katrina smiled. 'I'll be seeing you there, because I'm going to work for Matthew in the occupational therapy room at the clinic. I must go now and see if Matthew is back yet from the hospital. Goodbye, and good luck!'

'You'll need to borrow my car to get back, won't you?' Helga reminded her.

'Won't you be needing it? Our car, Dad's car, is on the hospital car park waiting for someone to tow it away for repairs, but I can always walk back.'

'It's a long walk. Take my car. I'll be too busy getting the house straight to need it.' With that, Helga handed her the keys and went with her to the front of the house to see her off.

Katrina drove the borrowed car very carefully to the end of the drive and waited there to turn into the road that would lead her back to Castle House. As she waited, her eyes on the bend in the road that followed the loch, she saw a vehicle approaching. The breath caught in her throat as she recognized the long, sleek, silver car belonging to Matthew, then her heart gave a lurch as her intent gaze picked out the figure of Matthew behind the wheel.

Had Matthew noticed her in the unfamiliar car? She did not know. All she knew was that he was safe. All she cared about was that he was safe.

After he had sped past she pulled out into the road and followed him as fast as she dared up the hill that led to Castle House. When she reached the entrance to the estate she saw that Matthew had pulled in there and was waiting for her. He must have recognized her after all. Her heart began to race as she got out of Helga's car and went to meet him.

How exhausted he looked, she thought with a pang. His face was stern, his lips compressed. Apprehension bit into her mind even before he spoke to her.

'What the hell were you doing at Daig Hamilton's place? Couldn't you keep away? And I'd been thinking that you would be at West Lodge waiting for me!'

She swallowed the lump in her throat that threatened to choke her. He was jealous, angry, disappointed in her, and he had got it all wrong because he was too weary to think straight.

'I have been waiting for you, and worrying about you, all day long. I was so afraid –'

Matthew scowled. 'What were you doing at Daig's place then?'

'I didn't go to see Daig, if that's what you think. I went to take his wife home because she came to Castle House looking for you.'

'Why should she go there today? She's not supposed to start her treatment until next week.' Matthew shook his head as if trying to clear his thoughts.

'She had had a message from Maggie MacTosh telling her she should come home at once. That Daig needed her.'

'Who the hell is Maggie MacTosh?' Matthew's voice was brusque with his tiredness and anger.

'Daig's housekeeper. Helga tells me that Maggie MacTosh has been encouraging her to keep going away to stay with her mother, or to have a drink to help her cope with things.'

'Why should the woman do that?' Again, he looked bewildered.

'Because she prefers to have Daig's house to herself; to have no interference with her sloppy housekeeping and her lazy ways. Maggie MacTosh is a trouble maker, Matthew. I know now that she was responsible for sending those two vile letters to me. I was so angry when I discovered that. Then when Helga arrived and told me how afraid she was of Maggie I knew I had to do something.'

'So what did you do?' His face was softening, she

saw with intense relief.

'I took Helga home, and let Maggie MacTosh know that she was not going to do any more harm to Helga or me. She did not deny she had sent the letters. Then, when she had gone, I left Helga to wait for Daig. I can only hope he'll be glad to see her, and that I've done the right thing.'

Matthew's eyes were grave. 'After what we've seen today, after what we've had to do today, Daig will need someone to help him forget. As long as it's not you, honey,' he finished, attempting to smile.

She moved closer to him and put her arms about his neck. 'Was it so bad, Matthew?'

He nodded. 'It was bad enough, but we were able to save most of the soldiers, thanks to the fire and rescue service.' He put his arms about her. 'You'll never know how glad I am to see you.'

She lifted her lips for his kiss, then drew away from him with a frown. 'Your eyebrows are scorched, darling.'

He slumped against her as utter weariness took him over. 'I'm so tired, honey. I've had enough of answering questions and making decisions. All I want now is to be quiet, and alone with you. Can you arrange that?'

She nodded. 'I'll let Dad and Mrs Muir know that you are safe, then join you in my annexe. We won't be disturbed there.'

Matthew smiled. 'Will you tell your father I want to marry his daughter?'

'I'll do that!' She got into Helga's car and started the engine.

'Don't be long, will you honey?' he begged.

'I won't,' she promised.

# Flower in
# the Snow

# One

It was the first cold morning of autumn and Lizzie was lost in thought as she walked across the yard, so it was Meg's howl of rage and furious barking which alerted her to the large Jaguar parked on the other side of the rickety farm gate.

She grabbed the scruff of Meg's neck and waited for the barking to stop before she spoke. The coldness of the morning filled her with a dread of the coming winter and she was tired after staying up late to do her accounts; she felt about as welcoming as Meg as she frowned at the man and the dog standing on the other side of the gate.

She decided as she looked over the man, his car and his dog that he was just the kind of person she disliked on sight.

The Jaguar was new and immaculate.

Probably loves it more than his wife, she thought, letting her eyes slowly take in the tall, lean masculine frame clothed in a dark suit and the man's broad shoulders and indefinable air of wealth and assurance.

His dog was a massive snarling Rhodesian Ridgeback – a breed she particularly disliked – with a collar and lead of heavy studded leather.

The dog surprised her somehow. The man was so tall and sophisticated, so powerful in a very non-aggressive way, that it was puzzling he should need a macho symbol like a ferocious dog. Her lips curled in a slight smile of derision.

But when he pulled his dog back and told it to be quiet it obeyed while Meg still snarled and barked, hackles stiff as a brush, even though Lizzie tugged and yelled, 'Meg, be quiet....'

Conversation was impossible. 'Wait here...' she shouted abruptly to the man and, securing her hold on Meg, marched surefootedly across the muddy half-frozen yard and shut the dog in an empty loose-box. Maybe he was a man from the Ministry or from the Inland Revenue; she couldn't think why anyone else would drive over the frosty moors to get to Ellis Ridge Farm on a cold and unwelcoming Monday morning.

She was aware of his scrutiny as she walked across the yard, of his eyes studying her in a way she was unused to. It was a long time since a man had watched her with that kind of intensity. She was uncomfortably conscious of her working clothes: dirty wellingtons, faded jeans and a large Aran jumper which had belonged to her father.

She suddenly realized she hadn't bothered to put a bra on that morning, her hands were dirty and her face clear of make-up.

Damn the man ... normally no one called at this time. She pulled back a strand of her long dark hair which had escaped from her ponytail and tried to smile welcomingly.

For what seemed like an age they just stood and stared at each other, then he broke the silence: 'How do you do. It's Miss Thornton ... isn't it?' His voice was deep and cultured. Some instinct told her that he wasn't from the Ministry of Agriculture or the Tax Office.

She frowned slightly, puzzled, as she tried to smile. He had opened the gate and was holding out a large brown hand to be shaken. She recognized him just fleetingly, and for a moment was sure she had seen his face before.

He certainly wasn't a man to be seen and then forgotten: tall, rangy, and as fineboned and powerful as a thoroughbred; he was undoubtedly the most attractive man she had ever met. And as she slipped her hand into his warm grip she chided herself for her moment of awareness, which made her pull her hand away a fraction too quickly for good manners.

OK, Lizzie, she told herself. So he's tall, blond and dangerous – but don't lose your cool!

His face was lean and intelligent with a hawkish nose. She found herself watching his mouth as he spoke, unable to take her eyes from the curve of his lips.

He was uttering some pleasantry about being sorry to call unexpectedly. She tore her eyes from his mobile, humorous smile and found herself looking into his eyes. They were very bright blue: the blue of precious stones or the Madonna's robe. Or, she thought distractedly, the brilliant hue of a mountain tarn on a clear, cloudless day: the lightest, brightest blue in the world.

He was waiting for her to speak. She moved away from him and said, more abruptly than she intended, 'Yes, I'm Lizzie Thornton.'

She was embarrassed because she was certain she had been gawping at him – unnerved by his attractiveness and the nagging feeling they had met before … but she couldn't for dear life remember where.

'I'm Guy Olafson. Peter Browne from the pub in Radcliffe told me you had some pups for sale.'

Olafson – a Nordic name. That explained his silver-blond hair and fine skin. She wondered if his ancestors had come over on a Viking long-boat. Despite his air of wealth and sophistication she could imagine him standing at the helm of a fighting craft, coming ashore to conquer and vanquish.

'Do you have some pups?' he asked again. She coloured slightly, frowning at him.

Peter Browne had been a life-long friend of her parents when they had been alive. Peter knew how fussy she was about the homes her puppies went to. Why on earth had he sent this man up to look at them? He was without doubt a town-dweller. Despite his tan and taut, atheletic body there was something about his clothes, his car, the timbre of his voice, which told her that he was not a country person.

She glanced down at his immaculate dark shoes and let her eyes travel up over his tall broad-shouldered body and expensive suit. Everything about him, down to the silk tie and plain gold watch, spoke of a world entirely different to hers.

He smiled at her. She noticed his eyes crinkling when he smiled, lightening the hawkishness of his expression and making him appear almost boyish.

Once again she was sure she recognized his face and had seen his smile before as he said softly: 'You are worried that the pups are from working stock and will need plenty of exercise – and I don't look as if I spend a lot of time walking.'

'That's right ...' she said, astonished that he had read her thoughts so clearly and determined to get control of the situation. 'They do make good pets – but not for someone who is out at work all day – they like company.' As if to prove her point Meg set up a pathetic howl of protest at being shut inside. Lizzie grinned at him. 'See what I mean!'

He smiled back and she was aware once again of an uncoiling of some exhilarating emotion – fear or excitement – she didn't know which.

'I'm looking for a dog for a friend who works sheep …
So may I see the puppies?'

She stared at him for a moment and he stared back,
looking straight into her eyes, waiting for her to speak.
She was aware of a strange electrical awareness between
them.

Come on Lizzie, so he's goodlooking, but so what?
she chided herself. She was, since her short, disappointing
engagement to a fellow student in her second year at
college, immune to men – however attractive.

'All right …' she said sulkily. She was still trying to
work out how she knew his face. Maybe he was an actor
and she had seen him on TV? It seemed unlikely because
she saw very little television, apart from the news,
which she always watched to make up for not having
time to read a newspaper.

Running the farm took up most of her time and she
enjoyed reading for relaxation when her chores were
done. But the memory of his face nagged at her and she
felt it must be connected with television.

Certainly he was handsome enough to be an actor.
The combination of light hair, tanned skin and bright
blue eyes was almost film-star material.

'They're in the barn. You'd better put your dog in the
car – Meg is very protective.'

'The dog's not mine. I borrowed the car and she
insisted on coming along. I was just driving around,
getting the lay of the land, it's a long time since I was up
here. I met Peter, he told me about the pups and I came
on impulse.' He looked down at his watch. 'I have an
appointment in Leeds at noon.'

She looked coldly ahead and her footsteps quickened
slightly.

'Yes, well ... I haven't got all morning either,' she said curtly.

When she opened the loose-box door she was aware that he was studying her with a questioning, half-amused look and she was suddenly ashamed of her rudeness. Most people would not have noticed it, but he had.

Meg, as soon as the door was opened, threw herself at Lizzie in a flurry of black and white fur and yelping barks as if they had been parted for hours.

'Come on then, Meg. Come and see the pups.' She was pleased to busy herself with Meg and to talk to the dog instead of the man. It gave her a few moments to compose herself.

Just because she felt at a complete disadvantage with him there was really no need to be so off-hand and rude.

'Here they are,' she said, opening the barn door and trying to smile. 'She had five this time and I may keep one – but I haven't decided yet. They won't be ready for a couple of weeks.'

The man crouched down and held his hand out to Meg.

'Come on sweetheart ...' he whispered. 'If I'm going to look at your puppies we had better be friends ... come on. ... good girl.'

As he continued crooning to the dog, in a deep voice which was as sweet as honey, Meg inched forward. Her ears were flat and lips curled in a snarl but to Lizzie's utter amazement, when his confident brown fingers touched the dog, Meg whined with pleasure and rolled over to have her tummy tickled.

'She wouldn't bite you.' Lizzie said shortly. 'Not while I'm here.' She felt an irrational annoyance, as if the dog, who normally hated to be fussed by strangers, had in some way betrayed them both.

Meg must like his aftershave, she thought with a smile. But she couldn't deny that his gentle hands and long sensitive fingers handled the pups delicately as he picked each one up and inspected it.

She thought that he might be a doctor... For the way he touched the pups had fired a memory of the past: of surgeons who had tutored her and obstetricians she had watched handling tiny, premature babies. They had had hands like his that seemed to have kindness in their very touch.

'They are a fine litter. I like the little bitch, she's nicely marked.'

'She's the runt.' Lizzie said rather sharply. 'Not that it really matters in a litter this size, but the other bitch would make a better pet. She's the bully already.'

Lizzie was aware of his relaxed, almost lazy smile, as he picked up the smallest pup and cradled it in his hands.

'She may be nervous, difficult to train...' she heard herself saying too quickly, because for some irrational reason she didn't want anyone else to have that puppy.

Guy Olafson smiled directly at her so that she was aware once again of the wonderful hue and intense clearness of his eyes.

'I think you've already decided this is the one you will keep,' he teased gently.

'The others pick on her...' she said, startled into telling the truth. 'I suppose I want to make it up to her and let her stay and become top dog when Meg retires.'

He laughed softly and the pup, responding to the noise and close warmth of him, squirmed closer and tried to lick his face.

'You're not the only one who likes a challenge and wants to champion the under-dog.'

He laughed again and Lizzie smiled stiffly, wondering if he was laughing at her. 'I'll come back and see them again if I may.'

'Of course.' She knew her manner was ungracious, almost aggressive, but she couldn't help herself.

As they walked back across the yard she noticed how he looked about him, observing everything. And she wondered with sick despair if there was an ulterior motive for his visit. Was he some kind of speculator? Had he heard on the grapevine, 'Liz Thornton at Ellis Ridge is having a hard time. She'll soon be going under…'?

But he didn't look like a farmer … and who else would be interested in a run-down hill farm? She was conscious of the sagging roof of the barn; the peeling paintwork on the doors and windows; the layer of mud and muck covering the cobbles of the yard; the abandoned tractor leaning drunkenly in the corner, now a roosting place for the hens.

There was a terrible air of decay about the whole place. Even the solid and respectable stone-built house which had been her mother's pride and joy now had grey windows and curtains that needed washing.

Looking at the farm through a stranger's eyes filled her with weariness and utter dejection. There was always too much to do … too many jobs waiting … too many animals to feed … too many bills.

Eerily, as if once again he read her mind, he turned at the gate and said gently, 'It must be hard work running this place alone, Miss Thornton.'

'I don't run it alone,' she interrupted abruptly. 'I have George.'

'Oh yes,' he said quietly, as if he knew about George already. Did he? Did he know when she said grandly, 'I have George.' It meant she had one rheumaticky old man who popped up for an hour or so when she had work like dipping and shearing which she couldn't do alone? Did he know that soon, very soon, unless the autumn sales went well, she wouldn't even be able to afford the pittance George accepted as wages?

It seemed in some awful way that he knew all this. And yet her reason argued he couldn't possibly know ... not even the bank manager was aware of the full extent of her problems. So how could this handsome, urbane stranger in his sleek, city clothes know anything about her?

This odd sensation that he could somehow read her mind and see all her thoughts and feelings was simply imagination. Caused, she told herself hastily, because no one had looked at her in the appreciative way he did for so long.

He was looking at her again with the same intensity and she was aware of his eyes searching her face as if his gaze burnt her.

'It's been a pleasure meeting you, Miss Thornton.' Her hand was again being held and shaken and she pulled away; acutely conscious of the contrast between his smooth, tanned fingers and immaculate white cuffs and her own work-roughened hands and frayed-edged jumper.

'I'll be in touch...' he said with a smile, as if he knew what she was thinking, his eyes sliding down the length of her body in a way that almost took her breath away.

She watched him get into the shiny car and drive away with something amounting to trepidation rising up in her.

After the car had disappeared she looked down at her grubby hands and broken, dirty nails and said, 'OH

HELL!'

She went into the washroom next to the kitchen and scrubbed her hands until they were sore, wondering as she did so where Guy Olafson was going in Leeds and what his line of business was. She could imagine him in a lofty, plant-filled office with a glamorous secretary; leaving at lunch-time with her for a restaurant or wine bar, laughing, joking, discussing the latest news.

She wondered if he looked at all women as he had looked at her: a look which caused intense awareness of one's femininity. And if his secretary blushed and twittered, warming under his gaze like a flower opening up to the sunshine. And she was suddenly heartsick for company and for some life other than the one she was living.

Damn the man ... she silently cursed. Why did he have to come riding up here in his smart car, with his city clothes, handsome face and devastating way of smiling? She didn't want reminding about the life the rest of the world was living.

If only, she thought with a rush of emotion that wrenched at her, he hadn't been so nice to Meg and the pups ... She recalled the softness of his voice when he had talked to them.

A question flashing into her mind, was instantly rejected, but returned and couldn't be kept out. Did he speak to women in that wonderfully caressing way, with his mouth curving in a half-smile?

Her mouth, she knew, wasn't curving in any kind of smile. She felt more dejected than she had for ages. The chill of the day, her frozen feet in her thin-soled wellingtons and her chapped, reddened hands, all seemed to be in conspiracy with the handsome stranger to make her feel depressed. And she had promised to go out that evening on a date with William Hoskins. She had regretted it after making the arrangement, but sometimes any kind of company was better than seeing and talking to no one but George. But William, with his tightly curled red-blond hair, bullneck and jovial, coarse manner, couldn't have been in greater contrast to Guy Olafson.

She felt eaten up with dissatisfaction. She didn't want to spend the evening drinking in the Black Swan with William and his friends.

She longed suddenly, with frightening awareness, for something she couldn't even put a name to. It was as if she were suddenly aware of all kinds of possibilities in relationships that she had never thought of before. She only knew with frightening certainty that she wanted more out of life and she didn't even know what it was! These feelings raging through her head made her feel treacherous.

For hadn't William Hoskins been an invaluable friend after her parents died, helping her with loans of hay and plenty of good sensible advice? He was a very capable farmer and a kind neighbour. He got a bit amorous sometimes after one drink too many, when she had to drive his Range Rover home, but she would probably be even more affronted if he didn't find her attractive enough to try to kiss good-night.

She studied herself in the small cracked mirror over the sink. Her face was thinner than ever, her high cheekbones giving her an angular, fine-drawn look. There were dark circles under her eyes, telling of too many late nights doing accounts and early mornings checking the stock. Her hair reached well below her shoulders and was thick and heavy; but the way she wore it, tightly tugged back, only accentuated the thinness of her face.

She pulled at the Aran jumper which effectively hid the curves of her figure. Guy Olafson must have thought her second cousin to a gypsy...

But there was no point wishing herself a different path in life. She had vowed when she gave up her studies to come home to run the farm that she would make a success of it and she was still determined to do so. This feeling of being caged, of wanting another kind of life, was just a temporary hiccup in the steady routine of running the farm.

And this heart-searching was all Guy Olafson's fault! She tried to feel bitter about the man's intrusion. But however much she tried to build on her initial dislike she would find that memories of his voice and his long brown hands would slip into her mind – and she couldn't find it in her heart to blame him.

Instead, remembering the way his mouth curved when he smiled and the intensity of his eyes became a treasured memory: a glimmer of light to ease the darkness of the day.

As Guy Olafson drove slowly down the rough track that led from Ellis Ridge Farm he smiled to himself and at one point laughed out loud.

He was thinking about the girl he had just met, and Marianne, a friend of his in London. Marianne ran a top modelling agency. They had been friends since university and had both become divorced at the same time, so it was natural that they should have become close friends. Props to each other, as Marianne, with her fund of good humour, put it.

Most of their friends presumed they were having a low-key affair: an assumption they had taken pains not to destroy – it seemed to suit them both to be protected from any further involvement. Their friendship meant they each had a partner to invite along when needed and a friend when in trouble. He took her teenage children to concerts and she helped him to buy his Christmas presents. He also enjoyed his evenings with Marianne because her world was so very different to his, and he was a man who liked to know what was happening in all areas of life.

Marianne, always enthusiastic about her work, had bubbled over as she had showed him the photographs of her latest 'find'.

'I hope you don't mind, Guy. I've invited her for dinner this evening, Toby's down from Oxford so I thought we could make a foursome.'

'Are you matchmaking?' He had asked, amused. Toby was her eldest son, an earnest and serious-minded boy whom Marianne laughingly called her 'chaperon'.

'No ... I thought you might like her. She's a real country girl...' Marianne had teased, handing him the portfolio.

He had studied the photographs.

The fashions were based on nineteenth-century rural styles: low-cut lace bodices, smocks and full skirts pulled high to reveal frothy cotton petticoats. The girl in the photographs was heavy-breasted with a pouting, sensual mouth.

'She's called Genivieve, isn't she sensational? A perfect Tess of the d'Urbervilles,' Marianne had enthused.

He had felt nothing when he looked at the photographs, and nothing when he met the girl. She was pleasant enough, but he had disliked her heavy make-up and her upper-class home-counties accent.

He thought again of Lizzie Thornton. And realized, with a deep sigh of appreciation, that today he had met a real country girl. Peter Browne had simply told him that a lady ran the top farm and that he ought to visit her because she was 'a rare un.'

For some reason he had expected an old woman with a craggy face, but instead it was that amazing- looking girl. He thought back to his first sight of her walking across the farm-yard. She was as straight-backed and graceful as a young tree. The memory of her full breasts, almost but not completely concealed beneath the heavy jumper, and her slim boyish hips and legs, made a smile of pleasure slide across his face.

She had been so totally unaware of herself. And with her brilliant violet-blue eyes and dark lashes, she had the kind of wild beauty Genivieve had been trying to capture. And much more than that – a brooding sensuality which could be seen when her mouth curved in one of her slow, rare smiles.

But what made him laugh aloud was her reaction to him ... she had looked at him with such thinly veiled hostility on his arrival. Her violet eyes had been shadowed with distrust, and her only concern had been whether or not he would be a suitable owner for one of her puppies.

Yet underneath her brusqueness he had sensed vulnerability. He had noticed the bluish smudges under her eyes and the state of her hands; she obviously worked very hard.

He stopped at the bottom of the track and looked back at Ellis Ridge Farm. It was the only house for miles around. A lonely grey cluster of buildings clinging to the hillside and sheltered from the gusting wind by a few blasted pines and deformed thorn bushes.

He was intrigued by the place and by the girl who lived there. He thought again of her dark eyes surveying him with unfriendly, almost analytical acuteness.

'I don't think Lizzie Thornton was impressed with either of us, Clara....' he said to the Ridgeback, who was riding along with her head on his shoulder, her cold nose nuzzling his neck.

'Don't dribble down my suit, there's a good dog,' he said gently, pushing her away. And he smiled as he drove, deep in thoughts of the girl he had just met.

# Two

'I'm going to get Charlie the tinker from Thirsk to come and clear up some of this rubbish in the yard. He might give me a few bob for it,' she told the surprised George.

'Nah ... not worth bothering with ...' he said disdainfully. The yard looked all right to him, he didn't see any need to clear it up. 'Wrong time of the year for spring-cleaning,' he grumbled, with a sour look at the windows of the house which she had cleaned until they sparkled.

She had refused to go out on Monday night with a rather startled William, who had secured her promise to go to a 'bash' at Radcliffe with him on Saturday. Instead she had spent the evening at home listening to music and making a list of what she could do to improve the house, farm and herself. She had looked at everything through a stranger's eyes and found it wanting.

She decided she would stop worrying about the farm accounts and improve her quality of life – and her appearance.

She had asked George to come up for two extra mornings, and spent the time cleaning the house. She tried to dismiss the thought that the next time Guy Olafson came to see the puppies she could invite him in for coffee without being ashamed of a grubby Aga and dreary curtains.

It wasn't anything to do with him really, she told herself, she was just fed up with spending all her time doing farmwork and never having time for the house. And anyway – he might never come back...

She remembered how house-proud her mother had been: the old grey-stoned farmhouse had always glowed with beeswax-polish, the rooms alight with flowers and fragrant with the scent of pot-pourri.

She cleared the china from the massive oak dresser in the kitchen and washed it carefully. For her mother it had been a weekly ritual. How long was it since it had been done ... weeks ... months? She tried to forget the painful memories of the loss of her parents in hard work as she washed walls, scrubbed floors and polished furniture.

The weather was too cold to get curtains dry, but she ignored her overdraft and took them to the launderette in Radcliffe. While there, she had her hair trimmed and bought herself some expensive hand-cream and a new black jumper.

Then she turned her attention to the farm and the yard. There was little she could do without spending money she did not have – but she did get Charlie the tinker to take away some of the rusting metal which littered the yard. At first he refused, insisting on payment, but she haggled with him until he cleared some of the rubbish.

Then she found a hammer and nails and straightened the sign on the gate which said ELLIS RIDGE FARM and mended the broken hinge with twine. It didn't look much better but anything was an improvement.

George watched her dourly. 'What's to do Missy? Thinking of selling up?'

'No George ... just tidying up. After the next sale I'm going to spend some money on this place.' George sniffed and didn't reply.

Sometimes she asked herself how her father had managed all the years he had run Ellis Ridge. Admittedly, when she thought back, she could see that there had never been much money around. They had never gone away on holiday, always going to visit Mum's sister, Aunt Emily, at Scarborough instead; but she had never been aware of the endless grind of poverty that she had experienced since she had taken over the farm.

Dad had always joked that two could live as cheaply as one ... maybe that was how he and Mum had got by. She thought of William's heavy-handed proposals which had been more in the line of 'Shall we combine our farms?' than 'Will you marry me?' and giggled at the irreverent thought that William would be very expensive to keep, which was another good reason for not marrying him.

She was more enthusiatic than she usually was about her date with him on Saturday. It wasn't the standard drinks at the Black Swan but a get-together at the Radcliffe Arms. William had told her which organization was holding it, but she had forgotten.

William was very gregarious and belonged to endless clubs like the Masons and the Round Table. He drank less on formal occasions, so she was less likely to have to drive him back and rebuff his attempts at being romantic.

She hurried through her jobs so she would have time to wash her hair and get ready. Her newly-trimmed hair fell in a gleaming bob to her shoulders, her new black jumper looked good with tight-fitting black trousers and boots, and after she had applied make-up and a scant spray of perfume she felt presentable.

William wolf-whistled his approval. 'You look nice ...' he said inadequately. 'Black suits you.'

'Shame about the coat,' she joked, pulling on her old

sheepskin jacket. Then, because she didn't want William feeling sorry for her, or telling her how much better off she would be if she were married, she changed the subject. 'Do you think this darned weather is going to keep up? We've had a hard frost every morning for the past week.'

They talked in general terms about farming. She could hardly bear to think about, let alone discuss, her fears that if they had a bad winter she might not have enough stored food for her flocks. 'I'm pinning my hopes on the sale at Radmoor ...'

She talked on to William, bragging away like any farmer, full of praise for her animals, discussing in detail her Dalesbred ewes and lambs and hiding her worries in bravado. The truth was that if she didn't sell her surplus stock at the last sale of the year she couldn't bring them home again. She didn't have enough food to supplement their diet of grass throughout the winter. She had barely enough for the stock she was planning to keep.

They followed the tortuous road which snaked down the valley until they reached the village of Radcliffe, which straddled the River Wye in a jumble of narrow streets and tall stone-built houses. High above, like a watchful guardian, was Radcliffe Castle, the home of the Ogilvy family.

At the centre of the village was an open market-square lined with ancient oak trees. William parked the Range Rover there, then he turned to her and said laughingly: 'You're turning into a real old woolly-back, Liz ... talking of nothing but sheep, just when you're looking so delectable too ...' He bent his head and tried to kiss her but she pulled away, laughing.

'I hope you're not going to suddenly decide to muscle in and send a lot of stock to Radmoor and bring the prices down?'

She was suddenly serious as she questioned him. With the cost of feed so high and the weather so bad she was worried that other farmers might decide to off-load extra stock and flood the market.

'Stop worrying, woman,' said William, giving up on his attempt to embrace her. 'Come and have a drink and enjoy yourself.'

The Radcliffe Arms was one of the oldest buildings in the village; built to serve travellers in the days when the ruined abbey at the top of the valley had been a thriving religious community. The abbey had been sacked during the dissolution of the monasteries in the reign of Henry VIII but the coaching house and village had survived.

Lizzie had to duck her head to walk in through the low-beamed door. From the bar in the front of the pub she could hear the juke-box playing and the sound of young voices. She thought it sounded cheerful and fun and she found herself smiling, glad that she had come out.

The meeting was held in a large ,warm, smoky room at the back of the pub and the strangest sensation hit her when she walked in. A surge of adrenalin made her heart race – because she knew with absolute certainty that Guy Olafson was there.

She tried to reason with herself. Because she could think of no reason why he should come to this gathering of local people who ran the organizations and charities of the dale. He was an outsider, a man who belonged to a different world.

Why on earth should he come to a Rotary Club meeting at the Radcliffe Arms? He had taken up far too much of her thoughts since his visit to the farm. But as the fine hairs rose on the nape of her neck her eyes searched the room.

She couldn't stop the disquieting thought that some motive other than the pups had brought him to Ellis Ridge to see her. Apart from the fact that he had upset her sexual equilibrium in a way no man had before, she couldn't help a thread of worry. Who was he? And why had he come to look at the farm?

'Drink?' asked William, as he shouted greetings to his friends.

'I'll have a glass of white wine, please,' she answered, although normally she didn't drink.

'Hey up, it's my lucky night tonight!' said William with a grin, and his friends joined in the joke, asking when the stag night would be and ribbing them both.

She forced a smile; and then across the room, through the blue haze of pipe smoke, she saw hair blonder than any other in the room, a fairness seen only in the Nordic races. And she knew before he looked up and met her eyes that it was him, and her heart began to thud, until she felt quite breathless, because her strange premonition had been right: Guy Olafson was here.

Her eyes met his in a look of unspoken recognition and greeting and it was as if the room suddenly fell silent. She didn't hear the good-humoured banter of the group of men surrounding her and she took the drink from William's hand with a 'thank you' that she did not know she had uttered.

She stood quite still and watched Guy Olafson walk across to her. He seemed taller and more distinctive in a room full of people.

This man, she realized suddenly as she watched people parting to let him move through the crowd, would never be a victim of chance. He was a man who would make things happen. No arbitrary forces of luck or coincidence would rule his life. And she was suddenly afraid, because it seemed that their lives had met and fused and she didn't know why. There was some reason why he was seeking her out, and knowing that aroused powerful emotions which she could not put names to.

'Hello ...' he said softly, his blue eyes looking directly into hers. She realized with a start that she had been staring up into his eyes and had not replied to his greeting, and she said hurriedly: 'I didn't expect you to be here.'

His smile was crooked as he grinned down at her and said, 'And I didn't expect to see you here either – it's a very welcome surprise.'

More people were arriving and they were forced to stand closer, when suddenly she knew where she had seen him before and why he seemed so familiar.

She looked up at him, her eyes widening as her hands lifted; they were so close that she could have touched him but instead her hand fluttered as her words tumbled over themselves.

'I've got it! I've just remembered where I've seen you before ... You've been on the television. On the news.'

'Yes ... notoriety at last. You must have a very good memory for faces, to have remembered me.'

'It's been bugging me since we met. I knew I had seen your face before and that it was in some way connected with television. I thought that you might be an actor.'

'Well ... being a lawyer and working in my free time for "Prisoners of Conscience" is a bit like being an actor. I live a lot of the time on bluff and counter-bluff.'

He was grinning at her. And she smiled back as she asked, 'You got the man in the news reports, the rights campaigner, out of prison, didn't you?'

'Yes … by the skin of my teeth.'

'So you live in London?' she wanted to know what had brought him to this remote corner of North Yorkshire – there weren't too many political activists up here.

'Yes, I have a small flat in London, but I'm not there very much. I spend a lot of time travelling, I have quite long spells in Africa and the States.'

'Oh…' she said, feeling unable to answer. He had the aura of a man who was a citizen of the world. She could imagine him at international airports, travelling light with a small suitcase. How boring she must seem.

The room was filling up. He moved nearer and she was disconcertingly aware of his closeness as he asked: 'Have you always lived in Wyedale?'

'No … I lived in London for a while but I hated it …' There seemed no point in lying. In fact, she disliked all cities thoroughly and had been miserably home-sick, almost desperate with depression and loneliness, during her first year at college.

'How refreshing …' he murmured in an amused tone. 'A girl who is truthful.'

She looked away, rather hurt, because once again she had the feeling he might be laughing at her.

She wished suddenly that she could have said she loved London, had millions of friends there, and thought nothing of popping down for a weekend to take in a concert or a play in the West End … But it wouldn't be true. The very thought of travelling on the Underground or driving through the streets of a city overflowing with people and buildings filled her with a desperate claustrophobia.

'You were a student in London?'

'Yes …'

'Where did you study?'

'St Thomas's … I did four years of my training but then my father died.'

'Come and sit down …' He took her drink and guided her to a corner seat where they were hidden from view. She was aware of his hand, warm and strong on her arm, and the curious looks from people who knew her. He seemed oblivious to the interest they had caused.

'Medical training?' he asked. She nodded.

'Tell me about it,' he said, leaning over the table so his face was closer to hers.

'You don't want to know about it. There is nothing interesting to tell,' she said stiffly, looking down and trying to avoid his eyes.

His hand moved across the table and touched her cheek, turning her face so she had to meet his eyes.

Her face flamed at the touch of his skin on hers. A ripple of awareness ran through her body, and she was suddenly terrified that she had actually shivered when he touched her and that he might realize how he made her feel. She scowled at him, jerking her face free.

'I want to know all about you, Lizzie. Tell me!' he commanded. And he smiled again as she bit her lip in confusion.

'Please Lizzie …' he said gently and she wondered how anyone ever managed to refuse him anything when he smiled in that certain way and said 'please'. And suddenly she found herself talking to him as she had spoken to no one else since she returned home.

'I wanted to be a GP. I had great plans for coming back to Wyedale and working. I had wanted to start an emergency unit for the dale: a LandRover equipped for accidents so patients could be treated on the spot instead of having to wait for an ambulance and then have a long ride to hospital.'

He nodded encouragingly. 'That sounds like a good idea. What happened?'

'Dad died very suddenly in an accident. The kind of thing an emergency unit would treat. He didn't get to hospital in time.' Her voice was monotonous, almost emotionless, as she continued.

'My mother couldn't manage the farm alone. So I had a year off to get things sorted out. But then Mum died. She'd never been very strong. She had rheumatic fever as a child and it left her with a weak heart. She never really got over the shock of Dad's death. And since then I've never managed to get the farm to a stage where I could leave it. Dad worked so hard for so many years. I feel I've got to make a success of it.'

She looked up into his eyes, he was listening intently to her, obviously he was a man used to getting people to talk, but even so she was appalled and shocked by her openness.

Despite this she found herself continuing, as if driven to tell him everything. 'I keep on thinking this next season might be the one that makes my fortune, or at least keeps me solvent.'

She gave him a wry smile as she continued. 'I've done what my Dad had started to do and bred some fine Mashams; they are a breed which is really taking off so I might make enough money to set myself up.'

'Fate has given you a rough time, Lizzie. You've not thought of selling up completely?' he asked gently.

She looked down at the table and gripped her glass of wine a little more firmly. 'The farm has been in the family for generations. We don't own the land – it's rented from the Radcliffe Castle Estate. Most of the land around here – in fact most of the dale – belongs to them. But I couldn't give up the house – not even if I were starving, it would be like cutting myself off from my roots.'

'Are you following in another tradition. Are there other doctors in your family?' he asked.

'No, all my family have been farmers. But my parents were one hundred per cent behind me.'

'Don't you think then,' he questioned gently, 'that they would have wanted you to finish your training and become a doctor?'

She looked up at him with troubled eyes. 'I don't know ...' she said bleakly. 'But my father spent his life trying to make a go of the farm. I feel I've got to carry on. I've never questioned it. It is just something I've got to do.'

'Even if it means sacrificing your life and what you want to do?' he asked suddenly. And she felt a vibration of some emotion, anger or confusion, radiating from him.

She drew back from him, she didn't want to think about it.

'Have you always wanted to be doctor?' he asked and he slowly and deliberately touched the back of her hand lightly with his fingertips.

How odd, she thought, he was a stranger and she knew so little about him, and yet here she was telling him everything about herself. And he seemed to care, as if it really mattered to him that she might not get what she wanted from life. There was something very comforting about the way he had touched her hand, a curious soothing warmth from their contact.

'Yes, I always wanted to be a doctor,' she said with a little laugh. 'The only games I ever played as a child were ones where all the dolls and teddies were ill and I would bandage them or mix up medicine.'

They laughed together, and his fingers slid over hers in a caressing touch, so that her hand was held inside the soft warmth of his.

There was a sudden silence between them as the laughter died. His face was very close to hers. He moved forward instinctively and she knew that if they had been alone he would have bent his head a little further and touched her lips with his own.

As it was they were frozen for a long moment and then he slowly, almost regretfully, ran a fingertip along the length of her lower lip. Then he said quietly, but with a note of urgency in his voice as if the time they had together was running out: 'The man you came with, is he a farmer too?'

'Yes ...'

'Is he a special boyfriend?'

He was looking at her intently and she answered with absolute honesty: 'No, a friend and neighbour.'

'So he wouldn't object if I asked you out for dinner sometime soon?'

'Well he might. But I wouldn't ...' she answered with a small smile.

And he laughed aloud as he said: 'I love your frankness, Lizzie. Do you always tell it like it is?'

'No ...' she said, watching his mouth as he laughed, fighting an almost overwhelming desire to touch him.

As if he were thinking the same thing he covered her hand again with his as he said: 'We must try to make it very soon.'

Yes, she wanted to say, make it soon before you go back to London.

He suddenly looked serious and said, 'Lizzie ... I ought to tell you ...'

Oh no! she thought with a sudden sense of foreboding. But before he could utter the rest of the sentence they were interrupted by a voice saying: 'Are you ready to start Guy?'

And he gave her a strange look, half-concerned, half a frown, and touched her hand again as if to say 'See you soon' or 'never mind' in body language.

He rose and crossed the room to stand in front of the assembly, which had inexplicably grown absolutely silent as he walked the short distance.

She sat lost in her thoughts. She felt as if every detail of Guy Olafson, his voice and what he had said to her – the whole atmosphere of the evening, even the sharp unaccustomed taste of the wine and the smoky warmth of the low-ceilinged room – would be printed on her memory.

She suddenly realized she had been listening to the notes of Guy Olafson's voice, the gentle deep melodious quality of it, without paying too much attention to what he was talking about. Something about it being an honour to be invited ... but suddenly, as if her mind were a radio slowly being tuned in, she began to put together what he was saying.

He was talking about the Baronet's son – Clive Ogilvy – who had been killed in a car crash the previous year.

'And although I know, as we all do, that Clive can never be replaced, I will try to fill the gap, to carry on the fine work of the Ogilvy family in the village of Radcliffe and the surrounding area. And in this enterprise I rely on you – the people of Wyedale – to support me.'

He paused, looking around the crowded room for a moment. 'For I know only too well that it is little use having a figure-head without a backbone that is strong and united.'

There was much clapping and calls of agreement

from the gathering, for this was a rallying cry that they could identify with.

In the hubbub his eyes met hers for a fraction of a second, and she could not help the wounded look of accusation which she shot at him.

For now she understood … now, at last, like a complicated jigsaw puzzle, the pieces were beginning to fit and a picture was emerging.

Sir James and Lady Ursula, who lived at Radcliffe Castle, had had only one son and heir. Clive Ogilvy had been a wild young man, often the ringleader in rampaging drinking parties and practical jokes. He had killed himself in his Porsche after an all-night gambling session.

She had half heard gossip, and remembered it only now, that the title, castle and estate had passed on to the next male heir; a nephew – the son of Sir James's sister.

Through the noise and fug of the room and beneath William's loud voice telling her to drink up and offering her another glass of wine, accompanied by much laughter from his friends, she heard again a voice in the village shop: 'Sir James has never bothered with them. She married a foreigner you know … they say the lad is very bright but a leftie…'

Words from the past seemed to be jumbled in her head, swirling through mists, going around and around:

'I will try to fill the gap.'

'It's Miss Thornton, isn't it?'

'Married a foreigner…'

'It must be hard work running this place alone …'

'I want to know all about you.'

'Bit of a leftie…'

'We must try to make it very soon.'

'I want some air…' she muttered to William, not caring

that he didn't hear or notice her slip from the room. She was too bemused and upset to care about William or where she went.

She took the first door she came to, thinking it led back into the main corridor of the pub and the refuge of the Ladies'. But in her confusion she had opened a way out and as she let the door close behind her she realized the night was cold and dark with an icy Arctic wind cutting across the dry-stone walls of the hillside.

The unexpectedness of the bitter chill took her breath away and she began to shiver as the coldness sliced through the thin angora of her jumper. She turned, thinking she would have to go back into the pub and retrace her steps, but before she could move, the door opened, casting her and the frosty grass in a sudden spotlight.

Then there was darkness again and strong warm hands holding her shoulders. Guy Olafson began talking with no greeting as if they could dispense with formalities. 'I'm sorry, Lizzie.'

'You could have damn well told me ...' her voice was angry, bitter with contempt. 'Coming and snooping at the farm ... What do you want with me ...?'

His hands on her shoulders pulled her nearer to him. She was aware of his closeness. Combined with the coldness of the nightwind it made her shiver uncontrollably.

His voice was little more than a whisper as he said softly, 'It's freezing out here and you haven't got your coat ... Come in here.'

He opened a door and pulled her gently, but firmly, inside. It was the pub's bottle store, a dark and cold stone room, but at least they were out of the biting ferocity of the wind.

After the shadowy moonlight the room was as black as a tomb and she couldn't stop a sharp intake of breath which told of her tension as he reached for her in the darkness.

His hands held her firmly and pulled her close to him. She couldn't see his face, but she could feel the masculine hardness of his chest and the slight roughness of his cheek as he held his face against hers for a moment.

'I am sorry Lizzie. I wanted to tell you. I was going to talk to you about it before the meeting started. But how on earth do you tell someone: "Oh by the way … I'm the new young master." '

His voice was resigned, almost sad as he said: 'That's what they call me, Lizzie, "The new young master".'

'Of course they do!' she snapped at him, her anger with him and with herself spilling over. 'Because that's what you are. There is no point being squeamish about it!'

His voice was suddenly bitter as he said, 'I don't like stepping into dead men's shoes. But how could I refuse Uncle James? He is old and sick and he wants to see the Ogilvy line continue. You of all people should be able to understand family tradition and loyalty.'

Was there a similarity between them? She had given up a promising career as a doctor to come home and run a crumbling hill farm. He had given up working for a living as a lawyer to come here to Wyedale and become the lord and master.

Suddenly she was lonelier that she had ever been in her life.

'I don't understand why you didn't tell me who you were when you visited my farm.' Hot tears of mingled anger and hurt were stinging her eyes.

His hands came up and cupped her cheeks. 'Oh Lizzie,' he breathed, his lips touching her face. 'I'm so very sorry, I didn't mean to upset you ...'

'I'm not upset ... I'm cross ...' she said furiously, but she could not stop the quiver in her voice and she began to shiver deep within from the touch of his lips, almost afraid to move or speak.

Damn the man, he always seemed to have her at a disadvantage. She tried to steel herself against the touch of his mouth, but she couldn't fight the tremors of desire and pleasure which were replacing her cold anger with him.

He murmured her name as his hands held her close to him. And the darkness, the thick, close blackness of the room, seemed to intensify her senses so that she was overwhelmed by the feel of his body next to hers, the warmth of him, the subtle scent of his skin and the velvet texture of his soft cord jacket beneath her fingers.

She reeled, inwardly, from the vibrations of pleasure which rose through her body from his nearness. She had, despite her studies into human anatomy and physiology, found her brief sexual experience during her short engagement a disappointment.

She had never guessed that being touched by a man could generate this kind of feeling. And when his lips gently sought hers she drew back – afraid he would know how she felt if he kissed her.

'Don't you want me to kiss you?' he asked, his voice low and gently teasing.

'No ...' she said, her voice a husky whisper.

'That's the first lie you've told me, Lizzie,' his voice was amused. 'And I thought you always told the truth.'

She tried to pull away from him, but it just seemed to

bring their bodies closer.

In a sudden moment with terrifying clarity she re-membered Ricky – the boy she had been engaged to – and the brief weekend when they had celebrated their engagement with a stay in a hotel in Brighton. Ricky had never made her feel like this...

Guy Olafson laughed, a low amused chuckle, as if he had waited long enough for her to realize the stupidity of her lie as his lips came down and claimed her mouth. He kissed her until she clung to him, weak and breathless, her arms around his neck.

And she felt as she had sometimes in dreams when she was falling over a high cliff and the world was spiralling away in slow motion. Utterly helpless.

Suddenly, into the secret intimate world they had created in the darkness, she heard William's voice, raucous and rather annoyed, saying loudly: 'I say! Has anyone seen Liz?' William must be in the corridor of the pub, on the other side of a door, and so close it was as if he had spoken in her ear.

She had a sudden terrifying vision of the door opening and light gushing in and a crowd of people standing and gawping at her – seeing her breathless and dishevelled in Guy Olafson's arms – but worst of all seeing the passionate expression of longing which she knew was on her face.

'I've got to go!' She wrenched herself out of Guy Olafson's arms and moved to the outside door. The moonlight seemed blazingly light after the darkness of the room. He followed her. She glanced once at his face as they made their way back into the pub room and before she made a dash to the sanctuary of the Ladies'. His face was set, inscrutable and aloof...

It seemed hard to imagine that this was the man who

had kissed her and breathed her name over and over again as if it were a litany. Maybe it had all been a dream...

# *Three*

She managed to contain her anger and confusion during the seemingly endless drive home with a surly William.

He seemed to sense something of her mood and didn't try to kiss her good-night. He mumbled something about getting in touch, and although earlier in the evening she had decided she would not go out with him again, the obvious brush-off he was giving her only fuelled her feeling of helpless fury.

What she hated was the sensation that she was not in control of her life. She certainly wasn't in control of her feelings about Guy Olafson. The memory of the way he had kissed her, and the way she had responded, made her shiver with emotion.

It was fear, she told herself, because she had been an awful fool. It had been a long time since her weekend away with Ricky, maybe she was suffering from sexual deprivation? But a small, cold inner voice told her that she hadn't known what sexuality was until she met Guy Olafson. He had unlocked an inner door in her body and mind and she was afraid to open it and look inside.

How dare he have kissed her like that? She touched her lips nervously. Who did he think he was?

And who did he think she was? Some little country girl who was going to fall down at his feet because one day he would be master of the dale.

Damn him, she whispered as she shivered. The kitchen was unusually cold and she realized that she had forgotten to stoke the Aga before going out. It would be a devil of a job to get going in the morning if it went out completely, so she riddled the ashes and threw coal on to the dying embers.

Orange flames began to flicker around the fuel and she left the Aga door open and watched the shapes in the flames. When Mum was alive they always had a fire in the sitting-room; she remembered how when she was a child they would make toast in there, pretending they could see pictures in the swirling white and gold heat.

She never lit the fire in there now, the last time had been the funeral party, it was enough work to keep the ashes in the kitchen emptied. But she had hoovered and dusted the sitting-room; placed a clean lace tablecloth on the heavy yew table; plumped up the cushions of the old chintz settee; laid a fire in the grate, carefully folded newspaper firelighters and chopped splinters of logs dry enough to bring the fire to a blaze with a single match … and all in case the tall blond-haired man had called again.

'You fool! You stupid, idiotic, immature fool!' she cursed herself aloud. Guy Olafson was no romantic stranger. Soon, if the rumours of Sir James's health were true, he was going to be her land-lord. Owner of the pasture and moor where she kept her sheep.

Kneeling before the warmth of the fire she retraced her memories of him. Obviously he had come to inspect the farm and herself and not because he was interested in the pups.

Why hadn't he been honest with her and told her who he was? And then this evening – why had he encouraged her to talk about herself? She hated the feeling that he had been researching the dale and she was regarded as a kind of species: as if he was the anthropologist and she one of a nearly extinct tribe.

She felt anger rising in her. How dare he have kissed and touched her like that? And as for suggesting they went out for dinner together – the very idea was unthinkable. The social strata of the dale was almost feudal in its rules. If she was seen out with the 'young master' everyone would assume one thing – that he was bedding her!

A hot blush rose to her face. That was what he had been suggesting in that kiss tonight! And she had given him every reason to think that she was of the same mind.

She didn't understand what was happening to her. She had dated a few men and never had any trouble keeping them at arm's length. And even though she and Ricky had read all the right books there had been something awfully clinical and uninteresting about their lovemaking.

She sat by the fire biting her fingernails; remembering the books she had read about the right partner, the magical someone who holds the key to your sexuality. 'Oh God …' she whispered. 'Don't let it be him …' Why had Guy Olafson stirred up these violent passionate feelings? And why, why couldn't he have been what she thought he was?

She sat and wept. For unconsciously all their talk of St Thomas's and his assumption that she should go back and finish her training had married together with the the fact that he lived for part of the time in London.

And born from those ideas was a misty picture, not even acknowledged but there nevertheless; a dream of her in London, a student again, the farm solvent, and her meeting Guy Olafson for dinner … The capital had suddenly seemed a much friendlier place for knowing that he lived there: it would almost have been like going home.

But while still in its conception, the dream had been stifled with no chance of life. Reality had stepped in. He was not what she thought he was and she was furious with him, and with herself, for the feelings he had stirred up.

She had been jogging along splendidly until tonight – thinking of nothing but the next sale and juggling the accounts. Her time and energy, her very existence, had been taken up with thinking about her sheep: which tup to use, which ewe to mate with him, which lamb to keep and which to sell.

Work, the farm, the animals, had filled her days and nights: keeping loneliness, grief, lost ambitions and any need for love, all held at bay. And now it seemed this man had called up all the hidden ghosts in the dark recesses of her mind.

She wanted so much more now: to finish her studies, to talk about something other than farming, to dress up, make herself pretty and go out. And, worst of all, she knew she wanted to feel Guy Olafson's arms around her again and the wonderful excitement of his mouth on hers.

She bit her lower lip as the tears brimmed over and trickled down her cheeks. She could forgive him for coming snooping up at the farm. She could forgive him pumping her about herself – without telling her who he was. But she could not forgive the great chasm of longing that he had opened up in her.

'Damn him, damn him …' she whispered. Why had he touched her? Until tonight she had been unaware of the electricity of attraction which could be generated between a man and a woman. She had read about it, witnessed it in others, even thought in academic terms about being in love; and for a time she had been sure that the respect and friendship she felt for Ricky was love.

But the way she felt about Guy Olafson was different – as if what she had felt for Ricky had been a shadow and this real flesh and blood. She didn't know it could hit you like this. That you could meet a man twice and feel an aching inside for the sight and touch of him just because he had talked to you and held you once in his arms ...

She was too fearful to analyse her feelings closely; she just knew that as she sat there sobbing she was crying for the loss of something that she had not even had a chance to understand. And all her pent-up emotions grew together as anger against him. It was almost as if, having decided she could not love him, she would hate him instead.

Finally, as the grandfather clock in the corner of the kitchen wheezed and chimed twelve, she dragged herself upstairs to bed. She dreaded the morning; for winter, coldness and hard work seemed to stretch before her in a never-ending cycle.

The cold weather continued. The hedges and fields in the lower part of the dale were a glittering silver-spangled mosaic. Higher up, at Ellis Ridge Farm, the stunted trees which grew crooked in the prevailing wind were grotesque, frozen shapes furred with frost. Each morning as she broke the ice on Meg's drinking water her heart sank. So much for the greenhouse effect, she thought ... Yorkshire seemed set to go into another Ice Age.

She kept herself busy from morning to night getting the best of her stock ready for the late autumn sale. She worked tirelessly and was rarely in the house, so she wouldn't have known if Guy Olafson had tried to phone her. For some reason that thought was not as comforting as it should have been.

She fought an inner battle with herself; at times having imaginary arguments with him when she told him what she thought of him, but then at times an impossible day-dream would start. Then she would find herself locked in hopeless fantasies of them together in some place that was not Wyedale and where he was not 'the young master' and she Lizzie Thornton.

Impossible to tell herself to forget him. It didn't seem to matter in her dreams if they were arguing or kissing; for it seemed that in some uncanny way he was now part of her, like the ticking of an inner watch, with her while she slept and worked.

The day of the last sheep sale was brilliant with sunshine, the sky a high, intense blue. Even the bitterly cold wind had a clean tang to it. She couldn't help but feel more optimistic about life as she watched the sun flood warmly through the kitchen window and make golden puddles on the quarry-tiled floor.

She dressed herself in her usual market clothes: faded corduroy trousers, her best Guernsey jumper and a tweed hacking jacket with plenty of pockets so she did not have to bother with a bag.

She always felt excited on market days. Even as a child they always had a special magic about them. Because she was an only child she had been allowed to trail behind Dad wherever he went; her own sheepdog pup trailing behind her on a homemade collar and piece of string.

The farmers, more so than their wives, had petted her and she had been like a mascot to them. She remembered that one year when her birthday fell on the opening day of the Great Yorkshire Show a group of her father's friends had clubbed together and bought a leather collar and lead for her pup.

'Come on Meggie,' she said, stroking the dog's silky black head, 'we're ready to go …'

She had trouble starting the Land Rover. She wiped the spark plugs and swore under her breath. It was overdue for a service, but she hadn't settled the last bill at the garage. How she hated owing money, but it simply couldn't be helped. 'I should have trained as a mechanic, not a doctor,' she whispered to Meg, who sat on the front seat watching her.

She eventually got the engine started and with a grinding of gears drove out of the yard. William had been explaining to her about synchromesh and the mysteries of double-declutch.

'Double-declutch …' she said to Meg. 'Sounds like a calypso.' She drove slowly down the unmade-up road, singing softly and smiling. She didn't know why she felt so happy, but the morning was full of promise.

Dry weather suited the sheep, they had looked good when she had helped to load them earlier that morning, their fleeces fluffy and their eyes bright and alert in their gentle black faces.

'Today I might make lots of money, then I can pay all the bills …' she confided in Meg. Then she changed the words of the calypso to 'pay all the bills'. And so they made their way down the dale on the twisty road which led to the market town of Radmoor. The dark-haired girl, her brown face alight and smiling, and the glossy collie whose eyes never left her face, bumping along together in the rusty Land Rover.

The narrow road was gated at intervals to keep the sheep from roaming from the moors. She had parked in the last passing place and was closing the gate when the post-van stopped.

'Glad I've seen you Liz, saved me going up that track of yours. If it gets much worse I'll send everything up by pigeon.' The elderly postman grumbled good-naturedly as he handed her a couple of letters.

'And I don't even want them …' she teased. 'They're only bills …'

'Nay lass, might be a love letter … pretty young thing like you. I'd write you one myself if I were younger.'

She nearly didn't open the letters when she got back into the Land Rover, tempted to tuck them into the AA book and leave them until later; but she couldn't place the one in a thick creamy expensive envelope as she could the others in their flimsy brown coverings.

For a while she looked at the typeface on the front. Then very slowly, not tearing the paper at all, she opened the envelope and took out the heavy sheet of headed note-paper.

She skimmed the page, her mouth tightening, then she carefully folded the letter and tucked it inside the AA book.

She drove slowly on, only now she did not sing or notice the sunshine shimmering on the frosty landscape. Her violet eyes were dark and shadowed and Meg, as if sensing her distress, leaned over and licked her hand whenever she reached down to change gear.

Radmoor was crowded, the narrow streets were full of cars with pedestrians spilling off the pavements. She was pleased to have something to take her mind off her troubles and negotiating the cumbersome Land Rover took all her concentration.

She knew many of the farmers gathered at the market. They called out greetings to her and she answered, her mouth curving in a smile. This was her world. She had grown up coming here to markets and shows. There was a feeling of continuity and security about it. Her father had done this before her, and before him her grandfather and great-grandfather.

She looked over her stock with pride in her eyes. Father would have been pleased to see them.

'You've done well, my lass,' he might have said. But not well enough, she thought sadly; remembering the letter in the heavy cream-coloured envelope.

'Young master's just arrived I see. Handsome young chap...' said Tom, the elderly farmer standing next to her.

At his words her heart seemed to stop beating for a second and she felt as if she could not breathe. To stop her hands from trembling she thrust them deep into the pockets of her jacket.

The next lot of sheep to be auctioned were hers, so she had to stand still. She tried to concentrate on the sheep; to think about what was happening around her, to watch to see who was bidding for her stock, to listen to the quickfire rattle of the auctioneer's voice. But all she was really aware of was the tall man, who because of his height and distinctive hair was clearly visible at the other side of the market.

Guy Olafson was standing next to a smaller, dark-haired man with quick-moving, bright eyes and an alert manner. This man, she noted dully, was bidding for her animals. The price was going up and up; she sensed the interest of Tom next to her.

'Tha's in for luck money today, Lizzie...' he whispered.

Normally she knew to within a pound what her sheep would get. Now, as the bidding ended much higher than she had ever imagined, she found she was doing sums in her head. She might be able to avoid financial ruin …Excitement was building in her. Today she had been on the point of giving up; but the sale had gone so well, far outweighing her expectations, that she could see hope like a tiny bright star in a dark heaven. She would be able to pay some of the bills … The money she had made would not solve all her problems but it was a much-needed financial boost and would help her to keep going until lambing and the summer sales next year.

Then she noticed that the dark man who had bought her sheep was talking to Guy Olafson and she heard Tom's gruff voice: 'It's the young master's bought tha sheep Liz. Paid through the nose too.' The old man cackled, pinching her arm playfully. She gazed at him - mute with surprise and horror.

Then anger began building like a white-hot fire in her and she turned wordlessly and made her way over to the two men who had paid such an unusually high price for her sheep.

She gave no greeting as she looked up into Guy Olafson's blue eyes and asked icily, 'Why have you bought my draft ewes?'

She was aware of surprise in the dark-haired man, but Guy smiled at her with the half-amused look she had observed before.

'I'm going to run sheep at Home Farm … Let me introduce you. Lizzie Thornton, from Ellis Ridge Farm - this is Tony McDonald, who will be head shepherd at Home Farm.'

'How do you do …' said Tony, shaking her hand and giving her the benefit of a dazzling smile. She briefly registered that he was either an Australian or a New Zealander; but she was taken up with her anger and Guy Olafson so she hardly replied to his greeting.

'Shall we settle up?' asked Guy, who now seemed a little puzzled by her set face, although it hardly altered his easy manner.

'Why do you want my draft ewes?' she repeated.

He smiled at her as he replied: 'It's an experiment. But I feel from what I've researched that there's plenty of breeding left in those ewes. We will keep them in during the winter and during lambing and on a high plane of nutrition to see if we can get several more sets of lambs from them.'

She stood silently as he took a roll of notes from his pocket and began to count out the money he owed her. She stood like a statue until he had finished and handed it to her.

'Thanks ...' she said shortly, as if the very word was torn from her. She turned to go but he held her back by saying her name softly.

'Lizzie ... I would like to come and see the puppies again.'

She wanted to walk away and to pretend she had not heard, to cut him dead and let him know she was not playing games, but he was not a man who could be ignored and so she turned back to face him.

Tom had come over and with the familiarity of the elderly butted in: 'If you're interested in puppies you want to see the mother working, then you'll know you've a good un. There's none better for breeding pups in the dale than our Liz.'

Guy Olafson's eyes were sparkling as he turned to the old man and said, 'Thank you, that seems like sound advice.'

He was, she felt sure, secretly amused, whether at Tom's barefaced eavesdropping of their conversation or the use of 'our Liz' as if she belonged to the whole of

Wyedale.

Guy Olafson was smiling at her. 'When will you be working the dog, Lizzie?' he asked quietly.

'In the morning, but I'm going by pony up to the top of the moor.' She couldn't have been curter and even Guy Olafson's smile faded for a moment. He seemed rather taken aback by her rudeness, and his blue eyes narrowed as he looked hard at her frowning face. There was a moment of icy silence between them but then Tom stepped in.

'Well no matter, lass! Haven't you that old horse of your father's?' He turned to Guy Olafson.' You'll not mind trekking on him. Will you?' he asked with rough good humour.

'Not at all. If that's all right with you, Lizzie?'

She would have liked to have said no; but being near to him and hearing his voice and now having his eyes searching her face made her feel quite weak. She wanted to sink to her knees and sob, or throw herself into his arms as she had done to her father when a child and beseech, 'Make it better, take away this awful pain.'

'All right – but come early,' she said sulkily, and turning on her heel walked off. Tom followed her and when they were a distance away he began to chuckle.

'There now, lass, got you proper set up. Here Chas …' he called out to another old farmer. 'Young master's going trekking with our Lizzie. Right taken with each other they are. Not that our Lizzie is letting on.'

She looked at him with barely concealed annoyance. 'What on earth are you talking about?'

'Aye …' rejoined Chas, his wrinkled face crinkling with amusement. 'Young master might have bought my ewes if I'd been young and pretty.'

'Or if you'd managed to find a better ram at tupping

time …' she added acidly. Both the old men laughed at this, as if they liked to see a spark of temper in a woman.

'Could do with some good blood stock in the line – married too many of their cousins they have …' said Tom.

'And seventy per cent of the breeding comes from the dam...' said Chas. And they chuckled away like two malicious cupids, enjoying her annoyed face.

'Time you was married, our Lizzie,' said Tom affectionately.

'Heaven forbid! Don't wish that on me. I've enough problems already,' she said, forcing a smile.

She was scared that some of the urgent devastating feelings which Guy Olafson aroused in her had been noticed by Tom, or worse still by Guy himself. She wanted to get away and to be alone for a while.

'I'll see you two later in the Wool Pack,' she promised the two old men. 'And as I've done so well I'll buy you both a pint.'

'Nay lass,' said Tom. 'You'll not waste your money on us. We'll buy you one for brightening our morning, sight of your bonnie smile makes the world a better place.'

She was oddly moved by the old man's words and felt sudden tears sting her eyes. For a moment she desperately wanted Dad back; for letters about the farm to be addressed to him and not to her, and for the precious roll of money in her inside pocket to be his to spend and save.

An aching loneliness filled her, and with it a cresting wave of fear, for tomorrow she would see Guy Olafson again …

# Four

In the inky darkness before dawn Guy Olafson arrived at Ellis Ridge Farm. In the kitchen of the farmhouse Lizzie was putting bacon and tomato to cook in the hot oven of the Aga and making a pot of tea.

She heard the savagery of Meg's bark soften to a yap and knew who it was. She moved to the door and opened it, shivering in the blast of icy air that cut through her clothes.

'Good-morning ...' Guy said pleasantly as he walked in. His blue eyes slid over her with an amused look.

She stared back at him. With his long legs in faded jeans and cowboy boots, and his broad shoulders in an ancient fur-lined flying jacket of faded softened leather, he was breathtakingly goodlooking.

The way her stomach catapulted at the sight of him made her aggressive.

'I said early morning, not the middle of the night!' she said sharply, closing the door and frowning at him.

He shrugged off his jacket and threw it over a chair. 'I wanted to talk to you ...' he said softly, and something in the tone of his voice, and the way his amused blue eyes looked at her, made her move to her coat which was hanging on the back of the door and say casually, 'I have to go out. Make yourself at home. Pour the tea if you like.'

'I want to talk now, don't avoid me Lizzie. I hate this feeling you don't even want to speak to me.' He moved across and two long brown hands circled her waist.

'Lizzie…' He turned her around to face him with effortless strength as if she were a child.

'Please don't scowl at me …'

She was shamefaced suddenly and raising her face to him smiled in what she hoped was a casual, friendly way.

His eyes gleamed with humour as he looked down at her. 'That's a bit better…' he said. 'I'd started to wonder if you would ever smile at me again. Why were you so cross with me yesterday? I want us to be friends. I didn't know the sheep were yours when I bought them, honestly.'

She could feel the closeness of him and the warmth of his hands and she was suddenly breathless as she tried to wriggle away from him.

'Hang on a minute,' he said, 'I just want to say, before hostilities begin again, that I have been arguing with the world all week and I'm sick of it. Can we have a truce – please?'

His face was so close that his mouth, curving in a smile, was only tantalizing inches from hers.

For a few seconds she just stared into his face, absorbing the silver blondness of his eyebrows and the fine lines around his eyes. There was a tiredness and tenseness in him, despite his goodhumour, which made her say quietly: 'OK, a truce.'

Once again she tried to move away from him, but he was laughing down at her, holding her effortlessly as if she were a butterfly caught in a net.

'If you will let me get my animals fed,' she said with as much dignity as she could muster, 'then I'll make us some breakfast.'

'Ah yes … The way to a man's heart is through his stomach …' he teased, his eyes moving across her face like a caress. He bent and kissed her very lightly on the lips, his warm mouth skimming across hers. It was one of the most chaste kisses she had ever received, but even so her heart leapt and her face flamed and she had to steel herself not to kiss him back.

For a long moment they just stared at each other; he was searching her face as if trying to decipher the conflicting messages of longing and fear which she was giving out. Finally she pulled away and made a dash for the door.

'I was thinking,' she said acidly, pulling on her coat and wellingtons, 'more of the saying "An army marches on it's belly".'

His laughter followed her as she closed the door with a bang.

But she did not feel like laughing as she let the hens out of the hen-house and threw down corn. Her thoughts were all of Guy Olafson. She realized she had thrown down at least three days' worth of food. She pushed her hair out of her eyes, feeling a irrational rush of tears.

Please God, don't let him know how he makes me feel, she prayed, as she filled the water trough. We can't be friends, it is impossible for so many reasons … She reminded herself again of the letter in the expensive envelope. She would just have to be cool and businesslike with him.

He was stretched out asleep in the rocking chair when she went back indoors. His long legs seemed to fill the room and she closed the door quietly and tiptoed around him. She waited until breakfast was ready and the table set before she bent over him and touched his cheek with her hand.

His skin was rough to her touch. He obviously hadn't had time to shave that morning. She stood transfixed, unable to move or believe that just touching him could cause such ricochets of pleasure to explode through her.

His eyes opened suddenly and he looked up at her. She pulled away as if stung.

'Thank you, angel,' he murmured sleepily. 'What a lovely way to be woken up…' Once again his eyes were teasing, and she turned away from his amused smile.

'If you're so tired you shouldn't have bothered to come!' she snapped, putting a plate of bacon and eggs before him as he sat down at the table.

'Well…' he said carefully, 'apart from the fact that I very much wanted to see you and sort out what was wrong yesterday, it is also an almighty relief to get away from the castle. I'm not flavour of the month at the moment with Lady Ursula; and I'm sick of living with guerrilla warfare and English manners.'

His hand moved swiftly across the table and gripped her wrist in a firm hold. 'Let us get one thing straight. Buying your sheep was sheer coincidence, Lizzie. Not a clumsy attempt at giving you a charity hand-out. Is that clear?'

'Yes … perfectly,' she said icily. The way he read her mind was disconcerting.

'Good …' he said, grinning at her. 'Now you can stop sulking and start being nice to me. I could do with some kid-glove treatment after a week at the castle.'

'I would have thought that after Nicaragua and the Lebanon you would have been tough enough by now.' It was her turn to tease him with a mischievous smile. Her memories of seeing him on the news had fallen into place.

'I think I'd rather face a couple of hand grenades than Lady Ursula in full spate. It wouldn't be so bad if she wasn't so bloody polite as I am hung, drawn and quartered.'

She was aware, behind his humour, of the tension in him, which was like a steel cord being pulled too tightly.

'What have you been doing to upset her?'

He buttered a piece of toast and looked across at her very seriously. 'I don't know how much you know already, but I am telling you this in confidence; the estate and castle are in a terrible financial state, virtually bankrupt.'

'Really?' she said curiously. She had been too absorbed in her own financial disasters to worry about Sir James and Lady Ursula at Radcliffe Castle.

'Like so many of these estates it has been running at a loss for years and the actual castle is falling to bits. We either start to run the estate like a business and make it pay for itself or when Uncle James dies, and the tax bill needs to be paid, the whole lot will have to be sold.'

'No?' she was unable to keep the surprise and horror from her voice. 'But who on earth would buy it? A whole dale and a castle?'

Guy stopped eating. 'Sweetheart, the world is full of Americans and Arabs who specialize in buying up places like Wyedale. What I think we should do is to run the place as a business consortium. I never thought I would be preaching capitalism, but it's the only answer.'

She sat very still, unable to eat or answer him, trying to keep her face from showing her feelings. She obviously didn't succeed, because he looked up at her and sighed.

'Please don't stare at me like that, Lizzie, you make me feel as if I've murdered someone!'

'Sorry …' she said with an attempt at a laugh. 'I'm just a bit surprised, that's all. You can't expect change to be popular in Wyedale. People here like things to go on in the same old way.'

'Why?' he asked with a stern look. 'I don't see that the estate has done much for the people of Wyedale or for the tenants. The prevailing attitude has been one of neglect and *laissez-faire*.'

'Yes … it has …' she admitted reluctantly. And then, because she didn't want the conversation to lead on to anything which might involve her, she asked: 'If the situation is so desperate, and you have a solution, why is Lady Ursula giving you a hard time?'

'That,' he said with a frown, 'Is what I don't understand. Uncle James is very keen on everything I've suggested, and if I can get him to palm the ideas off as his then she is happy.'

He passed a hand wearily over his eyes. 'It is quite heartbreaking, they are desperate for the estate to stay in the family. But everytime I open my mouth she contradicts me, and although I don't mind aggression and flak flying in my professional life I do like some peace at home. I don't understand why she seems to hate me so much. Unless of course it's my politics she can't forgive me for,' he added with a wry smile.

'It's probably because of Clive …' said Lizzie slowly.

'Clive?'

'Yes … I mean it must be awful for her, after Clive, to have you coming and sorting everything out for them.'

She blushed, because he was looking at her very intently, as if what she was saying was important, and she suddenly thought that maybe she shouldn't be talking so frankly about his family.

'Finish, Lizzie,' he said quietly.

'Clive was her son. It must be hard for her to have to face the fact that he would never have had the interest or intelligence to think about the estate like you are doing.'

She avoided his eyes and crumbled her toast, worried

that she had said too much.

'I hadn't thought of it like that. Families are funny – I never really knew Clive apart from the odd meeting at family weddings, funerals and christenings – but the official version is what a great chap he was and how everyone loved him.'

He looked at Lizzie's startled face and he leaned across the table and took hold of her hand so she could not rise and walk away, which was what she had been planning to do. He said quietly but in a voice which brooked no argument: 'And now – tell me the truth.'

'I hardly knew him …' she murmured, looking away.

'Spill – Lizzie.'

'It's not for me to tell you about the skeletons in the family closet.' she chided gently.

'Well, no one else is likely to do it. Tell me!'

'He was a lot older than me and I didn't really know him. We hardly moved in the same social circle. But you couldn't avoid hearing the gossip. He had the most terrible reputation, which I believe upset Lady Ursula.'

'And was it deserved – this terrible reputation?'

'It seems so …' she said slowly. 'I don't know how much of it was an act but he seemed to live only for pleasure: fast cars, fast horses, even faster women. Not even marriage seemed to slow him down. To be frank I imagine he knew all about the state of his parent's finances and simply didn't care. Wyedale never seemed to be very important to him. It must be like salt in the wound for Lady Ursula to find out that you care when Clive didn't.'

'Thanks Lizzie, you've helped a lot.' He stopped holding her wrist and, turning her hand over, stroked his fingers across her palm. 'I wonder if women are always wiser than men?' he asked musingly.

He looked up and smiled into her eyes. And she could hardly bear the intimacy between them. It was complete madness for her to feel such a great rush of love for him. She pulled her hand away and rose quickly to her feet. 'If I'm to check all the stock on the top moor this morning we'd better get moving.'

He was staring at her with an intense, enquiring look, as if wondering at her mood and trying to analyse her mixed feelings towards him.

They left the house as the first rays of sun were beginning to touch the lichen-covered roofs of the barns and out-buildings.

'The horses are in the barn.' She didn't add that she had spent hours the previous evening grooming their thick winter coats and kept them in overnight so they would still be clean and presentable this morning.

'Do you ride often, Lizzie?' he asked.

'No. I don't have the time. And Rosie is fine for trekking over the moors but we wouldn't pick up any points in the dressage. But I can't sell her. She's invaluable at lambing time and for humping hay in the winter. Everyone here has to earn their keep.'

She watched Guy looking around the barn. Her tidying up hadn't reached this far, so cobwebs hung thick at the windows and the floor was littered with old discarded tools, string, cat saucers and bales of hay and straw.

He stopped for a moment and stroked the large tabby farm-cat sleeping on a bale near the door.

'Sorry,' he said, looking up and meeting her eyes. 'I'm holding you up...'

'It's all right ...' she said, putting the bridle on Snowy. He came and stood on the other side of the horse, and they tacked up together in companionable silence.

In the yard she watched as he gathered up the reins

and mounted the silver-grey horse which had belonged to her father. He appeared to be a competent rider. But he was the kind of man who would do everything well.

'You're a good rider,' she told him as they walked the horses out of the farmyard together. He grinned across at her. 'I'll have to bribe you not to tell Lady Ursula. She wants me to follow family tradition and wear the red coat.'

'Don't you want to lead the hunt?'

'No.'

'Why not?'

They were riding close together; Snowy and Rosie, who were life-long companions, liked to be in step, so she could see the small frown on his forehead.

'I am prepared to give up my lifestyle and career to take over the title and estate, when the time comes, but I'm only doing it because I think that keeping the castle and the estate together I can improve the lives of the people of Wyedale.'

'As a benevolent dictator?' she asked innocently, and Guy laughed.

'No. That's not my style. There are plenty of people who want the trappings of power and as far as I am concerned they can have them. They mean little to me.'

He shot a questioning look at her. 'I am prepared to give up a great deal for the estate, Lizzie, but I can't turn myself into a different person.'

'I can't imagine why anyone should want you to …' she said quietly. And then, feeling she had said too much, she quickly changed the subject and started talking about sheepdogs.

While the horses picked their way over the rough ground she taught him the softly called commands and whistles she used to work Meg.

Then he watched while Meg circled the scattered sheep, bringing them close to the horses and then picking off the ones Lizzie wanted to look at more closely.

'How did Meg know you wanted that particular sheep?' he asked after Meg had cornered one ewe before Lizzie had whistled.

They had dismounted and tethered the horses, and Lizzie had caught the ewe which Meg had brought forward with the end of her crooked stick.

Lizzie finished inspecting the animal and let it go free. She stood up and smiled.

'A good dog knows what you are thinking. Sometimes I'm convinced she knows what's going on in my mind before I do. She sees me look, senses something, and that's it.

'That is why if you are going to work sheep well together a dog has got to feel really close to you and want to get inside your head.'

'A bit like falling in love ...' he said, with a sidelong look at her and she turned away from him, so that he would not be able to see her eyes, and pretended to check Rosie's girth.

'I wouldn't know about that,' she said curtly.

'You're not going to tell me you've never been in love, Lizzie ...' he asked mockingly.

'No... yes ... well ... not recently ...' she said slowly. Then she enquired abruptly, 'Are you married?'

'Divorced ...' he shot a quick look at her.

They untethered the horses and walked up to an outcrop of strange-shaped rocks which broke up the high slope of ling and rough grass.

As they rounded the rocks, skirting the tiny streams which tumbled down from a spring at the top of the stones, she deliberately walked in front to avoid his eyes.

Here the rocks fell away in a dramatic cliff. Below them was a sweeping hillside of silver-edged grass and frosted patches of heather and bilberry, and then the whole of Wyedale stretched away before them until it softened into a distant smudge of smoky-blue hills.

'What a wonderful view ... it's like being on the top of the world,' he said to her. And she smiled because this was a favourite place of hers.

'Some of the local people won't come up here. They think it is an unlucky place. The old name for these rocks is Satan's Stones and local folklore is that Satan threw the stones out from heaven when he was banished. But it's also known as Lover's Leap.'

'Why?' he asked.

They were standing beneath the high overhanging rocks which offered a shelter from the bitter gusts of wind which swept across the hill side, for there were no trees or walls to give cover and the keening wind moaned and whistled across the heather.

'Oh ...' she said with a smile, 'I think all drops like this are called Lover's Leap. But the story goes that one of the Baronets in days gone by got a kitchen maid into trouble. And to hide her shame the poor girl came here and threw her newborn baby over the cliff. Then, overcome with guilt, she threw herself over as well.

'Her ghost is said to walk the castle kitchens, and on cold winter nights the moor is said to be haunted by the wailing of the babe.'

Lizzie shivered suddenly and added, 'It's a horrid story ... and probably apocryphal. I don't think I believe it.'

She saw that he was looking away into the distance, his face brooding.

'You don't believe in unquiet spirits do you, Guy?' It was the first time she had said his name and she bit her lip as she did so, confused by her familiarity and by his sombre face.

'I don't know, Lizzie ... I wasn't thinking about ghosts but about the family and the estate.'

He looked across at her with a gentle smile. 'The Ogilvies have been a potent force in the dale and rarely for the good of the people. What with carting men off to wars, keeping all the houses and farms on leasehold and blocking any kind of change. To say nothing of what appears to be a family tradition of debauchery ...'

She hung her head – this would be the moment to talk to him – to tell him about her own financial troubles – but something tied her tongue and instead she said, in an attempt at light-heartedness, 'You can't blame it all on the men.'

He grinned at her. 'Oh yes I can! I don't agree with women's liberation.' They laughed together as they mounted the sturdy horses and made their way back to the farm.

'I haven't got time to look at the pups. I've a lunch engagement,' he said regretfully as they rode into the yard.

'I'll not let them go until you've had a chance to see them again.' She dismounted and took the reins from his hand.

'Thank you very much for this morning, Lizzie, and for breakfast.'

'You're welcome. Goodbye,' she said rather hurriedly.

'Lizzie –' his voice stopped her. 'I owe you a meal. Will you come out for dinner one night this week?'

'You don't owe me anything,' she said abruptly. 'And I'm sorry, I'm busy ...' She hoped her face was a cool as her voice, and that he would just leave it at that and go, but he stepped across to her and put his hands on her shoulders.

She might have been able to keep up her charade if he hadn't touched her, but the touch of his hands, strong and yet gentle on her shoulders, made her feel light-headed.

'Busy – all week – every evening?' he teased gently. But his eyes contrasted with his jokey tone. They were raking her face as if searching for some clue.

'Yes – all week – every evening,' she echoed like a child reciting a message she has been told not to forget. 'I'm sorry,' she added quietly.

'So am I. And I would like to know why. When I asked you at the Radcliffe Arms your reaction was very different.'

His tone was still gentle but she felt a surge of fear because his eyes were so very cold and searching. She looked into their icy blue depths and then pulled away from his hands.

He took hold of her again and said with more urgency: 'I've only got a few more days in Wyedale. Then I have to leave for the States. I am booked to do a lecture tour of American universities to promote the aims of Prisoners of Conscience. I shan't be back until Christmas…'

'I hope you have a good time,' she said stiffly, trying desperately to ignore his hands touching her shoulders and the nearness of his face.

As if sensing her weakness, he pulled her a little closer and said in a gentle whisper which made her heart beat faster, 'Please… Lizzie…' He was so close that she knew in another moment he would kiss her and if she felt the touch of his mouth she would be absolutely lost.

She jerked away from him. A feeling of falling and

losing control was making her feel weak and shaky. How easy it would be to lean to him and say 'yes'. She wanted to forget all the obstacles which separated them, close her eyes, let him kiss her and sink into soft darkness.

A voice inside her head was whispering, 'Christmas … you won't see him until Christmas … and maybe not then … You might never see him again. Or he will become an acquaintance, someone you see across the street or at the other side of the market. There won't be any closeness, or talking together; all that you will be left with is a fleeting glance, a wave of the hand, a brief acknowledgement that you are a girl he once knew…'

Her voice was husky as she said, 'I suppose you aren't used to having your invitations turned down… but you'll just have to accept I want nothing to do with you … apart from selling the puppy … and I'm only doing that because I need the money.'

His face was calm, but he pushed a impatient hand through his hair as he said quietly: 'I'm not asking you out as some kind of conquest. I would like to spend an evening with you. Sometimes we seem to be friends … and yet at other times you seem to hate me. Even now when you say "no" your eyes say "yes".'

'Well …' she said, with an attempt at humour. 'Sometimes I get fed up with only Meg to talk to. Farming can be a lonely business.'

'But not so lonely that you are prepared to have dinner with me?'

She met his eyes with a hard look. 'No.'

'Well. That's fine. Only one thing, Lizzie, I don't believe what you've just said. And I don't think for a moment that you do either.' He gave her an amused smile. 'Still – I'll be seeing you …'

'Is that a threat or a promise?' she asked lightly.

He bent his head and kissed her softly on the lips in answer. Another of his fleeting touches which made her ache inside.

She watched him walk away, feeling as if her heart was breaking in two with longing. She wanted to call him back and throw herself into his arms and pour out all her problems. He would help her, she knew instinctively that he would help anyone who was in trouble.

And he would offer his help more than willingly to her. Because there was something special between them. She could sense it and obviously so could he. And she knew she would only have to confide in him for him to solve all her problems.

But she couldn't do it ... Her pride wouldn't let her. It would be like trading on the light she had seen in his eyes the first day he had come to the farm, making capital out of the way he kissed her and selling the friendship between them. She would find another way to get out of the mess she was in.

She was black-tempered with misery all day. The weather, as if in keeping with her mood, changed abruptly and icy rain came down in grey sheets. As a kind of penance she spent the afternoon cleaning out the hen-house.

'Come on Meggie,' she said to the dog, when the fading light of the dismal afternoon finally sent them back to the welcome warmth of the kitchen. 'I think it's going to rain forever ...'

# *Five*

Later, after an early darkness had fallen and the world was frozen into a silent white world of frost and ice, the telephone rang. She felt as if her heart had stopped beating as she picked up the receiver and said her number, trying to stop her voice trembling as she did so.

It was Aunt Emily. Summoning all her reserves, Lizzie attempted to sound bright and cheerful as she told Aunt Emily about the sheep sale and the money she had made.

'But it won't be enough will it, dear?' The line went fuzzy.

Lizzie could feel exasperation growing in her. 'No ... well ... you know farming. There's never enough to go around.' She hoped she didn't sound as dreary and despondent as she felt. 'I'll manage,' she added brightly.

'I've been thinking about Grandma's garnets.'

'Grandma's garnets?'

'Well, I've never worn them, and I don't suppose you will. Muriel, my friend with the antique shop, says all that hideous Victorian stuff is all the rage at the moment...' Aunt Emily's voice disappeared for a moment as if one of the crows sitting on the telephone line had swallowed it up.

'Did you hear me Lizzie dear? Will that be enough?'

Lizzie gasped with amazement. 'Surely they are not worth that much? And do you really want to sell them?'

The line fuzzed over and then unexpectedly cleared

so that Aunt Emily's voice suddenly boomed, making Lizzie grimace and move the receiver away from her ear.

'Well if that's all right with you I'll send a cheque.'

'If you're sure.'

'I only wish it were more... Don't work too hard, I'll see you at Christmas ...'

She was still sitting by the phone doing sums. If Aunt Emily sent a cheque she would use half the money to get her overdraft down ... She was scribbling lists when the phone rang again and startled her.

This time it was a male voice, but not Guy Olafson, it was Tony McDonald, the new manager at Home Farm. 'I hope you don't mind me ringing you. We met at Radmoor Market. I've been very impressed with the ewes you've bred. I was wondering if we could get together ... have a chat about sheep ...'

He laughed good-naturedly when at first she made excuses. Her disappointment that it was not Guy was so great she hardly knew what she was saying.

After a few minutes of her stalling, he said, 'Look Lizzie, I know it seems a bit of a cheek, just phoning you up like this, but Guy will vouch for me being an OK guy. No strings ... I would just like to see you. There's a bit of a get-together on tonight. There'll be a crowd of us. Why don't you come along? It's nothing formal, just dinner at the pub.'

Put like that, it seemed churlish to refuse.

'All right,' she agreed reluctantly.

But after putting the phone down she wished she had asked who else would be there. Still, it was too late now.

Then she panicked about what to wear. Finally she got out her smartest and warmest outfit, a red angora jumper-dress with tiny mother-of-pearl buttons, and decided on that. The Radcliffe Arms was very draughty unless you happened to be sitting right in front of the log fire. The night was bitterly cold with a gusting icy wind and bone-aching chill that even had George grumbling when he called in later for his wages. He was rarely seen in a coat; even on cold days he wore an ancient string vest and open-necked shirt. Whenever Lizzie remonstrated with him about putting on a scarf he would tell her long involved stories of how he had started work at the age of five as a crow scarer, moving on to be a stone-picker at the age of six, and how he had never worn a coat to work in. But the biting Arctic chill that blew down the dale that night forced him to wear an extremely tatty donkey-jacket.

'Never known it so cold ... not since '47 ...' he kept on saying. And Lizzie frowned, wishing he would not call up that particular ghost. She had heard about that dreadful winter when the farm was cut off for six weeks and the animals froze to death in the fields.

As soon as the early darkness fell, a thin coat of ice covered the yard and the roads, so she drove slowly and very carefully down the twisting track. There was no heater in the Land Rover and she could feel Meg's breath warm on her hands.

She was pleased she had refused Tony McDonald's offer to collect her. She knew every bend and bump on the track but even so was finding it difficult to keep the Land Rover on course.

Her hands became so cold she couldn't grip the steering-wheel. She stopped and buried them in the soft ruff of Meg's neck. 'You're better than any heater ... aren't you?' she said to the dog. 'I'm going to be very late, and I'm not going to stay long. I hope Tony McDonald doesn't think me rude. I wish we'd stayed at home. It's a filthy night to be driving.'

When they finally arrived at Radcliffe she found it had changed into a glistening fairy-tale place. Above the castle's dark silhouette a sickle moon glistened and all the roofs had been turned to silver by the frost.

The pub was alive, with light spilling out through the open door and sounds of music and laughter. She felt her spirits rise as she settled Meg on a blanket in the back of the Land Rover. She had missed her conversations with William about farming and it would be good to talk to Tony McDonald.

He was waiting for her, hovering anxiously by the door, and she was surprised by the relief on his face when he saw her.

'I thought you weren't coming. Or that you had got half-way down and decided the road was too bad. It's black ice tonight isn't it?'

'Yes – it's pretty skiddy. That's why I'm late.'

'You look frozen,' he said, taking her arm and guiding her through the throng of people. 'Come and have a drink. The table's ready but I told them to wait for a while. Have something to warm you up. A brandy?' he suggested, giving her one of his beaming smiles. Disconcertingly, for a moment his smile reminded her of Guy. She shook off the eerie moment of *déjà vu*.

'No thank you, tomato juice with a dash of Worscester sauce, please. I'd better have a clear head for the drive back.'

When she heard a deep male voice behind her she thought irrationally that, like Tony's smile, she was conjuring up the presence of Guy Olafson from her imagination. He didn't only haunt her when she was alone. Here in a room full of people it happened as well.

She turned slowly and found that this was no waking

dream; Guy Olafson and a small fair-haired girl were standing behind her.

'Hello, Lizzie. We're pleased you managed to get here.'

His tone was pleasant, his smile welcoming, but his eyes were very cold. He turned from her to the girl by his side and said: 'Lizzie, this is my cousin, Eleanor. Nell to her friends. Nell, this is Tony's friend, Lizzie Thornton, who farms up at Ellis Ridge.'

The words 'Tony's friend' cut like a knife-wound. She shook hands with the girl, murmuring a greeting, hiding her eyes from his, in case he saw the naked hurt in them.

She began to feel panic-stricken, and when Tony handed her a drink she had to make a conscious effort to hold it in her trembling hands.

How stupid of her not to have asked who they were meeting! Now she was going to be spending an evening with Guy Olafson and Nell.

Gone was any pleasure at the thought of talking to Tony and of being in a cheerful pub and eating something she had not cooked for herself. The tomato juice alone was making her feel sick and she knew she would not be able to eat anything.

She realized Nell was talking to her and she forced herself to listen to the girl's questions and answer them.

Nell was younger than herself with a sweet, heart-shaped face, enormous china-blue eyes and blonde, child-like hair which hung in a delicate bob around her face. Her voice was very low and hesitant and she stuttered slightly. Despite this she chattered away, asking questions about the farm and listening with her head on one side like a small inquisitive bird.

Lizzie found herself relaxing as she spoke to Nell,

who had a little of the magic which made Guy so special. The ability to be a good listener, to draw people out and make them feel important.

'I want to help Guy all I can with the estate, it is such a lot of work for him. May I come and visit you at the farm? I would like to know more, then I could be of some use to him. I did a floristry course when I left school. I wish I'd done something more practical now.'

Lizzie stared at her for a moment. After all, it was only right that the family would want to rally around Guy and help him to run the estate. But there was something about the way Nell had spoken, and in the fond look she sent across to Guy, which made Lizzie stare down at the table, unable for a moment to think or speak.

The whole evening was beginning to seem like a nightmare. She looked across at Nell's pretty, vulnerable young face. She was as graceful as a flower-fairy, a child of the aristocracy through and through. A fitting wife for the future owner of Radcliffe Castle ... Nell would know all the right people ... all the right things to do.

Nell was talking, covering the pause that her silence had left hanging between them, and gazing at her with a slightly puzzled look, and she knew with shame that she had not been able to totally hide her confusion and pain.

'Shall we go and eat?' asked Tony, coming and taking her arm again. 'Are you OK? You're very pale.'

'It's just coming into the warm after being so cold,' she lied.

'Come and sit by the fire,' he said kindly, and took her over to the table. He sat with her on the side nearest to the fire, leaving the two seats opposite for Guy and Nell.

There was much bantering and teasing between the two cousins and Tony as they ordered their food. Guy and Nell were on very good terms with Tony, treating him as a friend, or one of the family, rather than the farm-manager.

She sat silently, wishing herself a million miles away. She ordered a prawn salad, despite Tony's attempts to get her to have a steak. Her hands were beginning to hurt from being so close to the heat of the fire and she felt very miserable.

She saw Nell shiver and, noticing that the girl was wearing a thin blouse, asked, 'Are you getting a draught from the door?'

'Yes, It's freezing here…'

'Do you want to swap places with me?' she asked without thinking. 'The heat from the fire is making my hands itch. I think I ought to defrost them slowly.'

'Oh thanks,' said Nell. It was only when they were moving and Lizzie saw Tony frown that she realized changing places meant she was sitting next to Guy and at the opposite end of the table from Tony.

She slid on to the bench seat carefully leaving a gap between herself and Guy. She hoped he didn't think she had offered to change places so that she could be next to him. But he moved up, closing the space between them, so she could feel his body next to hers.

'What's the matter with your hands?' he asked, reaching to take hold of her hand. She bit her lip with mortification. Her hands, roughened with work and with pitifully short nails, were scarlet from the cold. They were exactly the same colour as her dress and hideous, like red sausages.

'They are cold … aren't they?' he said matter-of-factly, reaching for her other hand and holding them both inside the cupped warmth of his long, brown fingers.

'It must have been a very cold drive,' he said, his eyes studying her face. And she knew the unspoken question between them was why  had she agreed to come out on a dangerous, evilly cold night to meet Tony McDonald when she had refused even to consider seeing him.

She pulled her hands away almost angrily.

'It's difficult to believe when it's as cold as this that it will ever be warm again,' he said gently, as she tried to hide her hands under the table.

His words echoed oddly through her. That was just how she felt, as if the coldness would never cease and she would never be happy again. Any emotion other than this terrible hollow pain of wanting him seemed as remote, far away and as unbelievable as next spring.

Their food arrived. She gave up any attempt to join in the conversation and simply sat pushing her salad around the plate.

Nell and Tony were laughing and talking together, having given up trying to get her to join in their conversation. Guy was sitting aloof and silent next to her when suddenly he turned to her and said sternly, 'Lizzie ... are you going to eat that?'

She looked up at him, startled and rather confused. 'I ... no ... I don't think I can ...'

'Why not?'

'I don't know...'

'Don't tell me having dinner in my company is putting you off your food?'

He leaned back against the bench seat, his arm resting so that it was nearly touching her. His face was turned to hers, and she found herself meeting the brilliant blueness of his eyes as he continued speaking.

'Since living in Africa and seeing starvation I can't bear to see food wasted. And I'm sorry you're not enjoying your dinner. Try to eat it, there's a good girl.'

His hand touched her hair briefly and she turned away, filled with confusion. She forced down her salad, although each mouthful was like sawdust.

They moved into the bar to have coffee, which she drank gratefully as she made a valiant attempt to talk to Tony and Nell.

'I hope you won't think me rude if I leave rather early,' she said later. 'I'm a bit worried about driving back.'

'There's lots of room at the castle if you'd like to stay over,' said Nell kindly. 'We're all going to be up very early because Guy has to be at the airport at some terrible hour.'

'The airport?' she asked, suddenly breathless. Guy had said that morning he had a few days before he left England.

'Guy's been asked to go out to China to represent some students. It's all very hush-hush.'

Nell flashed another devoted look in Guy's direction. 'Then he'll go on to the States to start his lecture tour. Do stay the night at the castle, Lizzie, it would be such fun.'

'Oh ... no ... thank you,' Lizzie said quickly.

Being in the company of Guy and Nell was painful enough. The idea of staying at the castle with them would be torture. She could imagine the scene of domestic bliss: Nell in a pretty floral dressing-gown pouring coffee and fussing around Guy, checking that he had packed his shirts and remembered his passport ... as a wife would.

And the news that he was to leave the country in the morning had thrown her into complete panic. China was not only the other side of the world, but it was dangerous. She bit her lip nervously, unable to even look at him.

'It wouldn't be any trouble,' said Nell persuasively.

'Really I can't. Anyway I've got Meg, my dog, with me.'

'Oh ... how lovely!' said Nell, clapping her hands like a little girl. 'Does she go everywhere with you?'

'Yes, she doesn't like to be left at home.'

Guy smiled and said, 'Meg is absolutely devoted to Lizzie. It's worth seeing them together, Nell. They are a perfect example of true, everlasting and unselfish love.'

Lizzie met his eyes, and said lightly, 'Well, a dog never deceives you or lets you down.'

Tony laughed: 'Wish I could say that for my dog. It had a chicken leg off my plate last week. It is the worst lying, cheating hound I've ever come across.'

'You obviously don't inspire devotion, as Lizzie does,' said Guy, and Tony laughed again. But she noticed Nell was looking at them rather intently, and she feared Nell had picked up on their emotional tension.

Lizzie insisted on leaving, even though Tony tried to persuade her to stay for more coffee. She liked Nell too much to want to upset her. Also, the news of Guy's imminent departure had thrown her into turmoil.

She realized that, deep down, she had implicitly believed that because he had said he would see her again it really would happen. Her mind was whirling with trying to sort out how she felt. She wanted to go home and be alone.

Nell insisted on everyone coming out to the car-park

to see Meg. So they witnessed her attempts to get the Land Rover started. The engine coughed and vibrated, but would not go. She could have wept with annoyance as she angrily lifted the bonnet and began to push at connections and wipe at plugs with the cloth she kept under the seat for emergencies.

'I think you'll have to stay after all,' said Tony happily. He had tried to persuade Nell and Guy to stay in the warmth of the pub and was acting as if he wanted a chance to be alone with her.

'Come on Lizzie,' he said, putting his hand on her arm in a friendly manner. 'Leave it and come and have a proper drink and enjoy yourself. You've been as nervous as a kitten all night. No wonder, with this old crate to get you home. It seems to me,' he drawled, 'that this old bus is ready for the scrap heap.'

She shook his hand away, trembling with cold, tension and anger. 'I'm not staying. I've got to get home. My Land Rover may look like a load of rusty old rubbish to you but it's all I've got and I can't manage without it!'

'Sorry,' said Tony, 'didn't mean to offend you.'

Guy silently fetched a flash-lamp from his Range Rover and began to inspect the engine. Tony, seeming taken aback by her outburst, bent to help him.

'Try it now, Lizzie,' said Guy, and to her relief the engine growled into life.

'Take care ... won't you, Lizzie?' called Nell anxiously. Lizzie slowly backed the vehicle out of the car-park, calling her thanks and goodbye to Tony. Guy stood silently, a tall shadowy figure holding out a hand in salute.

She drove slowly down the deserted, icy road. It was so cold that the windscreen was freezing up as she drove. That, combined with the tears in her eyes, made it almost impossible to see.

Why did I go? she kept on asking herself. It had been a miserable evening and she had finished it by being rude to Tony.

And knowing that Guy was leaving for China was terrible. She kept on thinking how tall and blond he would be compared to the Chinese. With his great height and silver-blond hair he would stand out wherever he went – a perfect target for a sniper's bullet.

She sniffed and wiped her eyes on the back of her hand, she didn't dare stop the Land Rover and find a hanky in case she couldn't get it started again. It was driving in a very jerky way, with sudden losses of power, so she had to keep on changing gears.

If she hadn't been so absorbed in her own misery she would have known that the Land Rover would not get up Christmas Pie Hill. Even on good days it had trouble making the long, slow ascent up the steepest hill in the county. Tonight it was impossible that it would get to the top.

As it was, the Land Rover didn't even make the first incline. She heard the engine die and in a moment of panic pulled off the road with a lurch.

She clambered out. Under the brightness of the starry sky the Land Rover hung drunkenly over the ditch. There was no chance of her being able to get it out, unless the engine started first time and she could shove it into reverse gear.

She clambered back in, cursing her skirt, the night and her foolishness at ever going out. She tried and tried to get the engine started, then realized that she was just wasting her time and energy. The sooner she started the long walk home, the quicker she would get there.

Fortunately she had some old wellingtons in the back

of the Land Rover and she changed out of her high-heeled shoes. She called Meg to follow her and began the long, slow climb.

It was bitterly cold and the coarse grass at the side of the road was thick and furred with frost. The icy wind rasped in her throat and stung her legs through her thin nylon stockings.

Then she heard the sound of an engine droning up the valley. It stopped. Whoever was driving must have been inspecting her Land Rover. Relief flooded over her. She would hitch a ride.

She waved her arm as the vehicle came into sight. It was only after it had stopped and Meg began barking a welcome that she realized who it was.

She moved forward slowly, so they met in the circle of light cast by the headlights. Meg had moved ahead, tail wagging, whining with pleasure.

Lizzie looked up at Guy Olafson and said with an attempt at light-heartedness. 'What brings you up here at this time of night?'

'Get in. I'm taking you home.' His voice was cold as steel, and his hand was firm on her arm.

'All right … You don't have to kidnap me. I was going to hitch a ride anyway.'

'I know you were, and that is one of the things that worries me. It could have been anyone driving up here.'

'Oh … I shouldn't worry, there aren't too many maniacs roving around Wyedale in the middle of the night when the temperature is about minus sixteen.'

'Don't be a fool. You know what I mean.'

She had seen him in several moods, and imagined him in many others, but she had never thought to see him angry. She looked at his face; his mouth, normally so curved and sensuous, could have been chiselled from stone and his brows were drawn together in a frown.

They drove up the dale in silence. The only sound was the purr of the Range Rover engine and the thud of Meg's tail as she wagged it in contentment.

The farm, even to her eyes, looked cold and desolate: a squat cluster of buildings clinging to the dark hillside. One faint outside light was the only sign that it was inhabited.

They got out of the Range Rover and the night was so still and frozen that the sound of their feet crunching on the frost broke the silence with almost unreal loudness.

They stopped underneath the lamp outside the kitchen door while she fumbled in her bag for the key.

'I'm sorry,' she said quietly, as she tried to fit the key in the lock.

'So am I,' he said shortly as he pushed the door open and guided her through – once again his hand gripped her arm.

She looked up into his angry face. 'I was bound to know anyone coming up the top road so late at night,' she tried to explain. 'Wyedale isn't like London, you know.'

'Switch the kettle on and make yourself a hot drink. You must be cold.'

She did as he asked. Her explanation hadn't made him less angry, if anything his face had tightened.

He waited in brooding, angry silence while she made tea and placed mugs and a jug of milk on the table.

Then she turned to him and said quietly, 'Would you like a cup of tea?'

His anger exploded, his face a hard-etched golden mask as he took two steps towards her. 'Damn the tea. I would like the answer to a few questions.'

He reached into his jacket pocket and brought out a

flimsy piece of paper. The kind of paper used for carbon copies in offices. He threw it down on the table and she knew what it was without even looking at it.

'Why, in the name of heaven, didn't you tell me about this?'

She shrugged her shoulders. It was a copy of the letter in the heavy, expensive envelope she had received on market-day.

'I didn't see that it was any of your business.'

Her voice was very cold. She would hate Guy to know how many times she had wanted to show him the letter and confide in him.

'Hell and damnation, Lizzie, that is not true and you know it. It's –'

She didn't let him finish. 'You came snooping up here! And then at the Radcliffe Arms you still didn't tell me who you were! And it doesn't matter anymore. I can pay the arrears now, and the rent in advance that your solicitor has so charitably asked for.'

'How on earth have you suddenly got that kind of money? You would have paid it before now if you'd had it! Do you realize you've only just escaped the county court?'

'Mind your own business!' she snapped back.

'The money you made from the sale will only just cover the arrears.'

'It's nothing to do with you!' she yelled in reply.

'It's got everything to do with me.' His voice was raised now. The atmosphere of rage seemed to sizzle between them.

Her voice rose in anger. All the pent-up emotion of the evening generated by being so close to him boiled up inside her and exploded. 'And now you know just where all your fancy ideas about running the estate like a business gets ordinary people. It gets us in court and evicted. It makes us homeless.'

Tears of anger filled her eyes. 'And now get out. This is still my house. I can pay all the money now. So get OUT!' she shouted at him.

He moved forward and took hold of her shoulders. She tried to shake him off but he held her firmly as he looked into her face.

'Surely you know that all this isn't what I intended. Yes, there have been policy discussions about the estate. But this is something which has been worked out without consulting me. I only guessed what the problem was because of something Tony said this evening. Then I went to the estate office and went through the files. The last thing in the world I want is for life to be harder or worse for people in Wyedale –'

'Then why don't you just leave us alone? Sir James may have neglected the farms, a perfect absentee landlord, but at least he didn't harass us. *Laissez-faire* does have some advantages…'

'And is it because of this letter that you wouldn't come out for dinner with me?'

'Oh, don't tell me your pride is still smarting?' she jibed at him. 'You surprise me, Guy, I wouldn't have taken you for a man who was interested in conquests.'

His hold on her tightened. 'Stop playing games with me, Lizzie … What I want to know is, if you were so incensed about the letter, why the hell didn't you tell me about it and get it out in the open?' His voice was tense as he continued. 'The money you made from the sale of the sheep won't cover all that you owe the estate.'

'It's none of your business,' she said quietly. 'I have some of my grandmother's jewellery that I can sell.'

'For crying out loud , Lizzie …' he was angry again.

'Why didn't you tell me?'

'I don't want tô have anything to do with you,' she whispered.

'Why the hell not? Because of inverted snobbery, Lizzie? Because I am heir to the estate? Am I to be deprived of the company of people I like because of an accident of birth and because Clive is dead?'

'You make it all sound so simple and straightforward, but it isn't,' she said breathlessly, aware that his anger was evaporating and that he was holding her very close to him.

The kitchen, which had seemed chilly, was now too warm. She could feel an insidious heat and languor stealing over her. Her anger was gone, she felt weak and rather dizzy.

His hands moved gently to caress her and she leaned against him, powerless to move. His fingers tangled in her hair, pushing her face up to meet his. 'Lizzie … Let me do one thing for you, please. Let me write off this debt.'

'No!'

'There is so much more I want to do. I don't like to think of you living here alone, working so hard and driving that beaten-up Land Rover. I'd change it all if I could.'

'I don't need anything changed. I don't need any help,' she replied irritably, trying to hide her pleasure at the nearness of his face, trying to stop her heart from tumbling and diving with excitement as he moved his head down and touched her lips in a gentle kiss.

'I've got to be at the airport in five hours,' he murmured against her mouth. 'Let's not waste any more time arguing, please Lizzie.'

And suddenly she could not fight her feelings any

more or hide how she felt. Her hands slid up to clasp around his neck, and he pressed her close to him as they kissed on and on with fevered desperation.

It was the chiming of the clock which brought them back to reality.

'I don't want to leave you,' he whispered.

'I'll be here when you get back,' she said, and her eyes suddenly filled with tears. 'Please be careful in China,' she begged, her hands clutching at his shoulders as she clung to him.

His hands came and held her face while he looked at the tears trembling in her eyes. Then his mouth came down and touched hers. 'I'd better go. I've still got to pack,' he whispered but he did not release her, or move his lips away from hers. 'You'll let me write off the debt?'

She pulled away. 'It's not fair to ask ... not now ... not when we're like this ...'

'Please Lizzie...'

'No.' She was vehement, pulling out of his arms, suddenly angry again. 'If you want us to be ... friends,' she said, stumbling a little over the word, 'you must let me do things my way. I value my independence. I must have it.'

He sighed. 'You are going to be responsible for me having sleepless nights, you know that don't you?'

She tried to smile. 'You won't have time to think about me,' she said, wishing once the words were out that they hadn't sounded so wistful.

'You'd be surprised,' he said softly. 'I'll see you at Christmas.'

'Please be careful,' she begged, unable to meet his eyes as her fingers clasped his hand convulsively for a moment. He took her face in his hands and brought her eyes up to meet his and slowly kissed her.

'I'll keep in touch, Lizzie,' he said gently. And then he was gone and the door closed behind him.

Christmas, she thought to herself. It seemed a lifetime away.

## *Six*

The next morning when she opened her eyes her first thought was that Guy was now out of the country, and she was filled with an eerie loneliness.

Then, as her mind retraced the previous evening, strange conflicting emotions filled her. Partly she was jealous of Nell for she had sensed a closeness between the cousins and, much as she liked the younger girl, she could not stop the nagging questions. Nell was obviously fond of Guy – who wouldn't be? But what were Guy's feelings for her?

What ever happened, Nell would always be his cousin. She would always be able to see and talk to him, buy him Christmas presents and fuss round him when he was busy. Lucky Nell, she thought wearily as she set about her jobs in the bleak farmyard.

November – the longest, greyest, dullest month of the year, passed by. She hated the short, dark afternoons when the sun never rose above the sombre height of Satan's Stones.

The miserable weather and her loneliness were relieved a little by the fact that Guy wrote to her. Almost every day a postcard or a flimsy air letter arrived. They were covered with scrawled messages – some obviously written in a hurry. But she treasured them for the glimpse of the world he was living in and for the 'love, Guy', 'missing you' or 'Good-night, angel' that he scribbled at the end.

Some days the happiness she felt when she read the postcards and letters frightened her. She had never felt joy like it before. Yet neither had she ever been lonely until Guy went away ... and her longing to see him didn't lessen as the weeks drew into months.

When he eventually got to the USA he gave her addresses where she could write to him. She felt the news she gave of the farm and the goings on in the dale were dreadfully boring, but he seemed genuinely interested and sometimes replied asking for more details.

Tony McDonald came up and bought two of the puppies. He phoned her regularly to ask if she was all right and if she would like to go out. She always refused, it wasn't that she was lonely for anyone's company – just lonely for Guy.

Then one afternoon in late December, when she was trudging across the yard, she found Tony waiting by the back door. Meg rose up stiff-legged at the sight of him, teeth bared in a splendidly ferocious example of a guard -dog. 'Is she all right?' asked Tony, backing off.

'Yes,' said Lizzie, taking hold of the scruff of Meg's neck and pulling her back. 'She's just not used to visitors.'

'A hermit, like her mistress,' Tony quipped. 'Guy told me to look after you. So I thought I'd better come up and check you over or he'll be chewing my ears.'

She couldn't trust herself to talk about Guy and so she smiled at Tony and asked, 'Come in, would you like some tea?'

'Have you had your invitation?' Tony asked her as he pulled off his boots and settled himself in a chair.

She laughed. 'Invitation ... which one? I have been inundated with them. It's enough to turn a country girl's head.' She pointed to the Welsh dresser which filled up one wall of the kitchen. There, amidst the china were carelessly placed two gold-edged invitation cards.

'Are you going to William and Fiona's engagement party?' Tony asked curiously.

'I might,' she replied non-committally.

'I'm going on my own, do you want to come with me?'

'OK. I really ought to go. It might look like sour grapes if I don't.'

Tony laughed, and then asked more seriously, 'Nell wants to know if you are going to come to the ball. She wrote the invites.'

'She has lovely writing,' said Lizzie with smile.

'It's the traditional Christmas ball at the castle and a kind of welcome home party for Guy. You will come, won't you?' questioned Tony. And, as she opened her mouth to speak, he added: 'Nell says, if you say you've got nothing to wear, there is a very good dress agency in Leeds which hires ball gowns.'

'You've got it all worked out, haven't you?' she said curiously, as she poured out the tea.

'We'd all like you to be there,' he said, giving her the benefit of his dazzlingly attractive smile. 'What have you been doing with yourself, Lizzie? We never seem to see you. It must be lonely living up here.'

'I've been studying. I wrote to my tutor at college. He sent me lecture notes and books. In a while I'm going to go back and finish my medical training.'

'You're wonderwoman,' said Tony with a grin. 'Running this place and studying at the same time. You really are something special.'

'It fills my time,' she said quietly.

'Come with me on Saturday. It will do you good to have some fun, you're too young and beautiful to spend all your time among sheep.'

'I haven't got a thing to wear,' she said doubtfully,

and they both laughed.

'And you'll hire a ball dress and come to the Christmas party?' He smiled persuasively.

'I suppose so ...' she said guardedly, knowing in her heart of hearts she would have to go. Her longing to see Guy was like a constant pain in her. Her waking and sleeping hours, her whole world seemed to be filled with memories of him.

'Guy has sent me some lovely postcards,' she said. Just saying his name to someone was a relief, a pleasure. 'His lecture tour seems to have gone very well. Not that you get much information on a postcard,' she added quickly.

Tony was studying her with an enquiring look. She bit her lip nervously, wishing now she had not ventured on to the dangerous ground of talking about Guy.

'You're lucky to get anything at all from Guy, he's a dreadful correspondent. I'd better get going. I'll pick you up at about eight o'clock on Saturday.'

'All right,' she agreed. And after he had left she wished she had asked him how long he had known Guy. They didn't seem to have the usual owner and farm-manager relationship but to be good friends. She decided she would throw caution to the winds and ask him about Guy the next time they met.

She followed her plan, and as they were driving down the valley road on Saturday night, she started questioning him. He looked at her with a smile and said: 'What a relief, I thought you were the only woman I'd ever met with no curiosity – I didn't know what to make of it' She blushed and fell silent but he continued with easy goodhumour.

'As you are a very special lady I'll let you into a little secret. Guy and I are half-cousins.' She looked at him with amazement as he continued. 'Which also makes me half-cousin to Nell and to Clive, not that he ever acknowledged it ... but that's another story.'

She didn't like to ask how or why. But he continued: 'You're too young to remember Sir Edward, Guy's grandfather, the grand old man of Radcliffe. He was a womanizer and a rogue and everyone loved him. He and Lady Lydia had three children; Rose, Nell's mother; Rowena, Guy's mother; and Sir James, father to Clive; but Sir Edward also had a long affair and an illigitimate daughter by a local girl called Mary Sayers, who was my gran.

'According to the authorized version of the scandal he might have had a few more who no one knew about, but he was apparently very fond of Mary, too fond for Lady Lydia's liking. After Laura, my mum, was born she arranged for them both to go to New Zealand. She couldn't find anywhere further away, apparently.

'I can't speak ill of Sir Edward, he insisted on maintaining and educating Laura. And Sir James inherited the responsibility of me. He rather likes to have me around. There's a tremendously rebellious streak in the Ogilvies – it appeals to his unorthodox side to air the family skeleton – but Lady Ursula hates me. I suppose I'm a constant reminder of the Ogilvy curse of whoring and begetting bastards.' He laughed outright then, and Lizzie laughed too, with relief because he was so light-hearted about it all.

'Guy is a fantastic bloke. We've been friends, like brothers, for years. He's got a lot of the Ogilvy rebel in him but he channels it very positively.'

'Did you know his wife?' she asked, her voice deceptively casual.

'Yes, I met them both in Africa when they were doing

VSO. She was a lawyer. They were far too young and idealistic to marry. But Guy had this idea that they were going to change the world together. Of course, she altered her ideas of what she wanted out of life and he didn't ... he has the most incredible social conscience.

'When they got back to England all she wanted was an expensive home, children and to move up the social scale. She was a terrible snob. Personally I don't know how he stuck it for so many years. In the end she found a stockbroker and now lives in Surrey, in a house with a swimming-pool. Of course, the irony of it is, she would have loved him having the title and being lady of the manor. I hope she's eating her heart out.'

'You really didn't like her, did you?' asked Lizzie, rather shocked by his vindictive tone.

'No – she gave Guy a terrible time. There are civilized ways of ending a marriage. She didn't choose any of them. I'd hate anyone who hurt Guy, he's my mate, and about the best friend any bloke could have.'

'It must be wonderful to inspire that kind of devotion,' she said almost to herself, thinking her thoughts out loud.

Tony laughed, and said teasingly. 'Lizzie ... You could inspire a hell of a lot more than devotion in a man, I can assure you ...'

'The Ogilvies often marry their cousins, don't they?' she asked. And Tony shot a questioning look at her.

'They used to, though anyone who knows much about breeding animals knows it's not a good idea. Sir James and Lady Ursula are second cousins. I sometimes wonder if that is why Clive turned out to be such a nutcase. Not that I want to speak ill of the dead. But I can't see Guy marrying Nell if that's what you're thinking about.'

He laughed at her mockingly as she said quietly, 'Why shouldn't he marry Nell?'

'A multitude of reasons, but you can take it from me he wouldn't. She's the kid sister he never had. She had the most awful crush on him when she was at school. He'd just got divorced and I really admired the way he handled her – letting her down gently and yet not hurting her feelings. So now of course she is devoted to him, but not in the marrying kind of way. Has it been worrying you?' he asked kindly, and she said vehemently, 'Oh no … I was just curious.'

'Now, Lizzie,' Tony said, as they arrived at the Radcliffe Arms, 'I'm going to make sure you have a good time tonight.'

'I will,' she promised, smiling at him. He had laid to rest her ghost of a worry about Nell and Guy And the letter from Guy which arrived in the post that morning had said he would be home on Boxing Day and that he would try to come up and see her. The whole world suddenly seemed a magical place and she enjoyed an evening of dancing, talking to old friends and holding on to Tony's arm.

The following week she made a special journey to the Leeds dress agency Nell had recommended. She went early on a Monday morning, hoping the shop would be empty. She was rewarded, for she was the only customer and the plump middle-aged manageress gave her total attention.

Lizzie's jeans and old jacket gave the woman the idea she was a student. So she was steered over to the economy rail.

'Is it for the Christmas Dance at the university?' the woman asked kindly, studying Lizzie's fresh complexion and dark hair and thinking red would suit her.

'No … the Christmas Ball at Radcliffe Castle.'

'Oh well, my dear, you don't want this disco stuff! Come and look over here. Now, for the castle we want something really exclusive. It doesn't do to arrive and find someone is wearing the same dress. Now, this would look very fetching.'

Lizzie looked at the price tag on the dress and the low-cut sleeveless line of it and frowned. 'I don't think I can wear something off-the-shoulder like that, and it's really too expensive. I've got to get a bag and shoes as well.'

'Why can't you wear off-the-shoulder, you've a lovely bosom,' said the lady, bustling her and several of the rustling silk dresses into the changing-room.

When she saw Lizzie in the first one, a tightly fitting black silk dress which was sleeveless, strapless and backless, she sighed.

'I see what you mean. I have this problem all the time with the girls who ski, you come home with lovely brown face and hands and white as milk everywhere else.'

'It's not from skiing … I work outside,' said Lizzie, looking down at her hands.

'You are nice and tall. I've got something upstairs, a model dress, never been worn and the only one. I'll go and get it.'

When she returned, a little breathless from climbing the stairs, she unwrapped a white silk dress from the dust sheet.

'It's not the latest fashion, but it was such good quality, I had to keep it.'

Lizzie hadn't the faintest idea what the latest fashion in ball gowns was, but she liked the simple, full skirt and long sleeves.

As the lady zipped Lizzie into the dress, she said, 'I thought it would fit you. You have the height and yet the slimness here. I have had lots of ladies who tried to get into this dress but couldn't, but you have the figure of a model.'

'It's shearing sheep,' Lizzie joked. 'It gives you a good waistline. Is it very expensive?' she asked.

'Not for you, my dear,' said the woman with a smile. She then found a tiny sequinned evening bag to match and some low-heeled kid shoes.

'How much will it be all together?' asked Lizzie, trying not to sound anxious.

When the woman told her the amount, she gasped in surprise. It was the same as the taffeta disco dresses, and yet this was pure silk, with a lace underslip. 'You do me a favour,' said the woman. 'You have a good time at the ball.'

'I'll try … I really will try,' Lizzie promised.

She was thrilled with the dress. It fitted so well and felt so right on her that she longed for Guy to see her in it. And so the days leading up to the the ball passed with agonizing slowness.

She did all her Christmas shopping and cleaned the house in preparation for the arrival of Aunt Emily, who was coming to spend Christmas Day with her.

On Christmas Eve she got up especially early and finished her work around the farm, then cleaned the kitchen and made stuffing for the turkey, a chocolate log and pastry for mince pies.

Aunt Emily arrived with a troupe of small dogs and a large ginger tom-cat in a basket, which sent Meg into a frenzy of jealousy,.

Lizzie was very fond of Aunt Emily. She was one of the few people who accepted others just as they were and didn't want to change them. She knew that Aunt Emily would never dream of asking how she had spent the money from the sale of the jewellery. Lizzie thought with a wry smile that Aunt Emily's cheque combined with the sale money had seemed such a fortune, but bills and the cost of living had eaten it up and her financial situation was now as bad as ever.

Lizzie rose especially early on Christmas morning. Her night had been broken with strange, vivid dreams of Guy. She was glad to have the turkey to put in the oven and the animals to look after. It stopped a strange mood of melancholy from taking hold of her.

She was milking Gertrude, the short-horned cow she kept, when she heard Meg bark. She was miles away, deep in thoughts of Guy and how she would be seeing him next day, lulled into peace by the warmth of Gertrude's soft flank under her cheek and the regular rhythm of milking. She dismissed Meg's bark, thinking that Aunt Emily was likely to be up by now and had probably let her motley crew of dogs into the garden.

When she heard her name she turned quietly, so as not to disturb Gertrude. And at first she thought her dream was coming back to haunt her, for Guy stood leaning in the doorway of the barn.

He was taller and leaner than she remembered. His hair was bleached to white-gold by the sun and contrasted with the bronzed planes of his face. He was wearing a crumpled lightweight suit and a summer shirt, he was unshaven and under his intense blue eyes were smoky shadows.

She smiled almost lazily at him and said, 'Hello…'

He walked across and, standing behind her, slid his hands over her shoulders. 'It's good to see you, Lizzie.'

Gertrude turned to look at him and tried to kick the

milk bucket, swishing her tail as if offended by the interruption. Lizzie soothed her and carried on milking.

'Can I try?'

'I hope your hands are warm, Gertie is very temperamental.'

'Aren't all females?' he joked, as she stood up to let him sit on the stool. She put her hands over his and tried to show him how to squeeze and pull at the same time. When he finally had the rhythm she stood behind him, her eyes drinking in the ruffled blond hair, the deep tan of his face and the magic of being only inches from him.

'I wasn't expecting to see you until tomorrow,' she said softly, giving in to her impulse and sliding her hands on to his shoulders as he had done to her. He smiled.

'I got finished early so I pulled a few strings and got an earlier flight. I've come straight here from the airport. I wanted to see you ... and to give you your Christmas present.'

Gertrude moved restlessly and Lizzie said, 'I should think she's dry now. You have to grab the bucket quickly or she'll have it over.'

She moved the bucket of milk and he stood up flexing his shoulders.

They moved out of Gertrude's stall and to the dairy. After she had finished putting the milk into the cooler she asked: 'Will you come into the kitchen and meet Aunt Emily?'

'No ... I've come to see you,' he said, taking her arm and leading her back into the barn. 'Anyway I've got jet-lag so I'm allowed to be anti-social. And I want you to myself for a few minutes.'

He closed the barn door and leaned against it, as if to keep Aunt Emily and the world at bay, then he pulled her into his arms.

'I've missed you,' he said, his voice husky as he bent to kiss her.

She had forgotten the extraordinary intensity of his kiss and her lips parted in instant response to his touch.

'I seem to have been away from you for ever. One soulless hotel room after another. It's been hell,' he murmured, rubbing the roughness of his cheek against the smoothness of her face.

He kissed her again, a deep kiss that told of his loneliness and their separation. She had always seen his life as being glamorous, and hers as very dull. Now suddenly to find that he needed her made every nerve end of her body cry out to comfort him. She hugged him close, returning his kisses, her arms tight around his neck.

She was lost in the pleasure of being close to him, drowning in his warmth and the musky male scent of his skin.

'There's a dog-fight in the yard,' he murmured into her ear.

She moved away from him breathlessly.

'Oh goodness … It's Aunt Emily with her pack of hounds. What if she comes in here?'

'Well... You will have to tell her I'm Father Christmas...'

He pulled her back into his arms. 'I think you're pleased to see me, so I've got what I wanted for Christmas,' he teased. 'And I hope you like your present.' He reached down for his jacket and took a long, slim package from the pocket.

'Wear them for me tomorrow. I'll come for you at seven o'clock.'

'Isn't that very early?'

'You can help me welcome everyone. I want you there next to me. We are going to have a night to remember and nothing and no one is going to spoil our evening… I've missed you, angel,' he whispered, as his mouth covered hers.

In the yard Aunt Emily was calling. 'Come on Growler, come on Tiger, here Spartan!'

Lizzie began to giggle. 'You'd think they were really ferocious, but Growler is a Jack Russell, Tiger a Peke, and Spartan a curly-tailed mongrel who is terrified of cats.'

They hid behind the door of the barn, holding each other close and laughing together like children until Aunt Emily and the yelping barks had retreated into the distance.

She walked with him to his car, his arm around her holding her close. And after he left she wandered around in a daze. Her reflection in the mirror showed her a different Lizzie to the one that normally looked out. Her eyes were extraordinarily bright, and her lips full and reddened from the intensity of his kisses. But more than that, there was a glow as if a lamp had been lit deep inside her.

Her mind was full of him, she had to force herself to cook and eat and talk to Aunt Emily. She was possessed by him as if he were in her veins like a fever. She was lost in happiness and so she did not think about or worry over his words: 'Nothing and no one is going to spoil our evening.'

It was as if no one existed in the world except her and Guy.

# Seven

The next evening he arrived late. She stood and stared at him for a long moment as they faced each other in the kitchen.

His dress-suit was starkly black and his shirt brilliant white – a severity which contrasted with the silver-blondness of his hair and the smooth tan of his face. Although he smiled at her his eyes were shuttered. She sensed a change in his mood from the previous day. He seemed formidable and rather unapproachable.

'Do I look all right?' she asked nervously, her hand moving to her neckline and touching the choker of black pearls – his Christmas present to her.

'You look wonderful. The dress is lovely.'

'The pearls are beautiful.' She touched the tiny matching earrings. 'Thank you very much.'

'A pleasure, Lizzie, they reminded me of you – dark and mysterious.' His eyes sparkled, brilliant blue for a moment with a familiar teasing gleam. But the moment died as he looked at his watch and said tensely: 'We mustn't be late. Come on, we should leave …'

She picked up the multicoloured silk shawl which Aunt Emily had lent her to wear over her dress.

'Are you going to be warm enough in that?' he asked, frowning.

'Yes …'

'I'll put the heater on in the Range Rover,' he said, taking her arm as they walked across the icy yard.

But there was no warmth in his touch – she could have been Aunt Emily. It was as if he were holding her away from him and making sure she did not get too close; and she felt a great gulf, like a wide uncrossable river, between them.

And as they drove slowly along the twisting track she wished, irrationally, foolishly, that they could keep on driving and not go to the ball at the castle.

She wished that the journey would continue until they reached the motorway which cut through industrial West Yorkshire and led on to places with strange unfamiliar names.

Maybe then, without the restraint of this formal occasion, familiarity would come back. They would relax as they drove through the night … sometimes silent, sometimes talking, sometimes touching; sharing a togetherness which would exclude the outside world as the warmth of the Range Rover shut out the bitter night air.

They could drive to London, to Guy's flat … Everything would be different in London. There they would be anonymous and the city would be alive in the special way that it was in the middle of the night; the strange world of sodium-vapour lights and ceaseless traffic.

She had always hated city nights in the past, longing for silence and the velvet darkness of the dales. But it would be different if she was there with Guy … they might find a kebab house and have supper, drink harsh retsina wine and laugh together. No one would care who they were or that they were dressed for a ball – in London no one bothered about such things.

She had always equated the space and isolation of the moors with freedom. But now she felt stifled by Wyedale and claustrophobic at the idea of spending an evening at the castle. She wanted to escape.

In London everything would be different between them. They could be equal … friends … lovers…?

She looked across at him. This handsome aloof man was a stranger. She felt a wave of panic overtaking her. She wanted to take hold of his arm and reassure herself that this was the same Guy who had kissed her with such passion and whispered words of longing to her. And she wanted to beg him to take her away – anywhere – but not to Radcliffe Castle.

'Not nervous are you, Lizzie, darling?' he asked, unnervingly reading her thoughts.

'No, not at all,' she lied.

He touched her hand briefly. 'Good. I want you to enjoy yourself,' he said, as he smiled across at her. 'Nell and Tony will be there and Aunt Ursula generally invites quite a few local people whom you are sure to know.'

She wanted to say, 'I won't know them, Guy … or at least, I might know their faces, but they will not be friends. The dale isn't a place where the classes mix.'

Instead she asked, 'Do your parents have do's like this? Will they be coming tonight?'

'The answer to both questions is no. My father is a university professor and very left wing. They have lots of friends who, to put it politely, are eccentric. Nell calls them weirdo's. My mother brought my father to the castle just once and he spent the whole time talking about the abolition of blood sports. It went down like a lead balloon with Aunt Ursula and the county set and they've not been back since.'

'They sound nice,' said Lizzie thoughtfully.

She wanted to say, 'Where do they live? Shall we go and visit them, wish them a happy Christmas, and forget the castle and the ball?'

With sudden clarity she saw an imaginary picture of Guy's home. A graceful but rather shabby Edwardian house in one of the old university towns. His mother dressed in a floral smock, her hair swept up in an untidy top-knot. His father, tall and greying with an intense intelligent face like Guy's.

They would welcome unexpected visitors, not caring what time they arrived or what they wore. The sitting-room would have lots of books, a grand piano and tapestry floor-cushions. There would be all kinds of different people: students, politicians, writers and artists. They would spill off the settees and armchairs and sit on the floor drinking wine and talking about books and paintings and what was happening in the world.

Everyone would be welcome. Guy would say, 'This is Lizzie, she runs a sheep farm.' The eccentric friends would all be very interested; wanting advice about wool for home weaving, descriptions of country life, or to know how the EEC regulations had altered the face of farming. She would be a novelty, someone rather special and interesting, someone with something important to say.

'Come on, Lizzie, my beautiful dreamer,' Guy's voice was coolly amused. 'Wake up ... We've arrived.'

She started, colouring with embarrassment. She had been miles away in the imaginary sitting-room belonging to Guy's parents, with his mother smiling fondly at her saying, 'You're quite the nicest girl Guy has ever brought home.'

She was shocked by how real her day-dream had been. It was as if she had really been there and had seen the flower prints on the wall, smelt the joss sticks burning in a brass holder on the Victorian fireplace. She had to mentally shake herself to get back to reality.

Reality was Nell, dressed in pink chiffon, meeting them on the steps, and saying breathlessly to Guy: 'Thank goodness you're back, Aunt Ursula's been having fifty fits 'cos you'd gone out. And Uncle's just had one of his dizzy spells and had to lie down.'

Guy looked down at the small blonde girl and said quietly, but with reproach evident in his voice: 'Our first guest has arrived, Nell …'

'Oh gosh, yes! Sorry! Hello Lizzie. How are you?' Nell asked. Then she turned to Guy and said vehemently,

'You can tell Aunt you are back. I've had enough of her shouting at me.'

Guy, ignoring her last remark, said, 'Nell, would you be good enough to show Lizzie around while I go to see Uncle James. No one will be arriving for at least ten minutes so there is no need to panic.'

Nell's voice was childishly treble as she replied crossly: 'I'm not panicking!'

'Are your parents going to be here?' Lizzie asked Nell, as they watched Guy's retreating back.

'Yes, but they're always late, they won't be here for hours.'

'Your dress is lovely, Nell. You look a dream in pink, and I love the little seed pearls and sequins.'

'Do you really like it?' Nell smiled shyly. 'Aunt has just been reading me the riot act and telling me she thinks sequins are vulgar. She is in the most foul mood. Not that Guy will care. He's the only person I've ever met who she can't annoy.'

'I expect she's worried about Sir James,' said Lizzie, as they walked up the wide carved stairway together. 'Worry makes people react in funny ways.'

Nell showed her where to leave her wrap and where

the bathrooms were. She seemed preoccupied and nervy, and Lizzie, picking up on her mood, felt apprehensive.

As they walked back down the stairs Nell pointed out the family portraits. 'And this is Sir Edward, grandfather to Guy and myself.'

'And to Tony,' Lizzie nearly added, but stopped herself just in time. She studied the portrait of the tall black-haired man with a ruddy face and laughing black eyes.

'He was an old rogue by all accounts,' said Nell, and then added, 'I always think he looks rather jolly.'

'Like a pirate,' murmured Lizzie, and they giggled together like schoolgirls sharing a joke.

Despite Nell's nervousness and her pronounced stammer, she still had a streak of what Tony had described as the Ogilvy rebel in her.

'Please, girls, don't stand on the stairs laughing. The guests are arriving.'

It was Lady Ursula, resplendent in muted silver lamé, standing at the bottom of the stairs watching them. Her manner was that of a disapproving headmistress and her eyes were as cold as pebbles as she limply shook Lizzie's hand.

'Good-evening Miss Thornton, a pleasure to meet you,' she said, in a voice which implied just the opposite.

Fleetingly Lizzie's eyes met Guy's and he smiled reassuringly at her.

Then Sir James joined them. He shook her hand heartily, gave her the benefit of a beaming smile, and made a jocular remark about all the prettiest girls coming from the dale. A remark which she was sure would not endear her to Lady Ursula, whose erect silver back was radiating disapproval.

She was not really sure what she was supposed to do.

She wished she had driven herself down and not arrived early. Guy, Sir James and Lady Ursula were all standing rather formally in a line in the marble-tiled hall waiting to meet the guests as they arrived. A butler was hovering, waiting for the great bell to clang, summoning him to open the carved oak door and announce the guests. Lady Ursula settled the question for them all.

She turned to Nell and said abruptly: 'Take Miss Thornton to the library, Eleanor.'

'Yes, Aunt Ursula,' said Nell and, turning, hurried away like a frightened rabbit.

Lizzie followed her, avoiding looking in Guy's direction. From what he had said, he had had visions of them waiting arm in arm, in a relaxed friendly way, with her introducing him to the people she knew from Wyedale. But the reality was very different. Lady Ursula would not have one of the tenants acting like lady of the manor in her house, and besides none of the people she knew well would be coming.

Guy had no idea of the social nuances and rules of the dale. Lizzie sighed. He would soon find out.

'The library is so gloomy. Let's go to the conservatory and see Uncle James's orchids.'

They passed quickly through the enormous dining-hall, which was ready with tables laid for the buffet supper, and through the drawing-room, cleared of furniture for dancing. The band were already assembled and were tuning their instruments with a jumble of discordant notes.

From the drawing-room an enormous conservatory had been built along one side of the castle. Lizzie drew in her breath with delight. Here, like an unexpected glimpse of the Garden of Eden, were tangled vines, gnarled peach trees and riotous creepers, some hanging so low that the foliage swept the top of her head. The air was heavy, moistly warm and sweet with the scent of damp wood-bark and growing shoots.

Then, as they walked slowly down the length of the conservatory, a new perfume filled her senses. 'Aren't they lovely,' she breathed as she and Nell stopped by the first group of heavily scented flowers.

The two girls walked slowly, not talking, just looking and touching, breathing in the heavy perfume.

Then the door of the conservatory opened and the noise of the party, voices and laughter and the band playing softly, came rushing in.

Nell's face lit up. 'Come on,' she said gaily. 'Let's go and find Guy, most people should have arrived by now.'

They found Guy, but he had Aunt Ursula, smiling benignly, apparently glued to his side.

'She's making him talk to all the eligible young girls, how horrid,' whispered Nell. 'Let's get a drink and have some fun. Tony should be here.'

Nell stopped a passing waitress and gave Lizzie a drink which looked like orange juice, but wasn't.

'Bucks Fizz!' said Nell, with a grin. 'Orange juice and champagne. I suggested having them. Much more fun than sherry. Uncle James thought it was a super idea.'

Nell, apparently not at all shy, whirled Lizzie through the rooms, introducing her to all the young people. Some of the faces and names Lizzie knew from pony-club gymkhana's and horse shows. None were people she would have called friends and no one seemed to remember her. And although most of them smiled and said 'hello' in a friendly enough way, she knew she was of no interest to them.

The girls soon gathered in busy, gossiping groups.

She didn't know the people they were talking about so she couldn't join in. And she wasn't glamorous or sexy enough for the young men to notice her. One look at her simple hair style and the high neck of her dress and their eyes slid away.

She understood now what the lady in the dress shop had meant about the latest fashion in ball gowns. All young women were either wearing flapper styles, like Nell's, with chiffon fronts to show off curves, or very dramatic low-cut dresses, favoured by girls with plenty of cleavage.

She began to feel ill at ease, and the champagne made her light-headed, so that she seemed to be able to see herself from a distance; standing tall and gawky, listening with feigned interest to a couple of girls and Nell laughing about schoolfriends and scandals.

She felt a hand on her back, and a deep voice whisper, 'Come and dance.' And she turned slowly, trying to stop her face from lighting up with pleasure, and her heart from turning somersaults.

Guy pulled her into his arms and on to the dance floor. Mainly older people were dancing and she was aware that, compared to the other couples circling the floor, heads nodding as they talked, she and Guy were holding each other very close: closer than necessary to dance a waltz. But any thought or care was swept away by the wonderful feeling of his arms around her and his body moving rhythmically against hers.

His eyes searched her face as he whispered, 'Are you enjoying yourself?'

'Oh yes,' she murmured quite sincerely, because she was – now he was with her.

'I had no idea it was going to be so formal,' he said softly. 'I'm afraid I've still got lots of people I must talk

to. But I will come and find you as soon as I can get away
and we will go in to supper together.'

The dance ended; they were at the far end of the
drawing-room, near to the conservatory door. And as if
the idea was born at the same moment, they looked at
each other with unspoken understanding.

'Let's escape for a few moments. Come and see the
conservatory.'

She didn't have time to answer, he took her hand and
led her through the door. The conservatory was dark
and very quiet after the lights and noise of the
drawing-room.

They walked together for a few moments. Then he
stopped and pulled her into his arms. For a few minutes
he just held her against him, as if exploring the sensation
of her nearness. Then his mouth came down and covered
hers in a kiss of such searing sweetness that she clung to
him, her hands sliding inside his jacket. Through the
thin lawn shirt she could feel the warmth of his skin, and
the sensation intoxicated her senses.

This was what she had been longing for since the
beginning of the evening. Her lips parted and her hands
moved up his body to fasten around his neck.

She had felt like a ghost before, unreal and ephemeral.
No one had been interested in her, their eyes had moved
over her as if she were not real. But the silken caress of
his mouth and the warmth of his body was healing her.
She felt strong and confident as his kiss deepened and
they clung to each other.

The conservatory door opened and slammed shut.
Before they could part a voice full of derisive amusement tore into them.

'Sorry...!'

Lizzie turned with hot cheeks to meet the stare of a tall

blonde-haired woman – it was Barbara Ogilvy, Clive's widow.

Guy's face could have been chiselled from stone as he briefly introduced them.

'I came to find you Guy, darling,' Barbara said with an affected laugh, 'because the Fitz Simmonds have just arrived and I knew you'd want to see them.'

'Really…?' said Guy nonchalantly, making no attempt to move.

But Barbara made no attempt to leave and instead turned to Lizzie with a show of interest: 'Nell says you live up at Ellis Ridge. What on earth do you find to do up there?' And so Lizzie found herself trapped in conversation, and being ushered towards the door and back into the drawing-room by Barbara.

'Excuse me,' said Guy. 'I won't be long,' he added to Lizzie, dropping a kiss on to her face and smiling at her. Then he walked off without glancing at Barbara and the two women stood silently watching him weave through the crowds. Everyone seemed to want him to stop and speak.

It will be hours at this rate before he gets back to me, Lizzie thought despondently, as she watched him being buttonholed yet again by another elderly lady.

'He's irresistibly attractive, isn't he?' said Barbara smoothly. Lizzie realized Barbara had stopped watching Guy and instead had been studying her. Lizzie tried not to show any emotion as she smiled in reply.

'Have a drink and do cheer up a bit,' said Barbara, as she took two glasses of red wine from a passing waitress and handed one to Lizzie.

Lizzie sipped it more out of politeness, and to avoid speaking to Barbara, than because she wanted a drink. She had seen Barbara from a distance on various occasions and, as usual, she was glamorously and expensively dressed in black; which suited her bright gold hair and creamy skin to perfection. Tonight she looked stunning in a strapless, figure-hugging evening dress covered in back sequins.

Lizzie wondered what Lady Ursula, who had complained about Nell's sprinkling of sparkle, thought of Barbara's dress; which glittered and twinkled with every sinuous movement of her body like a million cat's eyes.

'I'm the very merry widow,' said Barbara, drinking her wine too quickly. And Lizzie turned away from her, embarrassed. But Barbara's next words made her spin around and look the woman full in the face.

'Of course I married the wrong cousin.' Barbara finished her wine and gesticulated with her glass to the tall figure of Guy across the room. Seeing Lizzie's startled expression Barbara laughed and said silkily: 'Oh, come now, don't look so shocked! You country girls know all about the facts of life. But my advice to you, Lizzie,' Barbara drawled her name in a way that made her cringe, 'would be to marry the man who satisfies you in bed … I wish I had …'

Barbara's gaze was following Guy greedily like a predatory and hungry Siamese cat. She turned and smiled at Lizzie, her brilliant amber eyes slightly unfocused as she said gaily, 'Have another drink and drown your sorrows.'

'I don't have any sorrows,' said Lizzie quietly, trying not to sound stiff or unfriendly, but longing to get away.

Barbara took another drink and tried to hand one to her but she shook her head firmly at the waitress and handed it back.

Then to her relief Nell joined them. Her high spirits from earlier in the evening had disappeared and her small face was pale and marred by a small frown.

'Come and meet Lizzie, who doesn't have any sorrows,' said Barbara with a scornful laugh. 'Or none that she knows about yet … Shall we enlighten her, Nell, or just let her find out in the fullness of time. It hardly seems fair, such a sweet young thing …'

Barbara's voice continued mockingly, 'It amazes me that local girls like you don't know about the Ogilvy curse. I would have thought mothers would warn their daughters when they are in the cradle …'

'Oh shut up, Barbara,' said Nell, 'you've had far too much to drink. Don't you dare be rude to Lizzie, or Guy will be furious.'

'Guy will be furious,' mimicked Barbara, and then added with a gusty sigh, 'How lovely, I simply adore him when he's angry.'

Barbara turned as if to walk away. Lizzie never knew exactly what happened next. Nell reached across to touch her arm, saying, 'Come on, Lizzie …'

Did she move?

Or did Nell jolt Barbara's arm?

Or was Barbara more drunk than anyone realized?

Because suddenly, in dreadful slow motion and while Lizzie was rooted to the spot in terror and embarrassment, Barbara's glass of wine cascaded like a red fountain down the front of her snow-white dress. The dress which didn't belong to her, which she was due to return to the shop on Monday, which had been hired, for a ridiculously small amount, from the generous woman in the shop … who had kind-heartedly asked her to have a good time at the ball …

She stood, looking at the vivid scarlet stain spreading like spilt blood, feeling her hands trembling like leaves in a storm. And Barbara's laugh and muttered words,

'Oh dear, it looks as lf someone has deflowered the bride …' were mockingly loud to her.

The next few minutes passed in a blur of misery, with Nell repeatedly saying, 'Oh dear, it will stain … what should we do?'

And then Guy, his face kind, taking her hand and leading her upstairs.

He took her to his room. It was dark and oak-panelled with a four-poster bed, a very masculine room, with his books and papers cluttering the bedside table.

'Take the dress off, Lizzie, I'll soak it in cold water, we may be able to save it.'

She was shaking uncontrollably, with a mixture of shock and cold, as she unzipped the dress and stepped out of it.

'Poor sweetheart,' he said, as he scooped up the dress. 'It's gone through to your slip. Take it off, I'll give you my dressing-gown and then find you something to wear. We really must stop Barbara drinking wine by the pint,' he said with easy good-humour, but she felt sick at the sound of his voice saying Barbara's name.

He handed her his dressing-gown. It was towelling and soft and smelt of him: the warm smell of clean skin and a tang of cologne. She pulled it's warmth gratefully around her, her legs were weak and she felt sick. She sat on the edge of the enormous bed trying to fight back tears. The evening had been a disaster.

Surely Guy must see now that she was not part of his world. She had been ill at ease and out of it all evening. She didn't wear the right clothes or know the right people. Neither was she interested in the right things: she didn't go to Switzerland to ski nor London to shop.

Nobody was interested in a girl who had nearly become a doctor and who might one day go back to finish her studies. Everyone thought she was an oddity to be running the farm on her own. She had spent the whole evening hiding her hands and trying to ask questions so she would not have to talk about herself.

And now the poisonous seeds Barbara had planted took hold in her mind. So that when Guy came back and rescued the slip, which lay in a crumpled pale circle on the ground, she stared at him as if he were a stranger.

He sat next to her, puzzled by the pain in her eyes, and put his arm around her, but she flinched back as if he had hit her.

'It's all right, Lizzie, I'm not going to ravish you … although you sitting on my bed is a temptation,' he said lightly.

He pulled her into his arms. His eyes searched her face. 'Why so upset? You're not crying because of the dress?' His voice was questioning, his eyes wryly amused. 'I'll pay for it. Don't let it spoil your evening.' He lifted her face with one gentle finger. 'Come on, darling, don't look so tragic.'

He bent and would have kissed her lips, but she pulled away. He was so sure of her, so confident that all he had to do was touch her, calm her like a child … kiss her better. But she could not rid herself of the image of Barbara, with her golden skin and gleaming tigress eyes, touching Guy's mouth with full red lips.

Barbara's words were tumbling around in her head: 'I married the wrong cousin … marry the man who satisfies you in bed … I wish I had … mothers should warn their daughters when they are in the cradle … You country girls know all about the facts of life.'

Was that what Guy had in mind for her? Was she to be just another in the procession of woman who had shared his bed? Was she just to be a part of the familiar Ogilvy pattern?

It was all there, written into the pages of history and gossip: the bygone Baronet and the kitchen maid with her poor unwanted murdered baby; Sir Edward and the village girl Mary Sayers, who had been sent off to New Zealand by a jealous Lady Lydia. There was a familiar recurring pattern in every generation; and that was certainly what Barbara, her tongue loosened by drink, had implied.

'Please, Lizzie ...' His hands were warm on her cold arms. He was still trying to pull her close to him. 'What's the matter?'

His face was so close she could feel the heat from his body hot against the icy nakedness of her neck and shoulders. His kisses on her face were gentle, teasing tormenting caresses.

She could feel the weight of his body and the robe slipping. He was enjoying her reticence, as he had enjoyed cajoling Meg, as he enjoyed any challenge. His long hands were sliding inside the wide sleeves of the robe to touch her arms. He was comforting her even as his mouth covered hers and she felt passion like an invisible spark flare up as their mouths touched.

She thought of how in the past she had always responded to him, unable to hide the fire of longing he ignited in her. How simple and naive she had been... And how careless – like a child playing with matches. She pulled away; her hair tumbling down in a dark curtain hid her face as she put up her hands and pushed him forcibly away.

He stood up and looked down at her with ice-blue unfathomable eyes. It was impossible to tell if he was feeling displeasure, annoyance, or anything at all. The only sign of anything untoward was a tiny spot of red wine staining the front of his dress shirt and a lock of blond hair falling across his forehead. He pushed it back with impatient fingers.

'I'll find you something to wear and we will go back to the party,' he said quietly.

There was a knock at the door and he answered it, taking care not to open the door too far.

'Eleanor told me that Miss Thornton's dress has been spoilt. I have found her one of mine which I think will fit.' It was Lady Ursula, being the perfect hostess. 'Is the poor girl upset?' she asked.

'No.' said Guy abruptly. 'Thank you for the dress, we will be down in a few minutes.' And with that he closed the door.

'Put it on,' he said, flinging the dress down on to the bed. It couldn't have been a greater contrast to the dress she had arrived in. It was black, with a stiff skirt and an ugly lace top. She slipped it on quickly, fighting to do the zipper up. He came and helped her in silence.

'All right?' he asked.

'Fine,' she lied. She couldn't begin to tell him how she felt: like an ugly lace-clad crow, or worse still … ready for a funeral.

But it wasn't really the dress. She imagined how it would have been if Barbara's words had been left unsaid. She and Guy would have laughed together about the ugly black dress. He would have been kissing and caressing away the pain. She would have cared for nothing but his desire and being close to him.

But the dream was over. How could she have been so simple as to have ever dreamed she could be more to him than the most casual of affairs …?

After all, everyone knew that country girls understood all about the facts of life … And now reality, with the hard cold truth of the immeasurable gulf between them, was staring her straight in the eye. And as they walked down the stairs the tension between them was like a heavy curtain which could not be lifted.

Tony was waiting at the bottom of the stairs. His smile was rather forced as if he sensed the atmosphere of distrust between Guy and herself.

'Lizzie, I've been waiting all night for the chance to dance with you. Come on!'

Tony took hold of her arm and pulled her away from Guy who watched, silent and unsmiling, as she moved into Tony's outstretched arms without protest.

When they were safely anonymous on the dance floor Tony whispered: 'Have you enjoyed yourself, Lizzie? Truth now. Don't be polite.'

She looked into his kind brown eyes and tears swam in her own as she said softly, 'I've hated every minute of it. Will you take me home Tony?'

'Of course I will ... Come on – we'll go now. Do you need to fetch anything?'

'Yes,' she said with a wry smile. 'My shoes and bag and a dress soaking in Guy's bath.'

'What the hell have they been doing to you?' he asked with a grimace.

'I'll tell you all about it on the way home.' She couldn't trust herself to speak or she might start howling like a baby.

With her ruined dress bundled into a plastic bag, they were soon chugging up the hill in Tony's Land Rover. As if sensing she didn't want to talk, he simply told her that, like her, he'd had a terrible time at the party.

'It's been one hell of a night,' he said gloomily. Then he changed the subject and talked about New Zealand and problems with the native Maoris, whose lands had been taken when the island was first settled.

'I'm a bloke who likes a quiet life. I don't like trouble and arguments. Hell! I don't know where you have to go to avoid them...'

Just for an instant she was jolted out of her own misery to wonder what had gone wrong for him that evening.

When they arrived at Ellis Ridge to the welcome of Meg's bark and the dull glow of the kitchen light, he turned to her and said, 'Well Lizzie, Happy Christmas.' And to her shame she burst into a flood of weeping, because happy was the last word she could think of to describe how she felt or would ever feel again.

'Oh baby,' said Tony, folding her into his arms as if she were a child. 'It can't be as bad as all that ... Come on, tell me all about it. Maybe I can help. You didn't argue with Guy did you?'

The mention of Guy's name made her cry all the more, and he held her closer, his head bent over hers.

'Jeez ...' he said. 'You must have had a terrible evening,' and then, 'What the hell –?' as powerful headlights and the roar of an engine broke the stillness and darkness of the farmyard.

For a single moment they were caught in the full beam of head lights which cut into their faces like the glare of a search party or inquisition. She buried her head into his shoulder as they clung to each other like lovers.

The engine roared with renewed life, the vehicle turned, and they were again in peaceful darkness.

'Who was it?' she asked tearfully.

Tony was tense next to her and his voice low as he said quietly, 'I'm sorry Lizzie ... I can't be sure, but I think it was Guy ...'

# *Eight*

Tony's despair matched her own. He buried his face in his hands and swore softly.

'Was it Guy? Are you sure?' she asked.

'It was either Guy or someone driving his Range Rover. I didn't see the driver. I was dazzled by the lights. But it might have been Nell …'

'Nell?' she questioned. 'Why should Nell …'

'It's all such a bloody muddle' Tony exclaimed, his voice ragged with emotion.

'Come into the house,' said Lizzie. 'I'll make you some coffee.'

'Have you anything stronger?' asked Tony, as he slumped down in a chair, his head in his hands again.

Lizzie found an almost full bottle of brandy which Aunt Emily had brought for the Christmas festivities.

She placed the bottle and a glass in front of Tony.

'Are you going to join me?' asked Tony, pouring himself an enormous measure and swallowing it down as if it were medicine.

'No thanks.' She already had a headache from drinking wine and not eating. 'I'm going to make some tea. Tell me what is wrong, Tony.'

He sat silently, drinking his brandy in gulps.

'It won't help getting drunk …' she added gently.

Part of her wanted to scream at him to get back into the Land Rover and race down to Radcliffe explain to Guy, if he had been in the Range Rover, that the impression they gave – of lovers twined in each other's arms – was not a true one. But she was sensitive to Tony's mood and felt sure that he was in some kind of trouble.

Tony poured himself another drink as she filled the kettle to make tea. She put a loaf of homemade bread and goats-milk cheese on the table but he shook his head as she offered them to him.

'Do you mind if I have another drink?' he asked, smiling crookedly at her.

'No,' she said levelly, meeting his eyes. 'Finish the bottle if you want to – but it won't solve anything.'

'No, it won't. We're both unlucky in love, Lizzie. You with Guy, me with Nell.'

She blushed suddenly, biting her lip to keep back tears. With sinking embarrassment she realized that she had not been able to hide her feelings for Guy … Now the whole world knew what a fool she was…

'You're crazy about Guy aren't you, Lizzie?'

She sat looking at the bottle of brandy and didn't answer for a few moments. Then she said slowly, almost angrily, 'So what? He's not married or anything! And neither am I! We're both free agents.'

'Guy may not be married any longer, but then neither is he free … He's always been in love with his work. Jane, his ex-wife, used to say he was married to Prisoners of Conscience, not to her. And now he's got the estate as well … It will swallow him up, Lizzie. And you don't strike me as the kind of girl to play second fiddle to anything or anyone.'

He drank deeply, draining his glass, and she noted that his hands were unsteady as he refilled it.

'And anyway, Lizzie, we're not from their class are we? It's at "do's" like tonight that it really shows … Jeez, all those country deb types make me sick!'

She moved swiftly, removing the bottle from his reach, and saying curtly: 'For goodness' sake Tony, stop rambling on with this awful maudlin rubbish and tell me what's the matter.'

He looked up at her, his face working oddly. 'It's Nell,' he said brokenly, 'I've been in love with her for years. Ever since she was a schoolgirl and used to cry on my shoulder because she had a hopeless crush on Guy. I've loved her and wanted her and known that it was hopeless. But then tonight she suddenly kissed me and whole situation exploded … She told me she's in love with me …'

'Well …' said Lizzie patiently, 'if you're in love with her and she's in love with you, there doesn't seem to be much wrong. Why are you here getting drunk?'

'Don't be so bloody thick!' he said aggressively. 'We're related … And Nell doesn't even know. She just thinks I'm a friend of Guy's.'

'Yes …' said Lizzie, stung by his rude tone. 'But you are only half-cousins, and illegitimate ones at that, which is no bar to marriage, not on any grounds.'

'Marriage!' said Tony with a hollow laugh. 'Give me another drink, Lizzie, for the love of heaven.'

'No,' she said, moving the bottle behind her. 'You've had enough.'

Tony tried to rise to his feet and then sat down heavily, his face in his hands.

'I've had more than enough, Lizzie,' he said in a hoarse whisper. Then he looked up at her, his brown eyes squinting with a troubled frown. 'You must be in bigger trouble than I thought if you think Nell and I could marry and make a go of it. And don't give me any romantic clap-trap about love conquering all. I've had a bellyfull of that from Nell.'

She tried to speak, but he held up his hand.

'Let me finish, please,' he said with the dignity of the inebriated. 'Can you honestly see Nell as the wife of a farm manager: living in a run-down estate cottage; helping out with lambing and milking; rearing puppies and calves; mending the kids' jeans and driving them to the village school in a beaten-up Volvo?'

'She's not a snob!' said Lizzie hotly.

'For goodness' sake!' he howled at her. 'I love the girl. I worship the ground she walks on. I dream every night of making love to her ... But I'm not blind enough to think that Nell could adapt to my way of life. And do you know why?'

He stood up, towering over her, and for a second the fury in his face frightened her until she realized that his rage was with himself and not her. 'Lizzie, I know she couldn't do it ... Because as much as I love her I couldn't live her kind of life.'

'It's you who is the snob,' said Lizzie. 'Only yours is inverted snobbery.'

'I'm not a snob,' said Tony wearily. 'I just know that Nell's family and friends are not my kind. And, much as I love her, I know that Nell is not my kind either. She's not been bred to scrimp and scrape and work for a living. It's just unfortunate that we've fallen in love.' His voice sank to a husky whisper. 'I keep thinking maybe I should take her to bed, then maybe we'd burn it out of our systems, but I love her too much for a fling.'

He looked at Lizzie questioningly, as if asking for advice or absolution. She shivered suddenly with fear, thinking of herself and Guy. 'No ... don't do that!' she said quickly. 'You won't make it any easier.'

'And what about you and Guy?' asked Tony, suddenly more sober.

'I told you.' She forced a smile. 'I'm going back to finish my medical training. No involvements is my motto.'

'So it's just a fling?' questioned Tony.

'Yes ... just a fling,' she echoed.

'Well, I'm sorry if it was Guy who followed us up here. I'll explain it all to him. I'd hate to spoil your fun.'

'Fun?' she queried like a puzzled child.

'Yes fun ... Why else have a fling unless it is going to be fun?' he slurred at her. 'And now, can I have another drink to drown my sorrows?'

'No,' she said, suddenly so tired she could have wept with weariness. 'And you've had far too much to drink to drive back. Aunt Emily's bed is still made up, you can sleep there – as long as you don't mind dog and cat hairs on everything.'

'I like cats and dogs,' said Tony drunkenly. 'I don't mind sleeping with cats and dogs ...'

She tried not to nag him over breakfast next morning. He sat, elbows on the kitchen table, morose and unshaven in his crumpled dress-suit, drinking endless cups of black coffee and disinclined to move from the warmth and peace of the kitchen.

'You will explain everything to Guy, won't you?' she said for the fifth time.

'Yes ... I'll explain. Anyway, I doubt it was him. He wouldn't have left the ball at that time. It was probably Nell,' he replied dolefully.

'Well ...' Lizzie could feel her patience running out. 'Will you please explain to Nell?'

'Yes, if she lets me.' Tony frowned. 'If only I could make some money, then I could marry her. It's poverty I can't face landing her with.'

She sighed. 'Tony ... Life never seems bright the

morning after the night before …especially when you've got a hangover,' she added wryly. 'Go home, have a shower, get changed, then go to see Nell and tell her everything. I really think you've got to trust her a bit more. I know she's young but she's not a child. Why don't you give yourselves a bit of time together, a breathing space?'

Finally he left and she heaved a sigh of relief. But when the noise of the Land Rover disappeared, the farm seemed depressingly silent. And she found she was waiting anxiously for the telephone.

Surely Guy would ring? She found excuses for staying in the kitchen, anxious that she might not hear the phone if she went out to the barn.

She made a turkey sandwich for lunch but couldn't eat it. Then, with shaking hands, she found the telephone directory and looked up the number for the castle. She had to speak to Guy. She desperately needed to hear his voice and have some kind of contact, even if it were only to apologize for leaving the ball early.

The phone rang repeatedly until a woman answered.

'Just a minute, dear, I'll check but I think he left about half an hour ago.'

Lizzie hung up before the woman returned, unable to speak as the tears ran down her face. She was still sitting by the phone when it rang hours later, dry-eyed and staring into space.

It was Tony; he sounded tense and miserable.

'Nell isn't speaking to me. So it's been a bit difficult.'

'Was it her - last night?'

'No - it was Guy. Lizzie, I'm sorry, I was so busy trying to see Nell that I didn't get a chance to speak to him before he left. But I'll give you his London telephone number. He's sure to go back to his flat before he leaves

– ring him there.'

'Leaves – leaves for where?' she asked, her voice no more than a whisper. 'He didn't have any more trips planned, he told me so.'

'No, well, Guy never does. But these things seem to spring up out of nowhere – like tropical storms.' Tony's voice lowered conspiratorially. 'Look,this is top-secret but Nell thinks he's going into Afghanistan. Evidently one of his contacts from Pakistan phoned last night and Guy is flying out to Peshawar sometime today.' There was a long pause and he said: 'Lizzie ... Lizzie ... Are you still there?'

'Yes,' she whispered.

'If you've got a pen I'll give you Guy's number.'

'I've got a pen.'

After Tony had hung up she tried the number.

No one answered for ages. But then she heard a woman's voice saying the number breathlessly.

'I'm sorry ... I think I've got the wrong number.'

'Don't ring off,' said the woman authoritatively. 'This is Guy Olafson's flat. Did you want to speak to him? Just hold on a moment.'

She heard the woman call. 'Guy ... phone call. A girl.'

Then she heard his voice faintly in the background saying, 'Thanks, Marianne.'

An avalanche of longing made her hands tremble as she heard him say, 'Hello ... Guy Olafson speaking.' Then panic and pain took control and she replaced her receiver with a thud.

He had thought she was one of his clients. A girl from the Law Centre where he worked ... someone in trouble wanting his advice. Well ... she was in trouble, but it was of her own making and no one in the world could get her out of the mess she was in – least of all Guy Olafson.

She threw herself down on to the sitting-room settee, too hurt and angry even to cry. The cold dark dankness of the room, with unpulled curtains and unlit fire, reflected her mood.

Marianne ... who was Marianne?

She started to make up excuses, explanations, fantasies to take away the pain. Marianne was the cleaning lady who ironed his shirts, or a neighbour who looked after the key ... fed his cat ... watered his house-plants. But no ... none fitted. Marianne, with her light, well-bred voice, was someone close enough to be there when he came home unexpectedly and familiar enough to answer his phone and to know how to deal with whoever rang him.

Of course a man like Guy Olafson would have women in his life ... past lovers, mistresses, girlfriends. And there was no reason why he shouldn't have taken a passing interest in her. She hated herself with sudden fury. It was she who was at fault. He had told her 'I want us to be friends'. He had never told her she was anything special to him, said he loved her, or made promises.

Maybe she had imagined it all. The affection in his letters, the passion in his kisses and the tender, loving way he held her ... maybe none of it was real, it was a fantasy, a childish illusion. Reality was that she was nothing to him ... He hadn't even phoned to tell her he was leaving.

She turned her face into the soft feather-filled cushions. Somehow she had to find a way out of the maze of hurt and accusation which was poisoning her mind.

It had been horrible listening to Barbara, and suspecting that she and Guy had once been lovers ... might still be for all she knew ... But this new hurt went deeper.

She was angry with the whole world, seething with

impotent rage against her parents. Why had they died and left her alone? Why had they never had more children? She had no brothers or sisters to turn to … No one to care if she was in pieces. And Guy had so many women to love him: Nell, with her innocent devotion; Barbara with her lust; and the faceless Marianne with her cool, businesslike voice and proprietorial tone. So why should he care if a farmgirl from Yorkshire loved him too? He must be used to adoration, even Meg loved him.

Words from the past, from one of her college tutors, came back to her, cutting through her self-pity.

'No gain without pain … Take whatever life throws at you – learn from it – and in the end you will be a better doctor.' How young and naive she had been when she had gone away to medical school. Detached and aloof from reality and still arrogant enough to want to fight and win and never to lose.

And when she finally had been forced to grow up and face the reality of death, she had never let it hurt. She knew now that taking on the farm and managing alone was just a shield against her loss and pain.

You need time to grieve, Aunt Emily had told her. A time to grieve … she had not understood then. There were animals waiting to be fed, bills to pay, work to do … She had never grieved – just coped.

And now, for the first time, with bitter devastation, she faced up to how completely alone she was. There was no one to turn to. Nowhere to run to. Nowhere to hide. She buried her face in the cushion, her thoughts so dark she could not even face the room's dim light.

Then something cold touched her hand. She heard a low whine and looked up into Meg's faithful brown eyes. How strange, Meg had never been allowed into the sitting-room, her territory was the kitchen.

'What's wrong, Meg?' she whispered but Meg whined again and nuzzled with her cold nose and she knew then that she was the problem.

With slow, heavy movements she sat up. 'I know, it's milking time. Come and help me collect the eggs.' Suddenly her eyes filled with guilty tears. Why was she suffering this explosion of pain because a man had given her the cold shoulder? Why did it hurt so much to picture him lying in Barbara's arms, or lunching with the mysterious Marianne in London? Jealousy was the bitterest emotion she had ever felt. She was smothered, breathless, choked by it as she sobbed, 'Oh Guy … Why do I have to love you so much …?'

# *Nine*

The dale was gripped by the worst winter in living memory. Never before had the weather so echoed her mood as icy weather dragged on with interminable grey skies and flurries of snow.

She felt as lifeless and as chilled as the frozen dry earth, and as barren as the wind-tormented trees.

Her hopes of returning to London to continue her studies, and looking after the animals, filled her days and gave her a routine which nothing could destroy. It was at night that the longing for Guy became unbearable. She told herself resolutely that doctors don't die from broken hearts – they know too much about how hearts work. And she immersed herself in her studies, reading the latest immunology textbooks and even pharmaceutical trade magazines from cover to cover.

Tony rang her occasionally and once popped up for a quick cup of tea. He seemed despondent. All his usual cheerfulness had disappeared. He told her that he was thinking of returning to New Zealand and refused to discuss Nell. No one had any news of Guy. He had disappeared in Afghanistan.

When he saw the panic in her eyes at this news he tried to sooth her by saying: 'It is nothing new. He often disappears for months with no word. It used to drive Jane mad. I did try to warn you ...'

But his words were no comfort. The grey days merged together in a blur of hard work and fatigue until March

when the first snowdrops pushed their pale green and
white faces through the frost and snow.

'Thank goodness ... spring is coming,' she said to
George with relief.

'Winter's not finished yet,' grumbled George gloomily. 'We've more snow to come, mark my words.'

Tony phoned her. 'The long-range forecast is dreadful. Do you want to bring some of your stock down
here?'

She refused. The expected weather front might well
veer north and miss them. And she didn't want to move
her ewes now, it was too close to lambing time, and she
couldn't afford to lose a single lamb this spring if she
was going to sell up the stock and go to London.

But just as the first of the lambs arrived, the weather
became even colder and snow began to fall in a swirling
white blanket which covered the dale.

Tony phoned, sounding panicky. 'Are you all right up
there? The top road is impassable.'

'What's new? It's always blocked as soon as we have
more than a few inches of snow. I'm fine. I've got lots of
food, lots of fuel, and I don't mind the snow.'

'Ring me if you need anything, Lizzie.'

There was no post that day, and later, when she tried
the telephone the line was dead.

She saddled Rosie and humped hay up to the top
fields for the ewes, carrying a bale at a time. Then she
milked her goat, Tootsie, who had recently had a fluffy,
long-haired kid. She froze the milk, ready for any lambs
which might need bottle-feeding. She had been able to
match the few which had already arrived to their mothers
and ensure they had a good suckle before she left them.

She tried to reassure herself. So far everything had
gone smoothly. The weather was not good, but neither

was it bad enough to upset the lambing. Sheep fared better in light snow than in heavy rain, which could soak fleeces and drown lambs as they were born.

She was managing to get food to the ewes and considering the hardness of the winter they were in good shape.

So she tried to allay her anxiety as she made herself some lunch and fed the hens. It was probably just psychological because the phone was off, which was silly because days went by when it didn't ring and she didn't phone anyone.

Then large heavy snowflakes, as soft and light as goose-down, began to fall. The leaden lowness of the sky and the cruel wind whirling over the moors filled her with foreboding.

She forced herself to eat some lunch. She knew with sick certainty there was going to be a heavy fall.

Already the windows were filled with feathery whiteness which blocked the light and made the kitchen gloomy.

She wondered why the weather made her so ill at ease, because it wasn't unusual to have a fall late in the year and many lambs born in snow survived. Sometimes snowdrops, primroses and daffodils were covered in a sparkling white covering for a day – late snow generally didn't last long.

She decided to check the Mashams in the pasture below the house which would take her mind off the weather and her gloomy mood.

As she trudged across the yard her feet left deep imprints in the heavy whiteness. The wind cut across her face sending icy slivers of sleet into her eyes. She had only managed to walk a few yards, bending her head against the blinding force of the gale, when Meg stopped and growled a warning.

'What is it, Meggie?' she asked. 'Surely not visitors today?' she said in astonishment, as they watched a tall figure walking through the blizzard towards the house.

It can't be Guy, she thought wildly to herself, as she scrubbed the snow from her eyes.

Even when he stood before her she still stared, unable to believe it was him. 'Guy?' she asked in a bemused voice as if he might be a figment of her imagination.

'What on earth do you think you are doing by refusing Tony's offer of help and staying up here alone?' he asked in a voice as cold as the weather. 'Haven't you heard the forecast? This weather is coming from the States and there people have been dying in the streets from the cold.'

He had taken hold of her arm and was steering her back towards the house. They stopped at the porch. Meg leaned against his leg, her tail waving in a plume of welcome, her mouth wide as if smiling at him. Somehow Meg's instant delight at the sight of Guy drove her own feelings into rebellious anger.

'I didn't know you got world weather reports in Afghanistan,' she jibed bitterly, pulling away from his arm and stamping the snow from her boots.

It was as if the three months since they last met had vanished and the tension and brooding row between them then had smouldered and was now erupting.

His lean face was hard-etched with temper. And even through the dull mizzle of the snow driving in her face, she could see the blazing blueness of his eyes, as hard as chips of sapphire.

She looked at him grimly, her mouth set in a mutinous line as she continued angrily, 'I may not have the *Times* delivered, but I do listen to the TV news. And the idea that weather comes across the Atlantic is a fallacy.'

'Don't be an idiot,' he snapped. 'What do you call this – a lovely spring afternoon? Do you realize your phone is dead and the road impassable? I couldn't even get a Land Rover up your track.'

'So what? I don't need the phone or the road.'

His voice was clipped with suppressed rage as he asked: 'And what happens if you have an accident?'

'Oh well,' she said lightly. 'I shall just have to be extra careful until the road is open again, shan't I? Now, if you will excuse me, I have to go out. The door is open if you want to go in and make a cup of tea and get warm. I don't see why you should be worried about me. A snow storm in the Yorkshire Dales is hardly as dangerous as a week or two in Kabul ...'

She turned away but he took hold of her arm again.

'Cut the sarcasm, Lizzie. The weather is getting worse. I want you to pack some things and come down to Radcliffe with me.'

'I am not going anywhere,' she replied icily. 'I can't just leave the farm, especially when lambs are arriving.'

'I'll send a couple of lads from Home Farm up here to look after things.'

'Oh no you won't! In case you have forgotten, this is my farm and my animals! Don't patronize me, Guy. I am quite capable of looking after myself!'

He looked at her angry face and said more calmly, 'I know you are. I'm sorry to appear high-handed, let's go into the house and talk about it.'

'I've told you. I've got work to do.' She turned from him and walked quickly away, her eyes blind from tears which trickled down her cheeks and froze in the biting, chill wind.

How could he arrive and talk to her like this? As if he

had been away for a few days doing nothing very important. As if there was nothing between them but a landlord and tenant relationship? He had talked as if she were an incompetent child who couldn't be trusted to look after herself.

'Lizzie!' he called, but she walked quickly away, slipping into the barn and out through the back door, ignoring his voice, which was calling frantically now. She wouldn't let him see her cry …

The whole world seemed deadly still and unnervingly quiet as she stumbled across the first field and scrambled over a drystone wall. Her eyes searched in the heavy drifting whiteness for the sheep. She and Meg knew where to look because they gathered near wind breaks in bad weather.

Meg found the first lamb, cold but still alive.

There was no sign of the ewe, which must have wandered off, disorientated by the snow.

While they were searching for the ewe, Lizzie found a second lamb. She placed both lambs inside her coat, curving their skinny newborn bodies against hers to warm them.

She decided to get home as quickly as possible, because if the two scraps of life got a belly full of milk from an obliging Tootsie there was a chance they could survive.

It was dreadful to think how many more lambs and ewes may be buried beneath the snow … and newborn lambs stood no chance in such cold unless they could suckle.

The afternoon was now unnaturally dark. Greyness merging with the swirling snow made it impossible to see where sky ended and earth began. The whole world was full of white ice.

'Come on Meg…' she called irritably. But the normally

obedient Meg would not move. The dog's coat was so thickly matted with snow that she was practically invisible.

'Come on,' she called more urgently. But Meg ran in a circle, whining softly, and would not leave.

Moving cumbersomely, hampered by the two lambs nestling under her arms and snow caking her boots, she moved across to Meg. The dog was digging and sniffing.

'All right girl, let me see …'

Just under the top layer of frozen snow she found twin lambs. They were tiny, premature and only just alive. The ewe lay dead beneath them. She placed the two lambs inside her coat. Walking home carrying four lambs in a blinding snowstorm wasn't easy but she couldn't leave them to certain death.

The walk was a nightmare. Snow slid and dripped down her face, making it difficult to see, and her boots sank deeply into the soft whiteness so each footstep was an effort. The lambs were not only heavy but moved around and upset her balance. Once she sat down in a snowdrift and had trouble getting to her feet again.

An early darkness was falling when she arrived back at the farm. It appeared she had left all the house lights on and it guided her like a beacon.

She had never felt so cold. It had been impossible to zip her coat with four lambs sheltered inside and the vicious chill of the day seemed to have seeped into her blood.

She couldn't feel her hands, they seemed to be frozen to the heavy hump in front of her.

Guy was standing in the yard. 'Lizzie … Thank God you're back.' He must have been waiting the whole time for her. He was covered in snow and his face was grey with anxiety. 'What on earth?' He stared at her.

'Lambs … They've arrived in the snow and lost their mothers.'

'Let me help.' He unzipped his coat and began to put the lambs next to the warm lining.

'They're sticky, just been born … they'll make you mucky,' she said weakly.

'I don't mind,' he said. 'Where do you want them.'

'The barn. The goat will suckle them.'

She followed him, and watched silently as he took charge of the lambs, taking care that the smallest twins got first chance to suck.

She leaned against the wall, realizing how totally exhausted and cold she was.

'Come on,' he said, 'let's get you indoors. You are worn out.'

'Poor Meg,' she said, trying to stop her teeth chattering. 'You can only see her eyes, she's like a snow dog.'

'She'll be all right for a minute,' Guy said brusquely. 'Come inside and get warm.'

They stood for a moment in the centre of the kitchen looking at each other.

'You're nearly dead with cold.' His voice was low. 'I've been out of my mind with worry. Why did you walk off?'

'Sorry,' she said wearily. His face was swimming before her eyes, and she fumbled blindly as she tried to take off her gloves.

He moved forward and tried to help but the gloves were frozen hard. In the end he got a pair of scissors and cut them off.

Then he helped her to take off her coat, and she huddled over the Aga, nursing her hands, unable to stop shivering.

'I'll run you a bath,' he said, his face still tense. 'Go and have it while I get this snow off Meg and get her dry.'

Not even the bath, which felt red-hot on her frozen skin, warmed her. Guy met her outside the door with a mug of tea.

'Go and get into bed. I think you've given yourself hypothermia. Leave the tea until it is cooler before you drink it.'

He sounded almost angry. And she shrank from his gaze as she went quickly into her bedroom and huddled under the duvet, unable to stop shivering.

He came and stood beside her bed, looking down at her, and placing the mug on the bedside table he asked wearily: 'I don't understand why you didn't let Tony move your stock down to Home Farm. You must know that the weather can turn like this. Or was it just one more nail in his coffin? Couldn't you resist making him feel totally dispensable?'

'Go away and leave me alone,' she croaked miserably, burying her head under the duvet and trying to stop shivering. 'I don't know what you are talking about.'

With an oath Guy moved forward and pulled the duvet down so her face was exposed, she winced and refused to meet his eyes.

'Don't play the innocent with me, Lizzie!' he ground out between clenched teeth. 'I've never seen Tony so low – he's not interested in his job and he's drinking far too much. Why did you do it to him? You bitch! You gave him one night in heaven and the rest of his life in hell.'

She met his eyes with a blazing look. Suddenly she was as furious as he was.

'Tony is pining for Nell. On the night of the ball, when you thought he was having heavenly experiences with me, he was getting drunk and telling me how much he loves her. And I don't see what right you have to be so sanctimonious. What were you doing that night? Bedding Barbara or did you go down to London to Marianne?'

There, it was out – she had been unable to hide it. All her insane, unreasonable jealousy was exposed to him.

He drew in his breath and looked down at her with amazement on his face. 'Barbara?' he asked. 'What on earth has Barbara to do with us?'

'She told me … she said … I thought you and she were …' her voice trailed off; she was startled by the look of disgust on his face.

'You stupid little fool,' he said quietly. 'Do you really think I would have anything to do with Barbara? She epitomizes everything I dislike. What a wonderful judge of character you are, Lizzie.'

Tears began to fall down on to her cheeks. 'Go away!' she yelled. 'It has got to be my fault hasn't it? What about your judgement? You assumed I'd jumped into bed with Tony. Thanks for the vote of no confidence!'

He took hold of her shoulders and pulled her around to face him. She tried to shrug him off but he kept hold of her.

'Forgive me, Lizzie. I saw you together in the car, in each other's arms. And when he stayed the night here … I assumed … Well, I assumed that you had decided that he was the man for you.'

'Well, I've told you the truth,' she sobbed.

'Why the hell didn't you just ask me about Barbara? You never seem to trust me enough to ask even a simple question. It's been one long misunderstanding between us since we first met. I couldn't work out what was wrong with you at the ball … And Lizzie, I've been eaten up with jealousy ever since.'

'You, jealous …?' she questioned.

'Insane with jealousy,' he admitted with a rueful smile. 'I wanted to run away as far as I could go from you and Tony. But not even Afghanistan was far enough … And while I was there, shacked up in a hell hole of a refugee camp, I realized that all I had ever done in life was run away. My work has always been my refuge, a perfect escape … It has always been too damned easy to run out and lose myself in other people's problems. But Lizzie …' he took hold of her and buried his face in her hair. She could feel the ripples of emotion running through his body and she clung to him.

'I realized,' he said softly, his hands stroking her hair, 'for the first time I'd met a woman I couldn't forget. And once it was impossible to come back, I knew I should have stayed and fought for you…'

'Oh! How ridiculous,' she laughed through her tears.' You're talking as if you would have called Tony out for a duel.'

'I felt pretty murderous towards him,' Guy said, carefully wiping the tears from her face. 'I was out of my mind with rage at the thought of him making love to you. I'm sorry Lizzie … I never stopped to really analyse the situation and to ask myself if you would have done that. I'm sorry.'

She buried her face against his neck, breathing in the warm scent of his skin. 'I was jealous too,' she admitted in a whisper. 'I …'

He stopped her words with a kiss. 'Marianne is a friend of mine in London. When I go away she looks after the post and the flat … There is no one for you to be jealous of …'

He kissed her again. 'You're still so cold …' he murmured, his hands on her face, his mouth touching her lips softly.

'I don't think I'm ever going to feel warm again,' she whispered, trembling at the touch of his mouth.

'Oh yes you will,' he said swiftly, as he stood up and began to peel off his shirt and trousers.

'What are you doing?' she asked shakily.

He laughed. 'I'm going to get you warm. Body heat. If it works for lambs it should work for you.'

He slipped into the bed with her, folding her into the warm strength of his arms.

Outside the storm raged and the small window of her room was filled with silent whiteness. But secure in his arms she felt safe ... like a child who has come home.

He held her tightly to him.

'I love you, Lizzie,' he said gently. 'Come with me to London. Live with me there.'

'Yes...' she said, 'That would be nice...'

What a silly thing to say, she thought. But her answer satisfied him. He kissed her tenderly and slowly, with infinite patience, as if the world was theirs and theirs alone and the morning was a lifetime away.

And later he slept with his head against her breast, nestling into the curve of her body as the lambs had done. But she was too strung-out to sleep. She smoothed her hands across his hair, her eyes straining in the dim light of the room to study his face, which was softer and younger in sleep.

He belonged to her now. They were going to live together in London.

Nothing could come between them ... Not now he loved her. She drifted off to sleep, holding his hand tightly in hers.

# Ten

In the icy stillness of early dawn she disentangled herself from Guy's arms and slipped out of bed.

She washed and dressed in a daze caused partly by lack of sleep and partly by shock from Guy's sudden return. She wondered if she had really slept or if the night had been a waking dream.

Reality was coldness, the intense stillness of the morning, and shrouded windows. Outside there was an eerie silence: with no cockerels crowing or birds singing, or even a breath of keening wind to break the silent spell.

She pulled on her coat and gloves and whistled for Meg. Then she set off to try to find out how much damage had been done by the storm.

The world was a changed place. Everything which had been so familiar no longer was this morning. The abandoned snow-covered tractor was a strange, rounded mound and the farmyard a white wilderness. The small house seemed weighed down with snow, which had drifted against the northern walls and covered the ground-floor windows. The hump of the roof was the only landmark in a featureless sweep of hillside where track and trees had disappeared under a moonscape of snow.

She was filled with a strange sense of unreality. She was not the same this morning, and neither was the world.

She felt distanced from the world as if some other girl

were stomping through the snow crying because a lifetime's work appeared blotted out and destroyed by a freak blizzard.

She dried her eyes on the back of her glove and set to work. She fed the animals in the barn and hen house, there was little she could do on her own to try to find the stock out on the hillside. George would come up later and they could start searching for air holes in the snow, relying on Meg's sharp eyes and keen nose to scent out buried sheep.

As she walked back across the yard she saw a figure toiling up the hill, an ant figure, but one which grew larger by the minute, a small dark stain on the whiteness of the world. She knew with uncanny certainty the mission of the early-morning caller.

He had come to take Guy away from her.

She tried to recall the words of love which Guy had whispered to her in the night. She knew she shouldn't be counting them over like a miser with gold but she was frightened by the purposeful figure striding through the waist-high drifts.

He hadn't seen her yet, his head was bowed with the exertion of his journey. Childishly she wanted to run away and hide. Instead she kept on repeating to herself that no one could take Guy from her now. They belonged together ... she experienced a sharp pang of longing for Guy and wanted to run back to the house, bolt the door against the faceless visitor, and crawl back into her warm bed. But she stayed where she was, shivering with apprehension.

'Lizzie? Lizzie? Are you all right?'

She shook herself from her trance-like state. It was Tony, his face reddened by the long hard walk. His eyes were concerned.

'Is everything all right?'

'No. I should think I've lost nearly all my breeding stock and lambs.'

'Is Guy here?' There was a note of urgency in his voice, and she knew without a shadow of doubt that Tony hadn't come to find out about her troubles.

'Yes … Come up to the house … What's the matter?'

'The old man snuffed it last night.'

'What?'

'Sorry – Sir James had a heart attack last night, died in his chair.'

She hung her head, unable to speak for a moment.

'I'm very sorry,' she said at last as tears filled her eyes.

'Nell is taking it very badly. Lady Ursula has been expecting it. I just wish I didn't have to be the one to break it to Guy. I don't suppose …'

She looked at him with sudden horror. 'No – Tony! I can't tell him. Please …'

Tony squared his shoulders and didn't reply. She watched him walking up towards the house. Then she went into the barn and began sorting out spades and sticks. When George arrived they would have to start digging out the sheep.

She couldn't face seeing Guy or intruding on their family grief. Besides she had no words of comfort to give. She was filled with a terrible searing guilt because the same thought kept on returning to her: now Guy had inherited the estate he would not return to London – and now she had lost her stock there was nothing to keep her in Wyedale …

She kept on returning to her imaginary images of them together in London: travelling on the underground together and going to theatres and concerts; walking hand in hand along the embankment at night or visiting

Kew Gardens and Hampton Court at the weekends; being carefree and anonymous – a student and a lawyer who were lovers …

She could not put off going back to the house any longer. Guy was standing by the back door, his coat on, ready to leave.

'I'm very sorry,' she whispered to him. She couldn't say any more, she was dumb with misery.

'Tony will stay and help you with the sheep and I'll send the boys from Home Farm.'

'They'll be busy … the whole dale must be snow-bound.'

'All our stock is under cover. There will be roads and paths to clear but I'll send them up as soon as I can.'

He didn't attempt to touch her or kiss her and so they said goodbye formally and politely – as if they were strangers.

George arrived, wheezing and breathless. And for the rest of the morning he, Tony and Lizzie dug out as many sheep as they could find under the snow.

At mid-morning four young lads from Home Farm came to help and Lizzie retired gratefully to the barn, where she helped George match up ewes and lambs or foster orphan lambs on to other mothers. But despite their efforts, the frantic digging, and the warm goat's milk which they bottle-fed to the lambs, the pile of damp dead bodies outside the barn grew. Even hardy hillsheep could not withstand the ferocious battering the winter had sent.

After a hasty lunch of bread and cheese, she returned to the lower fields with Tony. Here there were more live sheep; fewer ewes had lambed too early, and more lambs had survived.

Tony and the boys became more cheerful and Meg

dashed about locating air-holes and barking joyfully when she found a sheep under the snow.

'We've saved quite a few for you, Lizzie,' said Tony and she smiled at him gratefully. She didn't want to tell him the truth; that her finances were so precarious that to lose any stock or suffer any setback signalled the death-knell for her plans.

The farm stock had been her capital, her only nest-egg. The money from the spring sale was to have provided her fare to London and money to live on until she could start her medical training; and, most importantly, rent for Ellis Ridge Farm while she was away. She had planned to qualify, then return to follow her dream of becoming a GP in the dale.

Fate, it seemed, had contrived to deny her all her hopes and dreams. Now none of it could happen.

She would probably never live in Wyedale again.

Someone else would rent the farmhouse and William Hoskins would take over the land. She knew he wanted it for a grouse moor. Thorntons would never live again at Ellis Ridge Farm and sheep would no longer graze on the bleak heather-covered hilltops.

Everything had changed … overnight.

She supposed she would sell up the furniture and go down to London as soon as the remaining animals were gone. She would find a job and a flat … And maybe it would be better never to return once she left. It would be terrible to see it all changed.

They stopped work when it was dark. Tony and the other men didn't want to stay for supper. They left with the promise that they would return in the morning.

When they had gone she was alone with the eerie silence of the snow-covered hills, sitting miserably in the kitchen, numb with fatigue and gloom.

Finally she roused herself to eat more of the bread and cheese which had been left out on the table and to fetch a drink of milk from the dairy. She was too tired and dispirited to be bothered to boil the kettle and make tea.

She busied herself with feeding three tiny lambs which she had brought into the warmth of the kitchen. They were too frail to be fostered to a ewe and she was going to bottle-feed them through the night. Tired though she was, the thought of nursing them gave her a moment of pleasure. It was a challenge to bring such fragile scraps of life back from the brink of death.

After sitting deep in thought, she got out a medical text book on obstetrics and sat down to read it, huddled over the Aga for warmth.

Guy opened the kitchen door without knocking.

Meg, deep in an exhausted sleep, had not heard his footsteps and still lay asleep in front of the Aga.

Lizzie, used to Meg barking at any noise, was so startled when the door opened she gave a cry of surprise and the heavy book slid from her lap with a thud.

'I'm sorry, did I make you jump...?'

'I was nearly asleep.' She fumbled with the book, embarrassed by the untidy room. The remnants of her meal were strewn across the table and the lambs were in a cardboard box in front of the Aga. Puddles from snow-caked boots dirtied the floor and there was hay scattered across the hearth. The air was pungent with the smell of wet animals, wellingtons and waterproofs.

'Move! Meg! ... You must be dry by now,' she said irritably to the dog. She pushed her hair out of her eyes, wishing she had bathed and changed out of her dirty jeans – or at least washed her face.

She looked around the room. 'I wasn't expecting company,' she said drily.

'Have you eaten?' he asked, looking at the remains of the bread and cheese on the table.

'Yes. Would you like a cup of tea … Or a drink?'

'A drink would be lovely. It was a long, cold walk.' He took off his coat and hung it on the back of the door and tugged off his wellingtons.

'It's either whisky or sherry.'

'Whisky, with some water, will be fine.'

He was still standing as she handed him the glass.

'I'm sorry about the mess … I …'

'It doesn't matter, Lizzie. I think it's rather nice, it looks like a nativity play with the lambs and the dog sitting around the fire.'

She stared at him silently. Despite the lightness of his reply and his smile, she thought he looked terribly tired, almost haggard, with a new look of strain around his eyes which she had not seen before.

She was appalled at her own selfishness. She had been so absorbed in her own troubles – seeing only the effects his uncle's death would have on her life that she had not spared a thought for him.

She could see by the sombre look in his eyes and the tight line of his mouth that he was suffering. His life would be changing. She was overwhelmed with sudden pity.

'I'm sorry about your uncle …'

'Thank you …'

The terrible formality from the morning was still there between them as if the room were full of people or their interview were being filmed.

'It will all be very different for you,' she said uncertainly.

'Yes. No more travelling. I'm pleased I decided that Afghanistan would be my last trip. I think I might have resented having a decision like that made for me by circumstance.'

'Yes,' she replied.

'Lizzie ...' there was an unspoken command in his tone which made her look up and meet his eyes. 'It changes things for us.'

'Yes.' She deliberately looked away to break the contact between them. She shuffled her feet, forcing herself to notice the hole in her sock and think about that rather than face up to any more dangerous emotion.

'Guy, you didn't have to trail up here to see me. I was just about to go to bed. I've got to start work at dawn. I know you must be busy.' She moved to the table and began to clear the dirty plates and cups.

'Leave that,' he said abruptly. But she ignored him and walked across to the scullery, her hands full of crockery, and pushed the door open with her foot.

'Lizzie ...' his voice stopped her. She stood uncertainly. The draught from the scullery was an icy blast and she shivered.

'I know you want to finish your medical training.' It was a statement, not a question.

She bustled in and out of the scullery, shutting the door briskly. 'Yes. It was you who made me realize I should go back and do it. You reminded me of how much Mum and Dad had wanted me to be a doctor and how proud they were of me. It's just as well I've got something else to do. My attempts at farming have been a complete disaster.'

'No one can help the weather,' he reminded her gently.

'No ... they can't.'

'Could you ... would you consider finishing your training in Leeds or Manchester?'

'Why?' she asked, startled. She met his eyes again. He looked concerned, with a small frown between his brows.

'I know it's selfish of me, but I don't want you to go down to London. Not without me. It's too far away. If you were studying at Leeds you could come back here at weekends.'

She leant against the Aga, bending to touch the lambs and hiding her eyes. Her voice was quietly reproachful. 'That's impossible, Guy. For one thing I can't afford to keep paying the rent here and rent somewhere in Leeds. And please don't tell me you will take care of it all because, as Tony once told me in a moment of drunken truth, I am not the kind of girl who is ... well any good at being' her voice trailed off uncertainly because she had caught sight of his face.

When he spoke his voice was very low ... dangerously quiet. 'What exactly do you think I am suggesting?'

'I don't know.' She was suddenly sulky, scared by his disapproval. 'I suppose...'

'Don't suppose anything ... I'll tell you. I'm asking you to marry me, Lizzie.'

'Marry you! Don't be ridiculous ...' She met his gaze, her eyes widening with shock.

He laughed, his bad temper chased away by her amazement. 'Why are you so surprised? I know we haven't known each other very long. But in relationships it's quality, not quantity which counts.'

He moved around the table and went to take hold of her but she pulled away.

'Guy ... you don't know what you're saying. You are going to be taking over the estate and title from Sir James ... *have* have taken over from him. You can't marry me.'

She bit her lip, 'Men like you take out girls like me for fun, for a fling, an affair. You don't marry them. The

Ogilvies are famous for seducing local lasses …' She didn't want to sound bitter but the words came out all wrong, not jokey and light-hearted, but serious.

She tried again: 'Barbara tried to warn me about it … she called it the Ogilvy curse.'

'Oh, what rubbish…' His voice was very low, he was watching her intently but making no attempt to take hold of her again. 'You don't believe in all that Victorian melodramatic nonsense, surely?'

'It's not me. What I think doesn't really matter. You belong to Wyedale now. Ownership isn't just a one-way business, you know. And you have no idea how conventional and dogmatic the people of the dale can be. They will be expecting you to marry someone who is suitable.'

'Well – I have no intention of marrying to suit a lot of tenant farmers and country squires,' said Guy lightly. 'And I always thought that my grandfather, Sir Edward, should have married Mary Sayers. By all accounts she was a warm-hearted girl, not like his wife, and she might have made him happy, which Lady Lydia never did … Even in those days people's memories were short I'm sure the people of the dale would have got over it – eventually!'

He looked across at her and smiled, his eyes gentle as he continued: 'If the Ogilvies have a curse, it is that the men in the family have never had the guts to marry for love.'

He laughed suddenly, catching her around the waist and pulling her close. 'The same cannot be said for the Ogilvy women! Tony has announced he is going back to New Zealand and Nell has told me she intends to follow him.'

'But what will her parents say? She's so young!'

'She says she doesn't care what anyone thinks. And she's telling the truth – she is absolutely determined. She says, quite rightly too in my opinion, that if she arrives destitute on Tony's doorstep he won't be so cold-hearted as to send her away, and he might wake up to the fact that she intends to marry him.'

He bent and kissed her mouth very gently. 'And I intend to marry you, Lizzie Thornton.'

'I haven't got a clue about looking after castles and being a lady,' she said with a small laugh. 'I will also want to work. You might get fed up with being married to a GP and getting woken in the middle of the night every time a baby is born in the dale ...'

'But I won't get fed up with you.' He kissed her deeply, his arms tightening around her.

'Now ... are you going to say "Yes" or do I have to bully you? The truth, Lizzie, is that I need you ... I need your strength and wisdom. I need you next to me. We are going to have a struggle. I have just inherited a castle with dry rot and a five-figure overdraft.'

'OK,' she said with feigned reluctance. 'You win ... Anyway, you sound as if you could do with a hard-working wife who knows something about farming.'

Guy shook his head ruefully, a smile curling the corners of his handsome mouth. 'I don't think your opinion of me has improved since that first day we met and you didn't think I was a suitable owner for one of your puppies.'

She hugged him, her arms tight around his neck, her face close to his.

'Oh, it has,' she teased. 'If I had been going to London I would have given Meg to you.'

'Why?' he asked with a laugh.

She was suddenly serious, holding him close, her body pressing against his as she whispered: 'Because she loves you so very, very much … And so do I.'